"Are you sure you want me in the same room with your daughter, Mr. Webb?"

Gifford Webb drew in a deep breath before replying to the younger man. "I don't," he said softly, "but I haven't got much of a choice. Dammit, McKay, my daughter's safety is at stake! You should understand how I feel—you have a daughter of your own."

When Cord McKay remained silent, Gifford continued. "I admit I was shocked to see you in my house this morning. I've still got a lot of raw edges from what happened eighteen years ago. But now I have to do what's best for Stacey. And it looks like *you're* what's best for her. At least temporarily. Till we can get another security man to be her bodyguard. Of course, I'll pay you whatever you want."

"What about Stacey? She doesn't know anything about me and—"

"No," Gifford interrupted, "and I don't want her to."

Torn, Cord wrestled with the situation. A deep, abiding sense of guilt had lodged somewhere inside him eighteen years ago and never left. How could he refuse to do something for the man he'd hurt so badly?

As if Gifford had read Cord's thoughts, the older man spoke in a tortured voice. "You owe me, McKay, and you owe Stacey."

ABOUT THE AUTHOR

Kathryn Shay grew up in a small town in upstate New York, very similar to the town of Canfield, New York, in which she set *A Suitable Bodyguard*. She kept her home-town in mind—the city streets, the places she'd lived, worked and frequented—in order to give a real sense of place to her novel.

In addition to being a high school teacher, Kathryn has two children of her own. The parent-child relationships described in this book reflect her own philosophy on rais-ing children. The hero is devoted to his four-year-old daughter and sacrifices a great deal for her. And the heroine has a special relationship with her father, who is supportive, interested in all aspects of her life and tries to make amends for past mistakes.

This is Kathryn's second Superromance novel. Her first, *The Father Factor,* received excellent reviews and has been nominated for several awards.

Kathryn, her husband, Jerry, and their children live in a small suburb of Rochester, New York. She would like to hear from her readers. You can reach her at P.O. Box 24288, Rochester, NY 14624-0288

Books by Kathryn Shay

Kathryn Shay

A SUITABLE
BODYGUARD

Harlequin Books

TORONTO • NEW YORK • LONDON
AMSTERDAM • PARIS • SYDNEY • HAMBURG
STOCKHOLM • ATHENS • TOKYO • MILAN
MADRID • WARSAW • BUDAPEST • AUCKLAND

ISBN 0-373-70709-6

A SUITABLE BODYGUARD

For my daughter, April, and my son, Ben, who are loved and cherished as much as the children in this book.

CHAPTER ONE

"LOOKS LIKE you've been stood up, darlin'," the bartender drawled.

Stacey Webb peered up at him as she nursed her glass of wine. "Yeah, Bobby, I guess it does."

"Think somethin' happened to Lauren?"

"No." *Mark Dunn probably wouldn't let her come.*

"She's been in here a couple of times lately with that jerk she dates. She doesn't look too good."

"I know. She doesn't."

Sighing, Stacey leaned against the high back of the stool while Bobby poured draft beers for two guys at the end of the mahogany bar. She glanced at the clock. Cutter's Bar and Restaurant was quiet, not unusual for ten o'clock on a Monday night. Nibbling on popcorn, she tried to watch the football game on the large-screen TV, but it didn't distract her from thoughts of Lauren. Stacey was worried about her friend, whose recent unreliable behavior was out of character.

The door whooshed open, allowing in the warm June air, and Stacey turned to see if Lauren had come, after all. But instead, a tall broad-shouldered man filled the doorway.

Surreptitiously, Stacey watched him as he scanned the room. His gaze landed briefly on her; he nodded in a common-courtesy way and took a seat several feet down the bar.

Cord McKay.

She knew who he was. Everyone in Canfield knew who he was. He'd been in the news about a year ago for saving a four-year-old boy who'd fallen into an abandoned well. McKay had maneuvered himself down the narrow shaft when efforts to coax the toddler into a harness failed. On the way up, with the child in his arms, his shoulders became wedged between the walls and one had been severely dislocated. The injury ultimately forced an early retirement—he was only thirty-six—from the police department he'd joined three years ago after he'd returned to Canfield.

Stacey had been impressed when she'd read about the rescue, and moved by the picture of little Timmy Malone hugging McKay in a death grip as they emerged from the well. But her father had had a strange reaction to the media-touted event . . .

Lord, her father! He'd never have gone on his business trip if he'd thought for one minute she'd be spending the night alone. Especially after all that had happened to her in the past few weeks. She'd promised him that Lauren would be staying at their house tonight.

"What can I get you, Cord?" Bobby asked congenially, as McKay settled onto a stool with the grace of a trained athlete.

"A draft."

"How's the shoulder?"

"It hurts."

"You workin' yet?" Bobby seemed oblivious to the other man's clipped tone.

McKay scowled. "No."

"Decided what you're gonna do?"

"Nope. Who's ahead?" McKay asked, his eyes flicking to the screen.

Stacey pretended to watch the game, but stole a few glimpses at the town hero. He wasn't exactly handsome, more craggily attractive, she decided. His thick hair—growing out from its regulation police cut—was the color of ripe wheat. In profile, his nose had a slight bump, indicating it had probably been broken. There were deep grooves bracketing his mouth; stubble lined his jaw.

"Want another one, Stacey?" Bobby asked, wiping the counter in front of her.

"No, I'll just sip this and wait ten more minutes for Lauren."

"The police ever catch the guys who slashed your tires?"

Stacey wasn't surprised at the question. There were no secrets in Canfield, a small upstate New York town in the Southern Tier, but she loved the place, anyway. She'd always felt safe here. Until now.

"No. It was probably just some prank."

"Your father didn't think so. Heard he raised a ruckus at the police station."

What Bobby *hadn't* heard about was her being followed, and the strange phone calls she'd received where no one had spoken when she'd answered. But Stacey had assumed they were all coincidences and hadn't reported them to the police.

"Well, my father overreacts sometimes."

"Your daddy just cares about you."

And, Stacey thought with reluctant affection, as CEO of Canfield Glass Works, her father was used to getting his way. Like insisting someone stay with her tonight.

Well, she'd tried.

Glancing down the bar, she saw Cord McKay take several long swigs of his beer, then stand up. His navy blue T-shirt rippled across his muscles, and Stacey felt a little jolt in her stomach. She tore her gaze away from him and fingered the ring on her left hand. She hadn't looked at another man since she'd gotten engaged to Preston Matthews six months ago. She was annoyed at herself for noticing McKay's sexy body tonight. If there was one thing she believed in, it was fidelity.

Unlike her mother, she thought bitterly.

Just then, Stacey heard the door slam. She waited a few minutes to ensure she wouldn't run into McKay as she walked to her car, then got up to leave, too.

"DAMN!" Cord McKay bent down to rescue his car keys from the mud puddle where he'd just dropped them. It was dark on Bridge Street, so he fished around for a few seconds until he came up with them. He'd been thinking about Stacey Webb and hadn't been watching what he was doing. Wiping the keys— and his hands—on his denims, he pictured her sitting alone on the bar stool, waiting for her friend. She'd looked worried. And what the hell was that about slashed tires?

He scrubbed his hands over his face. The last thing he'd wanted tonight was an encounter with her. He'd seen her around town a number of times. She was easy to spot, with her dark sassy hair, knockout body and wild clothes. He'd made a point of keeping his distance. Though she seemed blissfully unaware of his tension when they met, it coiled within him like a snake ready to strike whenever he was in her company. Thank God there hadn't been many incidents.

Tonight, he'd only stopped at Cutter's to take the edge off his restlessness. He'd been up for three consecutive nights with his daughter, Megan, who had a raging case of chicken pox. And his shoulder was giving him trouble again. He'd been too tired to sleep and needed to get out of the house for a while. So he'd left Megan with his mother and gone for a beer.

Just as he jammed the keys into the lock of his truck, Stacey exited the bar and headed straight for her small, metallic blue Miata without noticing him. He eased open the door and was about to climb in, when he glanced over his shoulder and saw a figure leap from the alley and dart toward Stacey. The man was dressed in dark clothing, with a ski mask over his face. About Cord's height, and as muscular, the guy quickly overtook her and slammed a hand over her mouth.

Pivoting sharply, Cord reached behind his back for his gun. He cursed when he remembered he no longer carried it. Unarmed, he bolted across the sidewalk.

Before he could get to her, Stacey twisted her body and elbowed her attacker in the gut.

"Bitch," the man snapped just as Cord hurled himself at them.

Headfirst, he clipped the assailant behind the knees.

"What the f—" The guy released Stacey and started to whirl toward Cord, but lost his balance and smashed face first into the concrete with a bone-crunching thud.

Cord straddled his prone body and twisted the man's arm behind his back. With a knee on the guy's spine, Cord yanked the attacker's head up by the ski mask. Though the position strained Cord's shoulder, he pressed and pulled mercilessly. Suddenly, a car screeched to a halt at the curb in front of Cutter's. Its headlights illuminated another dark-clad figure bounding from the alley.

Without warning, Cord felt something slam into his temple. His head exploded with bright colors and blinding agony.

Then the world went dark.

STACEY WATCHED Cord McKay toss his head on the utilitarian emergency-room pillow and listened to him moan low in his throat. After the doctor and nurse had tended to him and left, Stacey had suffered a delayed reaction and had been shivering for at least ten minutes. She was just now getting herself under control. Though there was no way she could rid herself of the ball of fear that had settled in her stomach like a dead weight.

She shuddered again at the thought of what could have happened if Cord hadn't been at his truck when she'd left Cutter's. She tried to stifle the panic that came when she realized tonight's attack probably meant the incidents of the past few weeks were not coincidences. Oh, God. Someone was after her!

Stacey forced herself to concentrate on her knight in shining armor. She picked up the ice pack the attendant had given her with instructions to apply it to Cord's head—ten minutes on, ten off—and gingerly placed it over the lump on his right temple, which was already turning purple around the raw spot where the gun butt had broken the skin. His body jerked at the touch, and his left arm flailed, socking her in the stomach. Recoiling, Stacey clutched her middle until she could take in more air. After a moment or two, her breathing evened out and, restraining his arm with her other hand, she reapplied the cold compress. He twitched, but was unable to strike out again.

While she held the ice pack to his head, she studied the curtained cubicle. Canfield's hospital was only about twenty years old, but its emergency ward was small, cramped and understaffed. Tonight, the ER was packed with victims of a highway accident. The white drapes that isolated them from the other patients were opaque and tattered with overuse. The smell of antiseptic, along with other acrid odors Stacey chose not to identify, stung her nostrils.

"What the hell..."

Stacey peered down at the source of the curse. Blue ice stared up at her.

He watched her for a minute, then said, "Would you mind letting go of my arm? The angle you're holding it twists my shoulder."

Surprised by his clipped words, she flinched and scooted back. "Sorry, but you hit me in the stomach when I put the compress on your head."

Dark blond eyebrows knit together. "Oh."

Not, I'm sorry. Not, thanks for the help.

Of course, she was the one who owed him, she reminded herself. Big time.

Stacey watched him brace his good arm on the mattress and push himself up. His biceps flexed beneath his T-shirt, and the tendons in his hand tensed, but he was sitting up in seconds. Leaning against the wall, he winced as he rubbed his shoulder.

"The nurse said to keep ice on that," she told him, indicating the goose egg.

He closed his eyes and grunted.

She leaned over and applied the compress again.

"Thanks," he said, not opening his eyes, but taking the ice from her.

As he relaxed fractionally, Stacey watched him. He was silent, breathing deeply, fighting the pain, she guessed.

"Why are you playing nurse?" he asked, still not looking at her.

"They're overcrowded and understaffed here."

"As usual."

"Well, there was a huge pileup on Route 17 just before midnight and lots of people were hurt."

He grunted again.

His attitude was abrasive. To be expected, Stacey thought, given the amount of pain he must be in. But she sensed something deeper. His responses to her were almost angry. Was he annoyed that she'd caused trouble for him? "Um...thanks for what you did," she said hesitantly. "Though I'm not exactly sure where you came from, or what happened."

Cord opened his eyes and scanned the curtained room, then looked at her. "I saw the guy jump you outside Cutter's." He scowled. "Last thing I remember is tackling him."

"But you're not a cop anymore."

"No, I'm not." His tone could have cut glass.

"Why didn't you just call the police? Why did you get involved?"

A storm of emotions passed through his eyes. "Beats me," he said flatly. "Look, tell me what happened when I passed out."

Stacey leaned against the chair and shivered again, remembering. Rubbing her arms up and down her thin windbreaker, she said, "Another guy jumped out of the alley after you grounded the first one. He hit you on the head with the butt of a gun. By then, some other people had come out of Cutter's, and I was screaming and yelling and kicking. The two men dived into the car that pulled up and got away."

Cord frowned.

Stacey stared at him, then said, "I've seen you around town, but we haven't formally met. I'm Stacey Webb."

"I know."

"How?"

"Small town."

"Yeah. So things like this aren't supposed to happen." Surveying the room, Stacey bit her lip.

"What's wrong?"

Her eyes came back to his. "Nothing."

"You bit your lip. What were you thinking?"

She waited a moment. "I was going to ask you what you think happened. Was it a mugging?"

"No, not with the car all set up. They were probably trying to kidnap you, though my guess is they were amateurs. They bungled it pretty bad."

Swallowing hard, Stacey clutched her hands together. She didn't want to start shaking again, especially in front of him. "I was hoping it wasn't so...premeditated."

"You suspected it wasn't just a one-time attack?"

"Yes."

"Why?"

Stacey told him about the other incidents, trying to keep her voice calm.

Cord arched a blond eyebrow. "Any idea why someone would want to kidnap you?"

"Daddy thinks it's probably to get to him," she explained. "There've been a lot of layoffs at the plant, for one thing, and this could be retaliation. Plus, in his position, he makes enemies for all sorts of political reasons. And he's got money."

"It sounds pretty serious. You need to work with the police on it."

"Yes, I know. I'm sorry you were hurt trying to help me."

"Yeah," he said derisively. "Me, too."

Unexpectedly, he swung his feet to the floor.

"What are you doing?" she asked.

"What does it look like?" He swayed before standing on shaky legs.

"You're hurt," she said as she stood. "You shouldn't be up. The nurse said . . ."

Cord wavered and reached for the first support he could get—her arm. He gripped it painfully. Bigger and stronger, he unbalanced her and they both tumbled to the bed, his body covering hers.

His weight felt...strange. He was a lot heavier than he looked. She'd grabbed his shoulders when they fell and his muscles strained beneath her fingers. His legs were much longer than hers. Originally, she'd guessed him to be her father's height, about five-nine. But he was closer to six feet. His chest was like a solid brick wall against her, except she could feel his heart thumping inside it. She found the sensation pleasant.

For a moment, he stared into her eyes, something akin to pain flashing through his. Once more, the look was gone before she could categorize it, and he eased off her to the side of the bed. "Sorry, I'm weaker than I thought." Sitting back, he leaned against the wall a second time and massaged his shoulder.

"That's okay." Stacey's reply was a little breathless. She scrambled off the bed and into the chair. "Sorry about your shoulder."

He nodded and waved his hand absently.

"So, you're a hero again!" Both turned to see two uniformed policemen standing in the doorway.

Joe Ferron, the officer who'd made the comment, was a former classmate of Stacey's. He'd been the all-American boy in high school, but Stacey still found it hard to believe he was a cop now.

Wayne Valentino, Canfield's chief of police, asked, "How are ya, Cord?"

"My head hurts like hell," Cord said irritably.

"Well, you're just as ornery as ever, so you must be okay."

"Hurt the shoulder any more?" Ferron asked.

"Some." His curt reply cut off any further concern from the men.

Pulling out a pen, Wayne took Cord's statement.

While the chief was writing his report, Cord watched Ferron and Stacey making small talk. The young cop fidgeted like a boy at a high school dance. His too-wide grin and his puppy-dog eyes clearly revealed his crush on Stacey Webb.

When Wayne finished, he called to Ferron, who turned to Cord and said, "Geez, you can't help playing hero, can you?"

"Just do me a favor. Keep it out of the paper this time."

"You kiddin'? The *Leader*'s already got the story. By tomorrow night, everyone in town will know about it."

Cord moaned audibly and Stacey mimicked it silently.

By tomorrow night, everyone in town would know that she'd almost been abducted.

Well, since keeping quiet about the other incidents hadn't helped, maybe public exposure would do some good. She hoped so.

Because for the first time since her mother, Helene, had left, Stacey was really afraid.

"WHAT TIME IS IT?" Cord asked as he awakened in the dim, unfamiliar room and saw Stacey Webb sitting next to him.

She blew her thick, chestnut bangs off her forehead. "Two in the morning."

"Why are you still here? They said *I* had to stay a couple of hours for observation, not you." He didn't try to control the edge in his voice. He wanted this woman gone.

"Because it's my fault you were hurt," she told him. "I'm not leaving you here by yourself." Her eyes, the color of hot fudge, scanned the cubicle. "I wouldn't want to stay here alone."

"Why not? Afraid of the dark?"

"Of course not," she murmured.

Her face was a dead giveaway. He'd only been with her a few hours, and he'd been dozing off and on, but already he could read her like a book. It gave him a slight twinge to think about how vulnerable she was. An innocent. Just like—

He cut off the thought before it formed.

"Where's your father?" he asked, and cringed inwardly as he heard his annoyed tone. "Why isn't he here after what happened to you tonight?"

"Out of town on business. I didn't call him." They were silent again, then she broke it by adding, "Besides, you should be glad I'm here. You scared all the nurses away with your surly disposition."

"No sass, lady." The edge slowly drained from his voice. Her pert features, scrunched into a mocking smile, were hard to resist.

He studied her outfit.

Tonight she wore hot-pink leggings and a long striped top, which emphasized her compact curves. She'd thrown on a purple jacket. She looked as if she'd just walked off the set of an MTV video, but he didn't comment. Best to keep this as impersonal as possible.

"You really should leave," he said gruffly. "You should get some rest." Again, the worried frown marred her face. "Isn't anybody home at your house?"

"No. Lauren, my best friend, was supposed to spend the night, but she never showed up at Cutter's."

"So you're afraid to go home by yourself?"

Her chin lifted. "Of course not."

"Sure."

She sat up straighter. "I'll admit that I don't particularly like being alone in that big house, but I can certainly handle being there on my own when I have to. You don't have to be so sarcastic about it."

He lifted the ice pack to his temple. "Look, my head hurts like hell and my shoulder's sore. You're right. I'm a grump. Actually, I've got a knack for sending women scurrying at the best of times."

"That's not what I heard." Her full lips twitched. "Seems you had quite a reputation as a lady's man before you left Canfield all those years ago."

His hand froze, and at the same time, sweat broke out on his forehead. She couldn't know, he told himself, or she wouldn't be this civil to him. He forced himself to relax the way he did every time he faced a criminal at gunpoint. "Don't believe everything you hear."

As he closed his eyes, fatigue washed over him. How bizarre, he thought. He was a big believer in irony, but being thrown together like this with Gifford Webb's daughter was a colossal example of the fates at work.

Images whirled through his brain. At the moment, he was trying very hard to block out thoughts of Megan. If he didn't make it home soon, she'd wake up this morning and not know where he was. She'd cry, until his mother calmed her with hot oatmeal, just as Nora McKay had done for him on those many mornings when *he'd* awakened missing his father. And worrying about the old man's safety. At four years old, Meggie's concern would be nebulous. But by thirteen, thoughts of what could happen to her dad would be terrifying for her. He knew because his own father had been a cop and Cord had experienced the fear. He'd come back to Canfield so that Megan would be spared all that.

I will not dwell on Megan, or the Webbs.

What was the old joke—trying to clear your mind of unwanted thoughts was like trying not to think about a pink elephant?

An hour later he dozed, and Stacey was resting in the chair next to him, when the harried doctor reentered. He checked Cord's vital signs, then said, "Well, looks like you're okay. I think you can go home now."

"Good."

This time, Cord eased himself to the edge of the mattress, rose slowly and let his equilibrium adjust.

He reached for the jacket that had been thrown over his bed, then looked at Stacey. "Ready to go?"

She stood and stretched. He caught himself noticing the way her top strained across her breasts and he forced himself to look away.

"I guess," she answered. "You need a ride somewhere?"

He stared at her. "Level with me, Stacey. You don't want to go home alone, do you?"

Averting her eyes, she picked up her purse.

"Is it because of what happened tonight?" he asked.

"No," she said, but didn't look at him.

"Most women would be nervous."

Her head whipped toward him, sending her short hair falling in soft curls around her face. "Well, I'm not like most women. I've never been like most women. I'm twenty-three years old, and I've had to grow up fast and deal with a lot of things on my own."

"Easy." Cord was stunned at the vehemence of her statement. "I didn't mean to insult you."

"Come on, I'll take you to your truck," she said, forestalling further analysis. "It's still at Cutter's. We left it there when the ambulance came. I followed you here in my car."

Ten minutes later, Cord started his truck as Stacey maneuvered her little sports car away from the curb. He'd known all along what he was going to do, but that didn't make it any easier. Cursing himself—and fate—he followed her across town, toward The Hill, the name given by town residents to Canfield's most upscale neighborhood.

They turned left onto Woodview Lane. She drove up to a house, and he pulled into the driveway behind her. His heart hammered in his chest as he took in the huge, brick home, with its big white pillars and a row of tall birch trees standing guard on the lawn. In the shadows, it loomed before him like a ghost from his past. Gripping the steering wheel until his knuckles were white, he willed away the memories.

Stacey was at his truck before he had time to panic. Pushing open the door, he got out.

"What are you doing here?" she asked.

"I came to make sure you're safe."

From the halogen light over the three-car garage, he could see her skin pale. Her lips parted slightly and her eyes widened. "They wouldn't be stupid enough to try again . . . would they?"

"They might. I'm surprised the police didn't follow you home."

"They were short on officers, just like the hospital, because of the highway accident earlier." She glanced at the dark foreboding house and shivered. "All right. Since you're here, maybe you should come inside with me. I'll check the alarm—make sure it's still on. You can leave after I get in and reset it."

A strong drive to protect her and an equally powerful urge to run like hell battled within him as he trailed her to the double front doors. Unlocking the dead bolt, she stepped into the foyer. He followed like a man going to the gallows. Memories swamped him, but he pushed them back and and tried not to look at the surroundings.

After Stacey dealt with the alarm, she turned to him. The foyer was dimly lit, casting her face in shadows. Her smile was genuine and it tugged at his heart. "Thanks," she said. "I feel better now that I'm inside. I'll be okay."

Cord glanced to the left into the mammoth living room, then to the oversize dining room on his right. Everything was black and silent.

Jamming his hands into his pockets, he sighed heavily. "Listen, my mother lives with us so she's with my little girl, and it's 3:00 a.m. Why don't I just stay here for the rest of the night?"

"Why?" she asked, her eyes wide with a different kind of fear.

"Relax. I'm only trying to help. I'm not coming on to you."

Stacey's chin lifted. "Of course you're not. I'm engaged."

To Preston Matthews. "I know."

"Small town again?"

"Something like that. Look, just grab me a blanket. I'll bunk on the couch in here." He tilted his head to the left.

Stacey bit her lip again, then whispered, "Okay. I guess I am a little afraid."

Giving him a half smile, she disappeared upstairs. He walked into the living room. Same high ceilings. Different carpet. Same silk couch and chairs. The wood smelled familiarly of furniture polish. He stood stock-still, staring at the walls. Before the memories suffocated him, Stacey returned with a fluffy pillow and two blankets.

Carelessly, he tossed them on the couch, then kicked off his battered Dock-Siders. "Go to bed, Stacey."

She stepped back and crossed her arms over her breasts. "All right. I just wanted to say thanks again. For saving me—and for this. Seems you've got a real hero complex."

"Don't give me credit for things I'm not."

Her eyes narrowed, but she turned and left the room without further comment.

Some hero, he thought as he pulled his T-shirt over his head and sank onto the couch. He closed his eyes to block out the house that reminded him of how wrong she was.

FOUR HOURS LATER, Cord was startled out of sleep by the angry rumble of a man's voice. Through bleary eyes, he looked into the mottled, enraged face of Gifford Webb. "What the hell are you doing in my house again, McKay?"

CHAPTER TWO

CORD STARED BLANKLY at Gifford Webb, the man who hated him with a long-standing passion. Though Webb was now forty-six, he looked fit and trim and even youthful. His suit was rumpled, yet its designer quality was evident, as always. But there were subtle changes—more than simply the gray at his temples. No, the real difference was in those eyes that were so much like Stacey's. There were creases of suffering etched around them.

"I asked you what you're doing here, McKay." Webb's skin stretched across his aristocratic cheekbones, belying the calm that filtered his voice.

Cord rose from the couch. Had he always been taller than this man? "I heard you. Maybe you'd better sit down for this."

"You bastard," Webb said with quiet venom. "If you've hurt Stacey, I'll..."

"Calm down, Webb. I...helped her out."

Fists clenched at his sides, Gifford said between gritted teeth, "Tell me."

"Somebody tried to grab your daughter last night."

"Grab her?"

"Abduct her." Cord scowled. "Happened outside Cutter's."

Gifford paled and grasped the edge of a table. "Who did it?"

"I don't know."

His eyes narrowed on Cord. "How'd you get involved? You're off the force, aren't you?"

Nodding, Cord hid his surprise that Webb had followed his activities since he'd returned to Canfield. "I was outside the bar around ten when somebody jumped her from the alley."

"You stopped him?"

"Yeah."

Shoulders slumping with the news, Gifford relaxed his grip and sank onto the sofa. "Tell me every detail."

Cord sat down again. He recounted the event in five minutes, finishing just as Stacey appeared in the doorway.

"Daddy!" she said, launching herself into his arms.

Gifford stood just in time to catch her. His eyes closed as he held her in a hammerlock. "Honey, are you all right?"

She nodded. Cord tried to tear his eyes away from the reunion, but he couldn't. Stacey was about six inches shorter than Gifford, but his muscled frame dwarfed her. The zebra-print nightshirt she wore peeked out from under the hem of a short, shiny purple robe.

Her father hugged her a minute longer, while she buried her face in his chest. Cord had a sudden image of Megan all grown-up. Then it was juxtaposed with a vision of Nathan McKay, who had never once held his only son in any kind of embrace. It wasn't the way men behaved.

Finally, Gifford stepped back but gripped Stacey's arms as he looked at her. "Are you sure you're all right?"

"Yes." She glanced over his shoulder at Cord. "I was just scared, that's all. Mr. McKay stopped those men, then offered to stay with me so I wouldn't be alone."

"You won't be alone again until this is settled," Gifford said, his tone stern.

Stacey's unlined forehead furrowed. "What do you mean?"

"We'll talk about this later."

"Daddy..."

Gifford glanced from her to Cord. Stacey's eyes focused on him, too. She stared at his bare chest so long that Cord became self-conscious and reached for his T-shirt. He pulled it over his head and found his shoes. He was struck by the contrast in her behavior. She'd seemed almost girlish around her father and yet she was all woman when she looked at him. Thrusting aside the observation, he picked up his jacket, and said, "I suggest you get in touch with the police."

"We will," Gifford said.

"You shouldn't ignore this like you did the other incidents."

"Stacey told you about those?"

"Yes. Slashed tires, someone following her and strange phone calls should all have been reported."

Webb's shoulders stiffened. "Thanks for the advice. We'll handle it. I'm well aware of the fact that there are reasons—because of my position at Canfield Glass—that someone might want to kidnap my daughter."

"Daddy..."

Cord looked at Stacey. Her mouth was pinched but it couldn't disguise the fullness of her bottom lip.

On a hunch, Cord asked, "What color was the car that was following her?"

"A dark sedan." Webb's voice was strained by a father's worry.

"The car the two guys jumped into was a navy blue Chevy," Cord said.

Stacey's face went chalk white.

All-business, Cord said, "Sounds to me like your daughter needs some protection. It might not stop at this."

Something shadowy passed over Webb's face. "I agree. We'll go back to the police station this morning."

"Yeah, but the Canfield P.D. isn't set up for this kind of thing."

"What are you talking about?" Stacey asked. He had to give her credit, her voice was low and even, he'd guess with great effort.

"Some major cities have divisions equipped with officers trained to provide special protection," he explained. "Like New York, where dignitaries and other important personnel often visit. Even in medium-size cities, like Rochester, the force has more police to assign to a case like this, and they've had training. Canfield has about thirty officers, but the department won't be able to spare anyone to protect Stacey full-time.''

"We'll have to get private help, then," Gifford stated.

"The police have names of agencies that handle surveillance and protection," Cord said. "Unfortunately, none of these are located in Canfield. You'll have to get somebody from out of town."

"In the meantime?"

"Don't let her go anywhere alone. Maybe the cops can provide some part-time surveillance. For a while at least."

"Maybe? I won't let my daughter's life rest on maybe."

Cord glanced at his watch. "Look, I've got to get home to *my* daughter." Shrugging into his jacket, he tried not to wince at the pain in his shoulder. As he faced Gifford Webb, he said, "Watch her," then turned to go.

When he reached the door, he heard her voice. "Dad, I will *not* let some stranger follow me around."

"Yes, Stacey, you will."

"And what if I refuse?"

Unable to stop himself, Cord pivoted. "Stacey?"

She looked over at him, a curious mixture of defiance and vulnerability in her eyes. "What?"

"Don't refuse."

"Why?"

"You could end up dead."

AT ONE O'CLOCK that afternoon, Stacey watched Cord McKay stride into the conference room at the Canfield police station and immediately felt better. She was still angry, upset and frustrated, but somehow his presence calmed her—though it looked as if this was the last place he wanted to be.

He'd shaved since this morning, and she could smell a clean soapy scent and woodsy cologne. He'd also changed into beltless, well-worn, white jeans and a black T-shirt. A large bandage covered his temple, a chilly reminder of the night before.

Slipping his hands into his pockets, he leaned against the bulletin-board wall. Ignoring both Stacey and her father, he addressed Wayne Valentino. "What's up?"

"Mr. Webb and his daughter asked me to call you in."

He looked directly at her father. A silent message telegraphed between the two. It intrigued Stacey.

"Why?" he asked Gifford.

"Ah..." Gifford raked a hand through his thick hair. It was the first time she'd ever seen her father at a loss for words. Finally he found his voice. "I need your help."

Something was wrong here. McKay looked as if her father had just asked him to sacrifice his firstborn to the gods.

"*I* asked for you to come," she put in.

"For what?" There was a hard look in his steely blue eyes.

Gifford had regained his composure. "We're having some problems ironing out what to do." He turned to look at his daughter. Stacey had seen that expression many times in the past: when she insisted on skipping breakfast, when she'd wanted to try out for the boys' lacrosse team, when she'd quit art school. "It seems my headstrong daughter doesn't want any protection."

With an exasperated sigh, Cord faced her and said, "You don't have a choice."

She straightened in her seat. "People always have choices."

Almost reluctantly, Cord glanced at Gifford. "Not always."

Again, Stacey's sixth sense was alerted. Something was going on between her father and Cord McKay. But what? Gifford was a good ten years older, so they couldn't have known each other in high school or college.

"Stacey, McKay asked you why you're balking."

She fidgeted with the strap of her purse. "Does it matter? The police say they can only provide minimal protection. Daddy's called several security agencies, and no one with any experience is available. So I think maybe we ought to just wait this out."

Cord scowled. "It's hard to believe you can't get someone from out of town."

"We tried, with money as no object," Gifford answered. "The best people are booked. It seems there's some big thing going on at the UN this month, and a couple of other events that require private protection in several large cities. Agencies in Chicago or Toronto could have sent one of their newer recruits, but I don't want a rookie. Obviously, a little harassment case in Canfield, New York, is very low priority for any of these agencies."

"Maybe I can help." Cord turned to the phone on the wall and picked up the receiver, to dial information.

"Give me the number of Anderson Security," he said.

As they waited, Gifford said, "McKay, that's not the only problem. Stacey doesn't—"

"Thanks." Cord scribbled something on the pad next to the phone, then punched the buttons again. "I'd like to speak to Tom Anderson." He waited. "Cord McKay... Oh, hi, Gloria. Yeah, fine. She's great. Yeah...loving small-town life... Okay... Hi, Tom. Look, I've got a problem here. Yes, Canfield has problems..."

Stacey listened to Cord explain the situation. Obviously he knew these people, and she wondered what he'd done in the big city.

"Not till then? Okay, okay, I know you would. You're sure he's experienced? All right, Saturday morning. You can contact the Canfield P.D. with the details. Thanks." He hung up the phone. "Anderson Security from New York can have someone here in four days. It's the soonest an experienced agent's available."

"Good work, Cord," Wayne said.

"Just luck. Well, if that's all..."

Stacey stood. "That's not all. Isn't anybody listening to me? I don't want this."

Cord crossed the few feet that separated them. "Stop acting like a spoiled brat. Your life is in danger. You don't ignore slashed tires and potential kidnappings. Believe me, I know, these things can get messy."

Jutting out her chin, Stacey said, "I'm not acting like a brat. I'm objecting to this imposition on my life. I have a say in what happens to me."

Cord stared at her, as if he'd gotten something he hadn't expected. *Good.*

"Smart people take advice from the experts," he said tightly.

"Oh, and you're an expert?"

"In a manner of speaking. I worked in one of those special divisions in New York for ten years."

Her jaw clamped shut.

"That's why you got some pull with Anderson's," Wayne said.

Cord nodded, his eyes never leaving Stacey. "Uh-huh. I worked with them and even did some training for their new people. So I know what I'm talking about."

Regaining her composure, Stacey took a deep breath. "All right," she said finally. "I believe you. But I can't live with some stranger dogging my every move." She looked to Wayne. "Especially if he's from out of town. Isn't there someone here who could stay with me?"

Wayne shook his head. "Sorry, Stacey. We just don't have enough resources. I could probably release one guy from the midnight-to-six shift for a while, but that's all." He glanced at Cord. "How about McKay? He's not doin' anything since his injury, are ya, Cord?"

The air in the room crackled. Gifford Webb's jaw tensed and every muscle in Cord's body constricted.

"I don't think that's a good idea," Cord said.

"Hey, yeah, it really is," Wayne went on, clearly oblivious to the tension in the room. "You got the experience, you're in good shape, except for the shoulder, and you're free."

Clearing his throat, Cord said, "No, I'm not free. I can't take on a case like this. It requires twenty-four-hour surveillance. I can't work those hours."

Stacey studied Cord McKay. Despite his high-handedness, she kind of liked the idea of being guarded by him. He made her feel safe. He also pulled at something inside her—something decidedly feminine. "Why can't you work those hours?" she asked.

"I've got a little girl."

"Oh, yes," Stacey said. "She lives with you and your mother."

"Maybe Nora could watch her till this is over," Wayne suggested.

Cord rounded on him. "No, definitely not. I came back to Canfield so I could raise Megan right. I'm not going to turn her over to my mother because of some *job*."

Gifford rose. His face was ashen and a muscle in his neck throbbed. "I'd like to speak to Mr. McKay alone, Wayne, if you don't mind."

"Ah, sure, I . . . I'll wait outside."

Turning to his daughter, Gifford said, "You too, Stacey."

"Me? Why?"

"Do as you're told."

"Daddy, I'm not—"

"Honey, please! Try being cooperative for once in your life."

Stacey nodded, startled by her father's unusual criticism. Though it was probably warranted. Somehow, she was always more petulant around him. It was something she wasn't proud of. She crossed to the door, but glanced over her shoulder before she left to see Gifford and McKay squaring off like boxers about to enter the ring.

CORD SAT in the Webb driveway trying to keep himself from sputtering. He was mad, mostly at fate, for dragging him back to this house, and to these people. How the hell had he let this happen?

But he knew the answer to the question. He could still see Gifford Webb standing in the suddenly too-small office, his features a study in conflict...

After Stacey and Wayne had left the room, Cord had turned to Webb. "We have nothing to say to each other."

"Since my daughter's safety is at stake, we have a lot to say."

"I'd have thought you wouldn't want me in the same room with her."

Gifford had sucked in a deep breath, then said, "I don't, really. But I don't think I have much choice."

Raking a hand through his hair, Cord shook his head. "Of course you do. Someone will be here Saturday from Anderson's."

"And until then?"

At a loss for an answer, Cord retreated. He stepped away and turned his back on Gifford, facing the chalkboard which spanned the length of one wall. Sometimes it hurt just to look at the man and remember all that had happened.

"Look, McKay. I'll admit I was shocked to see you in my house this morning. And I have to say that I've still got a lot of raw edges from eighteen years ago. But I've also come to see some things a little differently since then." Stacey's father spoke in halting words. "But that's beside the point. I have to do what's best for Stacey. And it looks like you're what's best for her. At least temporarily." When Cord remained silent, he added, "Of course, I'll pay you whatever you want. I'm sure you can use the money, now that you're off the force."

"What about Stacey? She doesn't know anything about me and—"

"No," Gifford interrupted. "And I don't want her to."

Torn, Cord wrestled with the situation. A deep, abiding sense of guilt had lodged somewhere inside him eighteen years ago and had never left. How could he refuse to do something for a man he'd hurt so badly?

As if Webb had read Cord's thoughts, the older man spoke in a tortured voice. "You owe me, McKay..."

Oh, yeah, Cord thought now as he looked at the Webb home through the truck windshield, guilt is the reason I'm here. With controlled viciousness, he yanked open the truck door and stalked to the front of the house. While he rang the bell, he assessed the surroundings with a practiced eye. The hedges would have to be cut—they were too tall and full and could hide an intruder. The lighting needed to be improved. He glanced at the garage. The glass window in the center would have to be boarded up because it probably wasn't connected to the alarm. Impatient, he leaned on the bell.

In seconds, Stacey whipped open the front door.

"Don't do that," he growled.

Her face went blank. "What?"

"Did you check to see who was at the door?"

"No, Daddy's expecting you."

"But it could have been the guy who's after you," he said harshly. "You've got to use more common sense."

Stacey's eyes narrowed and her cheeks turned pink. "Don't yell at me like I'm some child. I've never been stalked before, and I don't know all the rules yet."

"Well, you'd better learn them fast or you could end up dead."

She blanched at his bald statement.

Very deliberately, he gentled his voice, though he was no longer a gentle man. "I didn't mean to snap at you."

She shook her head, her chocolate eyes wide and bright. "No, you're right. I should be more careful." Then she stepped aside to allow him in. "Daddy's in the library." Her shoulders still tense, she led him through the large house.

Gifford Webb sat behind a huge oak desk in front of a set of French doors. Cord had only seen this room once or twice, and it looked unchanged. Rising, Stacey's father came toward him. "I'm glad you're here."

Cord nodded.

When they were all seated, Stacey turned to Cord.

"I really don't understand what made you change your mind. I thought you didn't want to leave your daughter."

"I won't be away from her for too long. I've arranged for the police to do sporadic coverage during the evening and overnight so I can still see Megan before she goes to bed and when she wakes up. And it's only for three days."

"She could come and visit," Stacey suggested.

"No, she can't. It's too dangerous."

"Of course. I wasn't thinking." Stacey glanced at Gifford and gave him a smile full of love and understanding. "Megan's lucky," she said, still looking at her father. "She'll have that special relationship with you all her life. It's a wonderful thing for a girl to have."

Cord coughed, uncomfortable with this personal glimpse into their father-daughter relationship. "I'm going to inspect the property right now," he said, "and make a list of everything that needs to be done to increase the security. First, there are some things we've got to get straight."

Cocking her head, Stacey said, "All right."

"You have to do everything I tell you. No sass."

"Are you always this rude?" she asked.

"Kindness doesn't catch kidnappers." Damn, she looked frightened. But better that than she do something stupid and pay for it with her life. "I've got to have your full cooperation."

"You'll have it," her father stated.

"I want to hear it from you." Cord addressed Stacey directly.

Stacey squared her shoulders. "Yes, you have my cooperation. You've scared me enough that I believe I'm in danger. Since the decision's been made, I'll do whatever I have to."

For thirty minutes, they discussed the schedule of the week's activities, who would be where when, then took a quick tour of the house. In the finished basement, Cord commented on the state-of-the-art workout machines. "You use this stuff?" he asked Stacey.

"Of course. So does Daddy."

By midafternoon, they were done with the tour and the briefing. Back in the library, Stacey turned to her father. "Dad, you'd better go. You're going to be late for your four o'clock meeting."

He shifted uneasily. "I thought I'd cancel it."

"Don't you dare. It's on the new processing-system figures. You've got to be there. Besides," she said, crossing to him and linking her arm with his, "that's why you're paying Cord all this money, isn't it?"

"Yes, it is. All right, if you're sure."

"Go ahead. She'll be fine," Cord added.

Gifford kissed Stacey's forehead, and glanced at Cord. He walked slowly to the doorway, then turned to face them. "I'll see you later."

"Don't worry, Daddy. I'm in good hands."

A look of such intense pain crossed Gifford Webb's face that Cord had to turn away.

"Did he?" Stacey asked as she leaned against the desk after her father left.

"Did he what?"

"Pay you a lot of money?"

"Enough. I'll put it away for Megan's college tuition."

"Hmm..."

"You work at the Glass Works, too, don't you?"

"Yes, I'm an accountant."

Cord checked his watch. "Aren't you going in today?"

"No, I took the day off."

"What do you usually do on your days off?"

"Relax, read. Spend time with my friends."

"What do you do to relax?"

"I bake."

He remembered Helene, standing at the counter, mixing batter, saying, *I hate to bake. But Stacey loves when we do it together.*

"How do chocolate chip cookies sound?" she asked.

"Good."

In the kitchen, Cord pulled out a chair and tried not to remember how many times he'd sat at this scarred oak table. Instead, he turned his attention to his charge, and watched her put softened butter in a bowl and mix it with sugar. He had to force back a grin at the difference in how she was dressed now and what she'd worn to the police station. There she'd had on a demure peach suit, with pearls and sensible shoes. It had made her look conservative and professional. Now, she looked wild and sexy—in cutoff denims with a sleeveless top made of sparkling gold. There were matching gold sandals on her feet. When she reached for a bowl from the cupboard, the shorts rode up to the top of her thighs.

Her legs were long and tanned. They were sleek and smooth and—he'd bet—soft.

"Do you actually have to be with me every minute?" she asked casually.

He whipped his gaze away from her fanny like a guilty teenager caught ogling a girl. "Trying to get rid of me?"

"Just making conversation."

"Not every minute. But it's a good idea, for a while, anyway. I *will* go to work with you this week."

"And stand watch." She added flour and other ingredients as she talked.

"Something like that."

"Won't it get boring?" Stacey dipped her finger into the bowl and brought it to her lips. Her tongue darted out and lapped up the batter.

Watching her mouth, Cord muttered, "Somehow, I doubt it."

She smiled and continued to stir. They made small talk as she finished with the dough.

After she put the first batch of cookies in the oven, she took a seat opposite him at the table. "Cord, I know you didn't want to do this. Because of your daughter especially. But I sense there's another reason. Does my father know you from somewhere?"

Through sheer willpower, he schooled his features not to change expression. "No, your father doesn't know me at all."

"Maybe it's the kidnapping attempt that's got him rattled. He's been acting strange."

Her perceptiveness made him nervous, so he didn't respond.

She pushed back her hair. "In any case, thanks for taking this on, despite your reservations. I'll try to cooperate, but nevertheless, I'm sure it won't be easy."

No, it won't be easy, he thought, surveying the kitchen where he'd sat eighteen years ago surrounded by the same scent of chocolate chip cookies. It would be torture every time he stepped foot in this cursed house, every time he entered another room. No it wouldn't be easy. But he owed them.

Because the last time he'd been here, his visit had ended one life, and almost ruined three others.

IN THE LIBRARY of his huge home, Gifford Webb glared at the headline in Tuesday night's *Canfield Leader:* Town Hero Strikes Again. He felt the familiar surge of frustration he thought he'd buried years ago as he read the account of how Cord McKay had saved Gifford's daughter from abduction. The irony of it taunted him, even as he tried to stifle the associations that bombarded him. In the end, he simply slapped the newspaper down on the table.

To outrun the demons of his past, Gifford crossed to the oak wall unit and uncorked a decanter of Johnny Walker Black. Pouring himself a generous portion, he leaned against the back of a wing chair, closed his eyes and sipped.

But the Scotch did nothing to calm his soul. Instead, behind his lids, he saw again the image of Cord McKay in bed with his wife.

Forcibly yanking his mind from that scene, he went to stand by one of the five floor-to-ceiling windows that faced south, and stared out. He recalled the day Helene had stood in front of this very glass, her stomach rounded with their unborn daughter...

Oh, Gif, look at the backyard. Perfect for a pool and playset. Are you sure we can afford this?

She'd been so excited, so naive. When had she turned into a slut?

Not fair.

No, it wasn't fair. And it wasn't true. Unfortunately, he hadn't know that when it mattered.

Without warning, his mind conjured another image—this time, Cord McKay stood at the windows, dressed like James Dean, complete with a black leather jacket. All expression fled his rebellious face as he listened to Gifford's tirade about what he, an up-and-coming executive from a prominent Canfield family, could do to Cord's working-class parents if Cord didn't leave town immediately.

And that was only one of the mistakes Gifford had made that afternoon. He couldn't bear to think about the others.

Was God paying him back now—after years of success—by threatening his daughter? And by making it his fault that someone was after her? *No, please, not Stacey.* She was his whole life. She had been for eighteen years.

Too much so. Judith, the woman he was seeing, told him all the time.

The doorbell rang, dragging him from the vile memories.

Gifford strode through the library into the marble foyer and opened the door.

Two people who were almost as close to Stacey as he was stood before him. Lauren Sellers, a small, thin woman with a perennially sad face, was Stacey's best friend. And Preston Matthews, tall and powerfully built, Gifford's protégé at work and Stacey's fiancé.

"Is everything all right?" Lauren asked as soon as they were in the house.

Gifford motioned them into the library, closed the double oak doors and turned to face them. "Sit down," he said.

When they had, Lauren spoke again. "Your message sounded urgent."

Lauren and Stacey had been close since they'd both attended St. Mary's Elementary School, though Gifford often wondered why. They were opposites in looks, demeanor and personality. Sometimes Lauren's involvement in their family felt a bit suffocating. There was something odd about her attachment to them both. But Stacey adored her, so Gifford never said anything. He'd already deprived his daughter of enough.

Looking up at Gifford with her big violet eyes, Lauren once again made him uncomfortable. "Is something wrong with Stacey? I'm worried about her," she added.

"I feel the same way," Preston put in as he sat back on the mammoth leather recliner. "With the tire slashing, and all." He scanned the room with shrewd, hazel eyes. "Where is she, anyway?"

"She's upstairs," Gifford said. "I'll call her in a minute. Since you two are so close to her, I thought you'd be able to help me convince her of something."

"That sounds ominous." Preston stood and tilted his head to the drink Gifford had poured. "Mind if I get one of those?"

"Help yourself."

"Lauren, would you like something?" Preston asked.

"No."

"I take it you two haven't seen the evening paper?"

Lauren wrung her hands together. "The paper? Um, no."

As he fixed his drink, Preston said, "I haven't, either. I came right from the airport. My secretary phoned me in Atlanta to tell me to come here when I got back in town. Why?"

"Someone tried to abduct Stacey last night."

Lauren gasped.

"What?" Preston's glass hit the bar with a thud and he whirled to face Stacey's father.

Gifford handed him the newspaper from the table. Lauren stood and crossed to Preston to read over his shoulder.

"Oh, my God, this is terrible," Lauren said, tears in her eyes. "She could have been…" Her voice trailed off.

Preston shook his head. "I can't believe it. Kidnappings aren't supposed to happen in small towns like Canfield."

"A lot of bad things have happened here. Tragedy doesn't know the size of towns or the families involved. No one, no place is immune." Gifford's voice was rife with meaning.

Preston asked, "How is she taking this?"

"You know Stacey. She's been calm, and brave. Too brave."

"What do you mean?"

"I had some trouble getting her to agree to protection."

"That figures." Preston ran his hand through his styled black hair. "She's so damn self-sufficient."

Lauren's shoulders straightened. "That's a good trait. I wish I were more like her."

"Well, I'd like to feel morc needed," Preston retorted.

"That's really not the issue," Gifford said abruptly. Preston and Lauren always seemed to be arguing, almost as if they were vying for Stacey's attention. "The reason I wanted to see you first was because I want you to support me on this. Stacey's reluctantly agreed to cooperate, and I want you two to reinforce that she needs protection."

"Are the cops watching her? I saw a patrol car at the corner." Preston's aristocratic features were set in a scowl. "I didn't think they had the resources for this kind of thing."

Briefly, Gifford filled them in on what had occurred at the police station that morning, and told them about Cord McKay.

"The guy from the paper?" Preston asked.

"Yes."

Lauren stood and began pacing. "God, I hope this doesn't bring back her nightmares."

"Nightmares?" Preston frowned.

"Yes. I'm surprised she hasn't mentioned them to you," Lauren said. "You're her fiancé, after all."

The implicit criticism in her words caused Gifford to intervene, though he also wondered why Preston didn't know about these stress-induced dreams. He said to Preston, "Maybe she simply didn't want to worry you." He turned to Lauren, "Why don't you go get Stacey?"

Lauren's expression softened. "All right."

When she left, Preston faced him, scowling again. "I don't like Stacey being around strange men, Gif."

"Believe me, Preston, I feel more strongly about it than you do."

Gifford looked down at the newspaper that lay open on the desk. Staring up at him was an enlarged photo of Cord McKay holding young Timmy Malone. McKay had a crooked smile on his face and grasped the child to his chest. Superimposed over that picture, Gifford saw the cocky grin and swagger of an eighteen-year-old boy.

Cord McKay's image would always remind Gifford of his own worst failure, as a husband and as a man.

CHAPTER THREE

"DO YOU THINK we can get out of here for a while?"
Stacey asked.

Cord was watching the ten o'clock news and glanced
over at her standing at the den window. The last two
and a half days were obviously getting to her. "I guess.
What did you have in mind?"

She looked at him hopefully. "Are you hungry?"

"I'm always hungry."

"Really? How do you stay in such great shape?"

Groaning inside, Cord stood to disguise his reaction. The woman had no sense. She'd been saying exactly what came to her mind, never thinking to censor
her words. It should have been refreshing, given how
most of the women he'd known practiced their timing
from the cradle. It would have been, if it hadn't made
him so edgy. Geez, she'd even told him how attractive
he was...

*Lauren thinks you're as handsome as Kevin Cost-
ner, but I think you're a much better-looking bodyguard.*

He struggled for an impersonal tone. "I stay in
shape by working out."

"Can you, with your shoulder?"

"I'm supposed to exercise more now."

"I haven't seen you do any since you've been here."

"I've done it at night at home."

"Cord, you can use our gym downstairs."

"I'm through here Saturday, but thanks, anyway."

Stacey frowned and swallowed hard.

"You'll be just as safe with the Anderson man," he said, picking up her anxiety. "Maybe safer. I haven't done this kind of work in years."

Biting her lip, she nodded.

He changed the subject. "Where did you want to go?"

"How about Checkers? It's such a nice night, we can get our food and sit outside."

"Checkers is okay, but we'll sit in the car."

Stacey finger-combed the bangs off her forehead. "Can we at least open the windows?" A tinge of exasperation crept into her voice.

Covertly he smiled. This was hard for her, but after her initial protests, she'd been a real trouper, showing a maturity that surprised him. Grabbing his keys, he said, "I think I can handle that." He looked her up and down. "You want to change first?"

She glanced down at her one-piece purple biking suit. Its shiny material clung to every curve, and its scooped neck emphasized her breasts. "Why?"

"Ah, you might be cold."

"We're staying in the car, remember?"

"Well, at least grab a jacket." *And cover up some.*

He berated himself as they made their way to the truck. He didn't want to admit that he found her attractive. She was thirteen years younger than he was. She was innocent and he definitely was not.

She was Helene Webb's daughter.

Catching a glimpse of her in the dim light of the cab, he shook his head. She couldn't have looked less like her mother. Helene had been tall and willowy, with long blond hair and a carefully made-up face. Stacey was about five-three, with a womanly roundness that her mother had never had. Her short hair fell around her face in curls; it was thick and looked soft. She used no cosmetics, from what he could tell.

All right, so he found her attractive. That wasn't a crime. He wasn't going to do anything about it, so it wasn't even an issue. And after tomorrow, he'd never be with her again. It only took a little willpower to ignore the dull ache in his chest caused by that thought.

Ten minutes later, they sat in the front seat of his truck devouring hamburgers, french fries and milk shakes. Cord stared ahead of him, trying not to watch her. But she kept talking. ''Tell me about your daughter.''

''What do you want to know?''

''Anything. You get this goofy, soft look on your face every time she's mentioned. She must be quite a kid.''

''She is.''

''How old is she?'' Cord glanced over just in time to see Stacey's white teeth close over three french fries.

''Um... What did you say?''

''How old is Megan?''

Cord forced himself to look away. ''She's four.''

''What's she like?''

''She's a pistol. Keeps her grandmother and me both hoppin' ''

"Where's her mother?"

His eyes narrowed. "Aren't we getting a little personal?"

Stacey laughed. "McKay, we've been practically joined at the hip for almost three days, now. I think I'm entitled to know a little about you."

He grinned in spite of his resolve to remain aloof, and suppressed the uneasy feeling that everything he did to keep his emotional distance from her seemed to be in vain. "Did anyone ever tell you you're a sassy broad?"

"Not in those exact words."

"I'll bet."

"Megan's mother?" she reminded him.

"Is dead."

"Oh, I'm sorry. Were you married long?"

Her tongue darted out to catch some drops of the chocolate shake. Then she licked her lips and he couldn't tear his eyes away from them. "We weren't married at all." When he realized what had slipped out, he swore.

"What is it? I'm not a prude."

"No, it's not that. It's just that I've never told anyone that. For Megan's sake. Canfield's a small town and I don't want her branded."

"As illegitimate?"

"I've legally adopted her."

Stacey reached out and squeezed his arm. He liked the way her fingers gripped him tightly. "I promise, I won't say anything. What happened?"

Cord's gaze strayed through the windshield. "I met Colleen, Megan's mother, in New York City. She was a waitress at the bar where all the cops hang out. We dated a lot. One day she just stopped coming to work. Six months later, she showed up at the police station with Megan in tow. Said I had a daughter. That she was mine now. Colleen had developed breast cancer—too far gone to be treated, apparently. I never knew for sure because two days later they found her in her apartment with her wrists slit.''

When he looked over at her, tears had pooled in Stacey's eyes. ''Poor Megan. I know what it's like. My mother died when I was five.''

Guilt slammed into Cord. He fought it, just as he fought the urge to lean over and run his knuckles down her smooth cheek.

''How did you ever cope with an infant?'' she asked.

A self-effacing grin tugged at his mouth and he relaxed back into the seat. ''I barely survived it. She was so tiny... so foreign. I was petrified. She cried nonstop for the first few nights. Thank God the Hermans intervened.''

''Who?''

''An older couple who had an apartment in the same brownstone in Brooklyn where I lived. The guy was my mentor on the New York City police force. He changed my life when I was twenty. His wife was a surrogate mother to me, and then when I got Megan, a surrogate grandmother. She took care of the baby while I was at work, but also taught me how to change diapers and fix formula.'' Cord shook his head. ''Sometimes, I don't know how we made it through those first few months.''

"Why did you come back to Canfield?"

Cord was surprised the hollow feeling inside him could still be triggered so easily. "Glen Herman was killed by a stray bullet in Grand Central Station one night on a routine arrest. Sarah Herman went to live with her daughter in Baltimore. Megan was six months old and I decided New York City was no place to raise a kid."

"So you came home?"

"Yeah. My father was dead, so I . . ." He looked at her and blinked. "Never mind. Anyway, Megan's the best thing that ever happened to me. Even though I did initially question if she was mine."

"Did?"

"Yeah. But my name's on the birth certificate. And you've never seen Megan, right?"

Stacey shook her head.

"She looks like me—exactly. And our baby pictures, except for the gender, are identical. Besides, I know in my gut she's my kid."

Stacey smiled wistfully. "I'm close to my dad, too. That's why this is so hard for him. And for Preston and Lauren."

Cord angled his body so he could look at her better. "Tell me about them."

"Which one?"

"Either of them."

Her eyes drifted to Cord's polo shirt, open at the throat, and her lips parted. Her breath speeded up a bit. "Ah, Preston. I'll tell you about Preston."

It was the first time Cord realized that the attraction wasn't one-sided. He cringed at the knowledge.

"Good idea. Let's talk about your fiancé. What the hell kind of name is Preston, anyway?"

"It's a family name. I like it. Just because it's not some tough-guy name like..."

He raised his eyebrows. "I'll have you know, I have a very religious name."

"Cord is religious?"

"No. My real name is Francis Xavier McKay."

"Oh my God."

"Yeah, I was glad I had a nickname."

"Where did it come from?"

He half smiled in remembrance. "Know what a whipcord is?"

"A tough, thin rope?"

"Yeah. When I was a kid, I was pretty hard to handle. My fath...someone called me a whipcord once and the name stuck. Even in high school."

"Let me guess. You were incorrigible."

"I was a hellion. I gave every single teacher I had trouble. Even the principal turned the other way when he saw me coming."

"Somehow, that doesn't surprise me."

He grasped her arm. "Be respectful of your elders, young lady."

"Oh, yeah, right."

He smiled. "Where did you get the name Stacey?"

She faked a yawn and said, "I'm a little tired. Maybe we should go home."

"No way, sweetheart." He held on to her arm, then slid his fingers to her wrist. "Confess."

"I'm named after my grandmother." She giggled. "Her name was Anastasia Keller Webb."

"Anastasia?" Cord hooted.

"I know, isn't it awful?"

"Actually, it's kind of pretty. Okay, back to Preston the Third. He works at Canfield Glass Works?"

Stacey stared at his hand around her wrist. His callused thumb was unconsciously fingering her pulse point. He ceased the motion immediately and let her go.

"Uh-huh," she said after a moment. "He's vice president of finance. I used to work for him. And he works for Daddy."

"Somehow, you don't look like an accountant, even though you seemed pretty proficient at work the last two days."

"Oh, what do I look like?"

He remembered her pictures taped to a refrigerator door long ago. "An artist."

Stacey frowned. "How could you know that?"

"Know what?"

"I started out at the Chicago Art Institute."

"How did you end up in business?"

"After a semester, I found out—" She stopped herself, then went on, "I decided the art world was too Bohemian for me. I transferred to the University of Chicago, got my CPA and went to work for CGW when I was twenty-one."

Cord shifted in his seat, uncomfortable with their easy sharing, their natural camaraderie. It was almost more dangerous than the physical attraction. "Well, as long as you're happy."

For a moment, something like indecision—or dissatisfaction—flickered across her face, then the look vanished. "Of course I'm happy. Except for all this stuff going on now."

A good out. "Speaking of which, we should get back." *And get the hell out of this truck that suddenly feels a little too cozy.*

"Okay, if you want."

The patrol car was at the house when they returned. "Well, looks like Ferron's here," Cord said when they pulled into the driveway.

She said nothing.

"Don't you like him?"

"No, it's not that. It's just that I don't feel as safe with him as I do with you."

A clutch of guilt got him in the gut. "Stacey, I need to be home for Megan when she wakes up."

"I know. I don't mean to complain. I hate the thought that I take you away from your daughter as much as I do. I really appreciate the time you *can* give me." Her smile was simultaneously so genuine and so seductive that it made Cord catch his breath. She leaned over and gave him a quick kiss on the cheek which just about stopped his air intake. "Thanks."

Opening the door, she climbed from the truck, just as Ferron exited his car.

Before she was out of earshot, Cord rolled down the window. Into the semidarkness, he called, "Good night, Anastasia."

She grinned back at him over her shoulder. "Good night, Francis."

A BRIGHTLY COLORED clown smiled at Megan and tweaked her nose, sending her scampering into Cord's arms. He scooped her up, cuddled her into his lap and nuzzled the long flaxen hair that he'd done in two braids. He savored its baby scent and thickness. "Are you enjoying your school's family fair, honey?"

"Uh-huh," Megan mumbled around the two fingers jammed in her mouth. "I wanna make a colored bottle."

"Sure. Lead the way."

As he put her down, his daughter stood and adjusted the straps of her red romper. Combined with her purple shirt and yellow sneakers, she was a sight. Even at four, Megan had decidedly unique tastes in clothes; she refused to wear anything sedate and insisted on picking out all her own outfits. Cord had learned that trying to dissuade her was a waste of time; besides, he wanted to show her he approved of her just the way she was. Not like his father, who'd always tried to change him.

"Hi, Cord," one of the preschool aides said at the bottle booth.

"Hi, Cindy." Benefit of a small town. Everyone knew everybody else.

"I read about you in the paper. You were great, again."

Cord smiled weakly, then glanced at Megan. "Thanks, but I don't think this is the place..."

Cindy Lasoto nodded. "Oh, sure. Megan's doin' fine at Time to Grow Preschool. She's the friendliest child here and seems so well adjusted."

At great cost. Although Cord never discussed it with anyone, leaving New York City to move back to a small town had been horrendous. The pace was slow, the work routine and unexciting—a tough change for a Big Apple cop. Then, when he'd gotten hurt and couldn't work at all... "Yeah, Megan loves preschool."

"You know, you're the only father who brings his child and picks her up. All the mothers talk about it."

"Fathers should take more interest in their children." His tone was cold, and he tried to lighten it. Nathan McKay's shortcomings were not Cindy's fault. "They miss out."

Turning his attention to the bottles, Cord fought the bitterness that welled inside him. To do it, his mind flicked to Stacey. Ironic that *her* father had time for her now. Eighteen years ago Gifford Webb hadn't been there for either his daughter or his young wife.

Not my business, he told himself. *Stop thinking about it.*

He could do that a lot easier than he could stop thinking about Stacey herself. Despite his resolve, he wondered if she'd left work yet. He glanced at the clock. Six-ten. Quickly, he reviewed her schedule in his head. She had a date with Matthews at eight, so she'd probably be on her way home now.

As he opened a jar of bright pink paint, he thought about the upcoming evening. Ferron was relieving Cord from five to eight tonight so Cord could attend the preschool fair with Megan, but Cord would be the one around for the date. At least until midnight.

That hadn't happened yet—Stacey dating and in need of a bodyguard, as Matthews had been out of town for two days. But Cord could handle it. This kind of situation was awkward sometimes, but he'd done it before. Mostly, he didn't care what two people did behind closed doors.

Yet he had to admit the image of Preston Matthews holding Stacey, touching her curves, shook him.

None of my business, he reiterated silently.

"Daddy, I want some cookies now." As she grasped his hand in hers, Cord teased Megan about her sweet tooth. They went over to the cookie booth where he let her have more treats than would have been allowed by Nora McKay, who was working at one of the booths. Cord and Megan made their way to a picnic table set up in the small gym. His daughter plopped down next to her friend Susie. As the girls invented a story, using the cookies as characters, Cord checked the clock again. Maybe he should call to see that Stacey had arrived home all right. No, that was stupid. Ferron was more than capable of guarding her for a few hours, even though Stacey didn't think so. It was typical in these cases for the victim to get attached to one person. Since Cord had saved her from abduction, she seemed to have more confidence in his ability.

Don't lie to yourself, McKay. She's attracted to you.

Well, that was typical, too. The movies were right, romance often developed between a bodyguard and his charge. They were also right in that it could be fatal—you got distracted, your timing was off, you got careless.

Restless, he stood and looked down at Megan. "Want more juice, honey?"

"Yes, Daddy. Susie does, too."

"Be right back."

On his way to the juice counter, he passed the phone. He shouldn't call her, he knew it. But he felt uneasy about something tonight, and a good body-guard never ignored his hunches. Before he could change his mind, he whipped out some coins and di-aled the Webb house, keeping an eye trained on Me-gan. He took a quick glimpse at his watch. Six-thirty. No answer. She could still be on her way home, he thought as he dialed her office just to make sure. No answer there, either. Damn, he should have insisted on a cellular phone for her car. He'd make sure the An-derson guy got one for her.

The Anderson guy was coming tomorrow to relieve Cord of his duty. He was thankful that he had only a few hours left of this job.

He *was* thankful.

It was best for all of them if Stacey had someone guarding her who didn't have any connection to the Webb family. Who didn't have to constantly fight his attraction to her sassy mouth, her curves and her quick wit.

Yeah, he thought as he returned to his daughter with two glasses of apple juice. It was best that he get out of Stacey Webb's life as fast as possible and return his own to normal.

STACEY GLANCED at the clock in her office for the third time in ten minutes. Six twenty-five. Where the hell was Ferron? She was meeting Lauren at seven and it would take at least fifteen minutes to negotiate the winding curves that led up to Canfield Community College where her friend worked as a secretary. Ordinarily, Stacey would have just called and canceled, but Lauren had telephoned at four o'clock and sounded really upset. Stacey knew it was man trouble, and not for the first time. Her boyfriend, Mark Dunn, treated Lauren like dirt, and Stacey lectured her constantly about it. But it was the old syndrome. Lauren had grown up with an alcoholic father, a weak mother, and now she was repeating the pattern. It happened all the time.

Except to Stacey. *She* certainly wasn't repeating any parental patterns. She was totally unlike Helene. *Thank God.*

No, Stacey believed in loyalty and being there for people. Which was why she'd agreed to meet Lauren. But at six o'clock, Ferron had gotten an unexpected call from the police station and had been summoned to the scene of a bad accident. He'd told Stacey to stay put until he returned.

Don't go, Stacey. Cord will kill you if you do.

She smiled at the thought of her reluctant bodyguard. He'd be furious if she left work unescorted. His temper would flare, as it often did, without much provocation. His blue eyes would blaze like the flame of a gas stove. All his upper body muscles would tense. She wondered briefly what it would be like to have that intensity focused on her for a different reason.

When she realized the direction her mind had taken, she stood abruptly and stomped over to the couch. With a thump she sat down and chided herself. She was engaged to Preston, and she had no right to erotic thoughts of Cord McKay. What's more, they appalled her.

You are not like your mother, Stacey. You're not like Helene.

She'd spent a lifetime proving it, too long to let burning blue eyes and a daredevil smile change that.

Stacey rose from the couch, claustrophobic with thoughts of Cord. To escape them, she made a decision which she knew was foolish, even as she switched off the lights, grabbed her jacket and left her office at Canfield Glass Works.

Unescorted.

Not hesitating, she walked down the newly carpeted hallway, noting that most of the building was dark. Here and there a light indicated some other employees were also putting in long hours. At the elevator, she pressed the button. Humming, she waited.

And waited.

Nothing happened. Checking her watch, she saw again that she was running late. Damn. What was going on? These elevators never malfunctioned. Her department was on the fifth floor of the glass tower that held CGW's corporate headquarters. Without a second thought, she strode to the stairway and was halfway down the first flight when she realized that it was dark, very dark, and very isolated. She clutched the iron railing, seeing that she'd placed herself in a situation she always avoided—dark, closed-in spaces. Her father had even installed two skylights in her bedroom because of her fear. She let go of the handrail and took the stairs faster, the clap of her pumps echoing up several flights. As she rounded each landing, she noticed the pipes jutting out of the walls, and smelled a faint musty odor hovering in the air. Quickening her pace even more, she flew down the rest of the steps.

She was breathless by the time she reached the bottom, and not from exertion. Reaching for the bar of the iron door that opened onto the ground floor, she was startled when it wouldn't budge. Her heart hammered in her chest at the thought of being trapped in this sinister stairwell. With her whole body as leverage, she pushed.

The door swung open, and Stacey practically toppled into the reception area.

Get a grip, she told herself firmly. Trapped! Sinister! She was being stupid.

Shoring up her confidence, she walked to the front door with as much poise as she could muster, bade the security guard good-night and crossed to her Miata, which was parked in the front, well-lit row, within sight of the security man. Cord had insisted she have this spot for safety.

Cloaking herself with bravado, she swung into the low car, started the engine and pulled out just as it started to drizzle.

"Oh, great, now I get the eerie atmosphere... 'It was a dark and stormy night...'"

Cord would yell at her for being flippant. Sexy, attractive Cord with the small scar to the left of his mouth...a mouth that would be demanding but... *Stop it, Stacey.* She decided to concentrate on her driving.

After work on a Friday night, even Canfield was hopping. She maneuvered through the town traffic, and managed to reach College Hill in minutes. Checking her watch, she hoped Lauren had waited.

The gloom was like a shroud. And the fog had begun to creep in. When the windows clouded, Stacey shivered, and flipped on the defroster. The gentle back-and-forth motion of the windshield wipers soothed her a bit, and she thought about turning on the radio. No, best to stay alert. All her senses were heightened and she didn't want to lose that awareness.

Watching the road carefully, she glimpsed the trees swaying ominously in the wind that had picked up. "Oh, sure, and any minute, they're going to talk... 'Lions and tigers and bears, oh my.'" At least she could still laugh at herself.

The grin faded when she saw the headlights behind her. It was only dusk, and even with the misty rain, it was too light outside for the bright beams the driver had on. Great! All she needed was some jerk behind her. The dark car came closer. She placed her foot on the brake. Maybe he'd pass her, though it wasn't the ideal road for it.

He didn't. Now he was tailing her closer.

The hair on the back of her neck bristled. All the muscles in her throat clenched and she gripped the steering wheel.

In a split second, she felt the first bump against her back fender. Oddly, it reminded her of being at Rose Land and driving the bumper cars as a kid. But this was no amusement-park ride, and it was surely no game. When the second thump came, she realized the driver meant business.

Stifling panic, she held on to the steering wheel, and let her foot off the accelerator slowly.

Bump. Bump.

Her little Miata swerved with the force of the car that was at least twice its size. Why hadn't she listened to her father and bought a bigger, safer car?

Because you didn't know some lunatic was going to try to run you off the worst road in Canfield.

Please, God, get me out of this. I promise I'll get a bigger car, I'll listen to what everyone tells me, I won't be so headstrong...

Another, harder thump.

That one did it. The sports car veered to the right and headed for the shoulder of the road. A line of old maple trees was directly in its path. She knew she was going to hit them. And maybe die.

Oh, God, no. She'd die before she got that promotion she wanted. Before she saw Paris again. Before she ever made love.

With a brief flash of insight, she pumped the brakes. The car spun right, toward the trees, but Stacey turned the wheel just enough to sideswipe them. She heard a crunch and the engine died. Her head pitched forward onto the steering wheel, even though she wore her seat belt. Pain sliced through her on impact. When she rebounded, she looked up to see the dark sedan whiz past her.

Inhaling deeply, she thanked God the man hadn't stopped. When she looked in the rearview mirror, she saw why. Another car whipped to the side of the road and came to a jarring halt behind her.

Leaving the lights on, a big, muscled figure stalked over to her car. Dazed, she held her breath, frozen by the thought that the driver of the dark sedan had an accomplice.

Suddenly, her car door flew open. The man dropped onto one knee, and Stacey stared into the face of Cord McKay. "Stacey, are you all right?" His voice was gravelly.

Eyes glazed, she nodded.

He reached in and touched the bump on her head. She flinched. "The bastard." His hand rested on her shoulder, then flicked open her seat belt. "Can you get out?"

She nodded again. Easing out of the car, she drew herself up, her hand braced on the door. She was trembling, and didn't even try to control it.

Stacey couldn't have said who reacted first. She didn't know whether she threw herself at him, or whether he stepped toward her. But suddenly she was engulfed in his arms. They banded around her and held her so tightly it robbed her of breath. Neither spoke; Stacey buried her face in the hollow of his neck—he'd lifted her in the embrace—and his mouth was in her hair. Closing her eyes, she savored the feel of him, inhaled his unique male scent.

"I was so scared," she murmured into his skin.

His grip tightened. "I know."

Stacey didn't let go immediately. After a few seconds of his wordless comfort, she drew back, though she kept her hands on his arms and his remained on her waist. She could feel them flex on her a few times. His face was drawn, the skin stretched tightly across his cheekbones, his jaw clenched. This man was controlling his anger, she reflected. At what had happened? At her?

"I shouldn't have left without Ferron," she confessed, her voice raspy and laced with fear.

His hands tightened at her waist. "No, you shouldn't have." Though the words were clipped, they, too, were uttered hoarsely, and gentled by his obvious concern for her. He lifted one hand and smoothed his knuckles down her cheek. His palm caressed her chin and she leaned into it. "Are you sure you're all right?"

It wasn't fear that trip-hammered through her heart. It was a strong surge of emotion for this man, and though her reaction horrified her, she couldn't make herself step away. Nor did she trust herself to speak, so in answer to his question, she nodded.

He stared at her for a long, meaningful moment, then pulled her into his arms again. "Oh, God, Stacey, when I saw that car..."

His emotional declaration undid her. Unashamedly, she held on to him as the tears came.

Tenderly he smoothed his hand down her hair. "Shh, baby, you're safe now."

She shook her head.

"Yes, you're safe now."

She shook her head again.

Easing back, he tilted her chin. "Tell me."

It came out against her will. As she hiccuped, she said, "I'm only safe when you're with me."

He started to protest, but she interrupted.

"No one else can protect me like you. You would never have left me at the office. I'm only a part-time job for Ferron. You'd have been there when I needed to get to Lauren. I'm sorry, Cord," she said, hating herself for her weakness, for the tears that streamed down her cheeks. "But I wish you didn't have to leave tomorrow. I know you need to, for Megan, but I'm afraid." Then she burrowed into his chest once more and he clasped her to him. "I'm afraid when I'm not with you."

CHAPTER FOUR

THE BLUE CHEVY TOOK a quick turn down one of the side roads off College Hill and came to a rumbling halt beside several trees. Safe, the driver switched off the engine and slammed his gloved hand against the steering wheel.

"Bitch!" the man raged into the empty car. The epithet echoed around him and he gave it the company of more pungent, more appropriate four-letter words. She'd escaped him again. That bastard bodyguard had saved her *again*. Where in hell had McKay come from?

As with the other three times, he'd planned it so well. First he'd slashed her tires, hoping to grab her when she left work, alone, late at night. He hadn't counted on the imbecile security guard helping her out. When he'd tailed her later that week, she met her father at a restaurant before he could snatch her. Ultimately, he couldn't keep himself from making the phone calls that had been meant to scare her. Well-deserved punishment for eluding him.

But Monday night was the last straw. He'd had her creamy white skin in his hands, dammit. He could still feel her soft flesh, her warm breath, her heart beating fast with fear. He'd *had* her and that son-of-a-bitch

hero had ruined all his well-laid plans. It was embar-
rassing. He felt like a bumbling fool. They were probably laughing at him right now.

Yanking open the door, he stomped out into the
drizzle and spat on the ground. Then he raised his face
to the darkening sky and let the rain soak him.

Now they'd both pay. It wasn't just for the money
anymore. After tonight, the person who had hired him
was out of the picture. Things had changed. He was
after Stacey Webb for a different reason.

He wanted revenge.

She'd pay for the trouble she'd given him. She'd do
her penance. He'd see to it. Leaning over, he slipped
his hand into his boot and fingered the blade hidden
there.

It made him feel better just touching it.

He'd enjoy using it to teach Miss High-and-Mighty
a thing or two.

CORD LOOKED AROUND the Webbs' library at the four
people comforting Stacey and her father. An ugly
thought was beginning to take hold. Everyone here
had revealed, in the course of Stacey's telling them the
story, that they'd known she'd be on College Hill tonight. And her relationships with at least three of them
seemed odd. Preston Matthews was protective of her
in what seemed a contrived way, as if he was only
playing the hero. Lauren Sellers was far too solicitous
of Stacey's well-being for it to be normal. Joe Ferron
seemed to almost idolize her. And Cord didn't know
much about Judith Johnson, Gifford's date for the

evening, and much more, if rumor around Canfield was true.

Settled into the crook of Gifford's arm, Stacey finished recounting how she'd been run off the road, how terrified she'd been and how Cord had rescued her again. As she told them about the stop they'd made at the police station to report the incident, she shivered many times and her words came out in halting phrases. Each one pierced the armor Cord was trying to maintain against her.

"What the hell were you thinking, Stacey?" Gifford asked, his voice harsh and driven by fear.

"Gif." Judith Johnson touched his arm soothingly. "I don't think Stacey needs to be reprimanded right now."

Her father hugged Stacey tighter and kissed her dark hair. It looked almost black now, still wet from the rain they'd stood in, while she'd valiantly tried *not* to beg him to stay as her bodyguard.

"You're right, Judith. But you were wrong about giving her some space. She took off for the college without an escort."

"I know," the older woman admitted calmly. "I was wrong." Cord watched her fold her hands, adorned with two thick, gold rings. They matched the gold at her wrists, neck and ears, and complemented her suit, the kind Cord had seen in the window of Lord and Taylor in New York. He made a mental note to find out how a high school history teacher could afford such expensive trappings.

"It...it's my fault," Lauren said from the other side of the room. She shrank back into a wing chair that dwarfed her, blending into the background, as always. "I asked Stacey to meet me, but I thought Joe would be with her." Watery eyes focused on Stacey's father. "I'm sorry, Gifford."

Gifford, not Stacey.

Joe Ferron stood. A former high school football star, he was about Cord's size, muscular and fit. Cord knew he worked out at Samson's Gym every day. "Aw, geez, Lauren, it's really my fault." He turned to Cord. "I...know I was supposed to stay with her, but I got this call from the department to report to the intersection of Routes 17 and 454. Only thing is, when I got there, there was no accident."

A pretend call? Or had someone been trying to get the cop out of the way? Cord wondered.

"Why didn't you go back to Stacey's office?" Gifford asked Ferron.

"I did, after I checked in at the station. When they told me nobody had called me from there about an accident, I high-tailed it back to the office, but she was gone."

Preston Matthews rose from the sofa, his face pinched with anger. "You're an idiot, Ferron. Stacey's safety is top priority. You should have called the station to check before you left her alone." Then he turned to Cord, his shrewd eyes blazing. "Which leads us to you, McKay. You're supposed to be such a hotshot. Where the hell were you when this was happening?"

Cord was tempted to knock out several of Matthews's perfect white teeth. Instead, he forced back the urge, leaned against the wall and crossed his arms over his chest.

Pulling out of Gifford's embrace, Stacey jumped up. "Preston, stop it! Cord made it very clear he couldn't be with me all the time. He was off duty. It wasn't his fault."

Matthews's gaze seared Cord for a minute. Then he crossed to Stacey and grasped her arms. As Cord watched Preston smooth back Stacey's hair, he gritted his teeth so hard they hurt. The man's other hand sneaked to her side and hovered just underneath her full breast. "I'm sorry, love, but I'm so worried about you."

Yeah, so worried you went out of town for two days.

Not your business, McKay. That rock on her third finger gives him the right to her.

"How did you happen to be on College Hill, McKay?" Gifford asked, breaking Cord's focus on Matthews.

"I had a hunch something was wrong."

"A hunch?" Matthews raised an eyebrow at Cord.

"Yeah, you know, one of those things where you have a bad feeling about something," he said sarcastically.

Easy, McKay. If he'd only take his hands off her. Turning away from the sight of Stacey wrapped in another man's arms, Cord finished, "I was at an end-of-the-year function with my daughter at her preschool. I called Stacey from the school. When I got no answer, I tried here and then Lauren's house. Finally, I reached Lauren at work and she told me she was meeting Stacey at the college."

"How'd you get to her so quick?" Ferron asked.

"Luckily, my mother was at the preschool, too. She took over with Megan, so I left right away."

"With not a minute to spare." Matthews didn't try to disguise his reproachful tone.

Drawing away from him, Stacey said, "Preston, he saved my life tonight. Stop criticizing him."

"I'm your fiancé, Stacey, and I'm concerned about your welfare. I have a right to be critical."

"This isn't helping," Gifford said as he stood. He turned to Cord. "Where do we go from here?"

Carefully avoiding Stacey's eyes, Cord replied, "The Anderson man will be here tomorrow to take over. I'll spend the night on the couch just in case, but you'll all feel better once you have a security expert here."

"I know *I* will," Preston said, sliding his hands into his thousand-dollar suit pockets.

Stacey looked longingly at Cord but bit her lip.

To keep from begging you to stay. To let you go to Megan.

"Stacey, are you all right?" Gifford asked.

"Yes, Daddy, I'm just scared."

Gifford watched her for a minute, then his gaze went to Cord. "Maybe this Anderson thing isn't the right choice. Maybe McKay should stay as your bodyguard."

"I don't think that's such a good idea, Gif," Matthews said.

Gifford faced Matthews abruptly. "This is Stacey's life we're talking about, Preston. She needs the best."

Then he turned to Cord. "Listen, McKay, if it's more money—"

Slowly stepping away from the window, Cord hoped his voice was more controlled than he felt. "It has nothing to do with money." Involuntarily, his eyes scanned Stacey's rumpled yellow linen suit, mud-caked shoes and tear-stained face.

"It's because of his daughter, Daddy," Stacey said, her voice strained. "We can't take him away from her. I only wish there was some way he could do both."

"Maybe you could make arrangements for Cord to spend time with Megan," Lauren suggested. "Occasionally. Frequently."

Gifford followed up with "I understand how you feel about your daughter, McKay. But try to understand how I feel about mine..."

Again, Cord felt the guilt ripple through him. He owed this family.

The jangle of the phone made everyone jump. Gifford plucked the receiver from the antique telephone on the desk, spoke into it, then handed it to Cord. "It's Tom Anderson."

Another hunch hit Cord in the gut. He knew he didn't want to take this call. "Yeah, Tom. McKay here."

"I have some bad news," his friend said, not wasting words. "The operative that was supposed to be in Canfield tomorrow got hurt stepping off the plane in New York. Broke his foot. Ironic, huh? He faced down terrorists for three months without a scratch."

"Then send somebody else."

"There's a lot going on in New York this month," Anderson told him. "The only guy I have is a twenty-two-year-old rookie."

"Pull a man off another case."

"You know I can't do that." Tom sighed audibly. "Look, McKay, you're better than any guy I have and you're free. Why don't you just take the case?"

Cord wondered what Tom would do if he told him outright that he couldn't take the case because every time he looked at the client, he got hard. And he couldn't do anything about it because he'd slept with her mother eighteen years ago, and really messed up everybody's life.

Which was why he had to help them now, he concluded.

Tom would probably tell him how *ironic* it was.

Ironic, hell, Cord thought as he replaced the receiver none too gently and faced a wide-eyed Stacey and a stone-faced Webb.

It was just plain unfair.

STACEY KEPT TAKING deep breaths—she hoped discreetly. It was the only way she could calm herself after the terrifying incident on the road, though she had to admit she felt a lot better now that Cord had agreed to stay as her bodyguard. That he was going to be sleeping in the sitting room that connected to her bedroom also helped.

"Nice place," he said, scanning the interior of the suite she'd occupied since returning from college three years ago. "Was it always like this?"

"Like what?"

"Did you grow up with it like this—your bedroom, a bathroom and a living room?"

"No. When I came back from college, we converted this wing into an apartment with a separate entrance. It's very private, since Daddy's room is at the other end of the house." She looked around sadly. "Originally, the bathroom connected two bedrooms. It was supposed to be for a brother or sister, but of course I never had one."

Cord's blue eyes were so bleak she wanted to hold him. It didn't help her state of mind to admit that she'd wanted to touch him ever since they'd returned from College Hill.

"You never had any siblings, either, did you?" she asked.

"No, one child was all Nathan McKay could handle. And he didn't do a very good job of that."

His uncontrolled bitterness shocked Stacey. "Everyone says your father was a fantastic policeman."

"He was." Cord's face shuttered. "Look, let's check out these rooms, okay?"

"What do you mean?"

"I want to secure the doors and windows, that kind of thing."

"But didn't you do that three days ago when you inspected the house?"

"Yeah, but I want to be sure." Watching her, the harsh lines of his mouth softened. "Sit down. A stiff wind could blow you over right now."

Obediently, Stacey sank into a comfortable armchair.

He disappeared into the bathroom, and then presumably into her bedroom. She could hear him rattling window locks and doorknobs. Stacey laid her head against the chair back and curled her legs under her.

"You must be exhausted," Cord said.

She nodded. "I am."

"I'll finish fast." He went to the far right-hand corner, where a door opened to the outside. A long flight of stairs led to the backyard. "I don't like this."

"You don't like private entrances?"

"Not when you're being stalked."

Stacey felt herself blanch.

"I shouldn't have said that," he told her. "I'm not very tactful, I guess." He stared at her until she wanted to squirm under his keen scrutiny. "You've had about all you can take, haven't you?"

Again Stacey nodded, too tired to talk.

Turning back to the door, he yanked several times on the handle. "I want this permanently locked. No one is to go in or out. We can't risk it being accidentally left open." When she grimaced, he said, "Sorry. If Matthews usually uses this door, he'll have to come in the front way."

"You don't like Preston much, do you?"

"The feeling's mutual, I think."

Stacey couldn't argue. When she'd walked her fiancé to the door earlier, Preston had been tense...

"I don't like McKay being around you this much, Stacey," he'd said.

"What do you suggest I do, Preston? I need his protection. I was run off the road tonight. I'm scared."

He'd reached out and pulled her into his arms. Although they were sheltered from view, she'd felt self-conscious, and didn't want to be held.

"I don't like him, Stacey," Preston had said, tossing his head toward the library, where Cord and her father sat talking. "He's too rough."

Stacey had remembered the tender way Cord had wiped her face with his handkerchief, how he'd held her hand all the way home...

"Stacey? Where'd you go?" Cord asked.

"I was thinking about the drive home tonight."

Not responding to her comment, he took one last look around. "I think things are okay for now, but tomorrow I'm going to have a lock put on the two doors that lead from the main house to this suite."

"All right."

Slowly, he came across the room and stood above her. He'd pushed his now-dry hair back with his fingers so it was off his face. The style emphasized the angularity of his jaw and his high cheekbones.

"I'm sorry you ruined your clothes," she said, pointing to the mud-spattered navy-and-white-striped shirt and tan Dockers he'd worn to the family fair at his daughter's preschool. "Do you want to borrow some of my father's clothes?"

Cord looked as though she'd asked him to put on a dress. "No, thanks. I had a gym bag in the truck, and pulled it out when I locked up. I have what I need tonight in there. Tomorrow, we'll get the rest of my stuff."

She frowned. "I'm sorry for taking you away from Megan. It's a horrible thing to do to both of you. Maybe this isn't the answer..."

"Let's not talk about any of this tonight," he said. "There'll be a lot to say tomorrow. You're whipped." When he reached out his hand, she took it and he tugged her up. "Go on, get changed and into bed."

Tilting her head toward the green-striped couch, she said, "That pulls out to a bed. Lauren stays over a lot and says its really comfortable."

"I'll be fine. Go to bed."

Despite his order, he didn't let go of her hand. She squeezed it, then let go, missing the feel of his callused fingertips. "All right." Tears welled, but she willed them back. God, she'd never been the weepy type. That was Lauren's style. Her voice husky, she said, "See you tomorrow. Thanks again."

Slowly, he lifted his hand to graze her cheek. In contrast to his fingertips, his knuckles were smooth and soothing. Stacey couldn't decide which she liked better on her skin. She smiled, crossed to the bathroom, then went into her own room.

HOURS LATER, from the depths of his sleep, Cord heard a noise. He roused, ready to check on Megan. But his elbow jabbed the arm of a couch and he came instantly awake. He wasn't home and the sounds hadn't come from his daughter's room. Megan was safe with Nora McKay at Cord's house. He was staying at the Webbs'.

Moans, and desperately spoken words, were coming from Stacey's bedroom. Bounding off the pulled-out sofa, he raced through the bathroom, swearing when he hit his hip on the edge of the vanity. Slowing down only minimally, he crossed the doorway and was at her bed in seconds. Her arms were flailing, her legs trying to kick their way out of the sheets. He bent his knee and braced one hand on the mattress, then shook her shoulder. "Stacey, wake up, it's me, Cord."

"No, no, no...please, Mommy, please don't leave me." Her words were wrenched from her, and for a minute Cord thought he was eighteen again, on the outskirts of the cemetery, listening to a five-year-old child's crying at her mother's burial.

"Stacey, wake up." Still no response. Just the thrashing of arms and legs. He leaned over and subdued both arms. "Stacey, sweetheart, you're okay."

Instead of releasing her, Cord covered her and pinned her body with his. Because of his weight, she was forced to still her motions, though she was strong and keeping her down strained his shoulder. In minutes, his full body contact seemed to calm her. Eyes closed, her mouth opened slightly, she gasped for breath. Her chest heaved and the bright pink nightshirt she'd worn to bed was soaked from exertion. Sweat dampened her hair. He stayed on top of her until her breathing evened out. When he eased back, her body jerked and she whimpered. At a loss, Cord lay down and pulled her close. Sound asleep, she plastered herself to him from her head to her waist, still kicking at the imprisoning sheets. He moved the lower part of his body nearer hers. Her arms went around his waist and she nuzzled into his chest. The sweet scent of talcum assaulted him. He could feel her breath on his bare skin and he felt his nipples bead. When her mouth accidentally brushed one, his erection surged against the soft cotton of his sweatpants.

He swore softly, but Stacey had settled in and was finally quiet. Quietly repeating every curse he knew, he lay still as long as he could. Then he tried to pull away—and got the same jerky reaction. Two more times, with the same ending. At which point, he resigned himself to a sleepless night. But he found her nearness a comfort as well as a stimulation and sank into sleep before he could worry more about the circumstances.

CORD AWOKE and glanced at the red numbers on the bedside clock. Six-eleven. Stacey was still wrapped around him like a pretzel. She felt soft and warm from sleep. But she was beginning to rouse, too.

"Cord?" Her whole body stiffened but she didn't look at him.

"Shh, it's okay," he said, stroking her hair. It felt like heavy corn silk and smelled like lemon. "You had a bad dream."

She stiffened even more.

"I swear, I'm not putting the moves on you. You—"

"It's not that." Her voice was early-morning husky. After-sex hoarse.

"What?"

Stacey looked up at him then, her expression a curious mixture of trust and seduction. If it weren't for his past, he would have kissed her. But he knew that would be another step on the path to damnation, though the devil probably had rights over his soul by now, anyway.

"The nightmares are back," she whispered.

"Back? You've had these before?"

She nodded.

"When did they start?"

Again she went board-stiff. Her warm brown eyes narrowed. "When Helene left. I was five."

Cord had to consciously control his breathing. "Helene?"

"My mother." The phrase *choking on your words* came to his mind as she made the identification.

Like a person with a sore tooth, he couldn't stop himself from probing the injured area. "Why do you call her that?"

"What?"

"Helene."

Stacey's face went blank. "I don't know. I always have."

Not always.

Cord shook his head, wondering if he'd lost his mind to be questioning her like this. "Tell me about the nightmares."

"The psychologists Daddy hired said they were induced by abandonment. My five-year-old psyche couldn't cope with losing someone so important in my life. Though I don't remember being close to her. Actually, I don't remember her much at all. Thank God."

He wanted to object to the statement. Apparently, he knew more about her mother—and her relationship with Helene—than Stacey did herself. But, of course, he said nothing about that and only murmured, "I'm sorry."

"Don't be. I had a wonderful childhood and adolescence. Daddy was the only parent I needed."

"Have you had the nightmares all along?"

"No, they stopped after I got used to Helene's absence. They started again when I was ten and Daddy had a skiing accident. A textbook case of fear of losing him."

"Those were the last ones?"

She shook her head, her hand sifting through his chest hair. "Nope. Lauren got pneumonia when we were seventeen and almost died. They came back for a while then, too."

Absently, Stacey moved closer. He inched back, trying to hide his throbbing state of arousal.

Stacey talked on, thankfully unaware of his reaction. "They stopped when Lauren got better, just as they did once my father came home from the hospital. Seems the incident has to be solved for the nightmares to go away."

He couldn't keep himself from asking, "But your mother..."

"Died. No, that was never, ever solved. I must have outgrown it." Both were silent. "Cord?"

He stroked her hair again. "Hmm?"

"I could have these bad dreams until this thing is over." Her voice trembled and so he pulled her closer.

"It's okay, Stace, I'll help you through them."

Saying nothing, she settled into him. After a few minutes, he felt her breathing even out again. Fully awake now, and sanity returning, he stared up through the skylights and absently continued to stroke her hair. He'd see her through these nightmares. He owed her that much.

Since it was his fault they ever began.

CHAPTER FIVE

STACEY AWAKENED languorously a few hours later to the chirping of the sparrows outside her window and the delicate rays of the sun glinting through the uncovered glass behind and above her. She lay on her side, her hand gently grasping the pillow. When she nuzzled her nose in it, she inhaled a familiar, comforting, woodsy scent. Then she remembered the dream—and Cord.

As if she'd conjured him, he appeared in her doorway with a steaming cup in his hand and an amused look on his face. He braced one arm against the frame, revealing a long line of bare torso, and muscles that bunched against his weight. Gray sweatpants rode low on his lean hips, revealing a white scar just above the drawstring. Jerking her eyes upward, she saw his blue gaze focused on her. "Good morning, sleepyhead."

Propping up pillows, she lazed back on them. "I'll be your slave forever if that's coffee you're holding, and it's for me."

Dark, sexy emotion crossed his beard-shadowed face. Then he smiled, and the look got even sexier. "Now I know why you have the coffeepot in there." He inclined his head to the adjoining sitting room.

"Don't make me beg."

His Adam's apple convulsed. "How do you like it?"

"Like what?" she said, her gaze furtively darting to his chest, then back to his face.

"Coffee. This is black, but I'll put something in it for you."

"No, I'll take it any way I can get it."

He looked at her assessingly. *Damn,* he was reading things into her words.

Cord crossed the room and handed her the cup. She took it, sipped twice, then scooted over and patted the side of the bed. "Sit down. I think we're a little past the formality stage."

His thick eyebrows arched as he sank onto the mattress. "You remember?"

She looked at his hair. It had always seemed a dark blond, but this morning the sun highlighted the golden strands that shot through it.

"Stacey, do you remember the dream?"

"Yes." She gave herself a firm mental shake. "And that you stayed with me."

"You were inconsolable . . . and every time I inched away, you whimpered."

"Whimpered? I've never whimpered in my life."

The sexual intensity that flashed through his eyes turned them almost a navy blue, making Stacey squirm.

"Whatever," he said, waving his hand in dismissal. "I had to stay with you, Stace."

That nickname again. No one ever called her that. When he said it, the word was a harsh whisper, curling inside her like a velvet fist. Feeling close to him, she reached out and squeezed the hand that had soothed her hair and rubbed her back all night. "Thank you. I get...terrified when I have those dreams."

"You told me. We talked."

"Yes, I remember."

He turned more fully toward her. "Do you remember anything about the dream?"

A little girl in a knitted coat, crying, and holding on to a large hand.

"No," she lied. "I don't remember anything." She sipped the coffee. "I never do." *At least until today.*

A shrewd gaze examined her, as if it detected the falseness of her words. Then Cord stood. "All right. I'm going to take a shower. There are a lot of things we have to do today."

"Like?"

"Go to my house and get my things." His eyebrows knit deeply. "And I'll have to talk to Meggie. I already called her this morning and smoothed over why I wasn't there, but I need to explain all this in person."

Pushing the hair off her face, Stacey said, "I'm sorry you have to leave Megan."

"Yeah, me, too." He sighed heavily then sank back to the bed, bracing his arms on either side of her. He seemed unaware of the intimacy of the position. "Stacey, there's something else we have to do today."

"What?"

"Go shopping."

"Shopping?"

He wasn't teasing; she recognized the no-nonsense set of his jaw.

"I'll be carrying my gun from now on and I'll need some shirts and blazers to conceal it. Since I left New York, I haven't needed those kinds of clothes."

"Oh." The stark reminder was like diving into the backyard pool in early May.

"I know it brings home the situation, but you need to keep in mind how serious all this is—how important it is for you to be careful. No more solo escapes like last night's."

"All right."

"Promise? No matter what the provocation?"

"I promise."

TWO HOURS LATER, she sat in Nora McKay's modest living room. The house on the north side of Canfield was in an old but well-kept neighborhood, with tree- and flower-covered lawns. Inside, the living room was warm and cozy. Two oversize stuffed couches, frayed around the edges, were flanked by a TV. A doll dressed in psychedelic colors lay on the coffee table, and two trucks peeked out from under a big recliner. Alone, waiting for Cord to get Megan, Stacey ran her hand over the upholstery and wondered if Cord had ever necked with his girlfriend on this sofa. Chagrined at her line of thinking, she stood, wandered to the big bay window and looked out.

She shouldn't care who Cord had kissed—and where. She shouldn't have had the kinds of thoughts about him she'd had this morning, when her defenses were down, either. In the cold light of day, Stacey felt ashamed of her feelings for him and how much she thought about him. The *way* she thought about him. Preston should be the only man she had these kinds of thoughts about.

Okay, so she was attracted to him. She'd admitted that a while ago. But it didn't help to indulge in fantasies that censors would attack with relish.

"We're here."

Stacey pivoted. Behind her, Cord held a little girl in his arms. The first thing that struck Stacey was the resemblance between the two of them. Their hair was the same multicolored flaxen, and she'd bet if she touched Megan's, it would be rich and thick, like his. The child's, of course, was longer—much longer, falling in thick waves almost to her waist. Similar blue eyes inspected Stacey.

"Megan, this is Stacey Webb."

The innocent eyes narrowed on her, making them even more like Cord's. Megan looked Stacey up and down. "I like your skirt," she said without preamble. Squirming out of Cord's arms, she crossed the room. With tiny hands, she reached out and stroked the shiny navy blue wraparound miniskirt Stacey had donned with a matching tank top. "It's soft." Her gaze traveled up Stacey's body. "Wow. Neat necklace."

Stacey smiled.

"Can I touch it?"

"Sure." Stacey perched on the edge of the chair so Megan could reach the jewelry. She was a bit surprised—but pleased—when the child climbed up on her lap. Megan was a compact little bundle and her weight felt good on Stacey's knees. Once she settled in,

Cord's daughter ran her fingertips along the chunky stones adorning Stacey's neck, the palm of her pudgy hand skimming Stacey's bare skin. Then Megan looked up at her face. "You got earrings, too. Daddy won't let me have any. He says I don't need holes in my ears."

"Maybe when you're bigger," Stacey said, fingering one of the three holes in *her* ears and glancing at Cord. He was smiling at them, and something shifted inside Stacey when she saw it.

"Your hair's pretty short," Megan commented.

Reaching out, Stacey smoothed down the child's long blond locks. The scent of lemony baby shampoo clung to them. "My hair used to touch my waist, just like yours." Now, where had that come from? Stacey hadn't thought about that in years. Her hand remained in Megan's hair for a few minutes, its coarse thickness wrapping around her fingers. "Maybe some day you'll let me do your hair for you," Stacey said.

Megan cocked her head. "Will I see you again?"

Stacey looked to Cord for the answer.

"Megan, this is the woman I'm helping out. The one I'll be with, like I told you upstairs."

At the reminder, Megan climbed off Stacey's lap and flew to Cord. After she catapulted into his arms, she buried her head in his neck again. "Don't want you to go," she said.

Straightening, Stacey's heart plummeted. This man shouldn't have to leave his child for her.

Cord sank onto the couch with Megan, closed his eyes and kissed the top of her head. "I know, honey. But Daddy's got to go away for a while."

Without warning, Stacey experienced the quick flash of an image before her eyes. It was almost like the glimpses one got when switching channels with a remote. She saw a woman, with long blond hair, bending over, tears shimmering in her eyes. *Mommy's got to go away—just for a little while.*

Suddenly, Stacey couldn't breathe. Her hands got clammy and spots clouded the vision.

Then it was gone.

Unnerved, Stacey grabbed the edge of the high table near the chair and gulped for air. When she glanced at Cord, he was so intent on Megan, he hadn't seen what had happened.

What *had* happened?

Before Stacey could figure it out, a door banged in the kitchen, and Nora McKay came to the archway wiping her hands on a blue-and-white flowered apron. ''Hello.''

Again, there was the family resemblance between Cord and his mother. Though streaked with gray, Nora McKay's hair was blond like his and full around her face. Blue eyes stared at Stacey with almost as much wariness as when Cord looked at her.

''Hello, Mrs. McKay.''

''Nora, please.''

Stacey nodded. ''Nora. I'm sorry about all this.''

''Not your fault someone's after you.'' She turned to Cord and Megan. ''What do you think, peanut? Just you and old Norna for a while?'' she asked, using the nickname Megan always called her by.

Megan looked at Stacey again. ''Daddy says someone wants to hurt you, and he's gonna 'tect you.''

Well, they certainly did believe in being honest with the child. Somehow, Stacey had assumed you'd keep something like this from her.

As if he'd read her mind, Cord said dryly, "We believe in telling the truth around here, as much as we can."

"I see." Stacey looked at Megan. "Yes, your dad's going to protect me."

"I can visit him some, not a lot."

"I'm glad you'll visit some. Maybe you can see me, too."

Megan eyed her necklace. "You got lots of necklaces like that?"

"Tons." For the first time, Stacey noticed Megan's outfit. She wore a black bodysuit, with a long white-and-black flowered skirt and black ballet slippers. Around her neck she had fashioned black-and-white ribbons into makeshift jewelry. "You know, I've got a black-and-white necklace that would go great with that outfit. You can borrow it sometime."

Megan's eyes sparkled. When Stacey sought Cord's, she saw that his were watching her with unabashed approval.

It shouldn't have felt as good as it did.

When they were ready to leave, Cord hugged Megan tightly and whispered into her ear before he set her down. Stacey had to beat back the tears forming in her eyes. Cord didn't say anything all the way to the truck, but when they got in, she reached out and touched his arm. Still, he stared ahead.

"I'm sorry. I'm responsible for this," she said simply.

"You're not." His voice was hoarse. When he turned to her, and she saw the telltale moisture in his eyes, she felt a swift gush of panic sweep through her. How was she ever going to keep her feelings for this man in check?

"COME ON, Stacey. A little harder."

"*Harder?* You've got to be kidding. I hurt already."

"Aren't you woman enough to take this?"

She sputtered. "All right, McKay. Harder. Whatever you dish out I can take."

As he reached to adjust the tension on her exercise bicycle, Cord looked down into her red face. By now, after twenty minutes, sweat was pouring off her. She grunted but pedaled steadily in reaction to his challenge.

After another five minutes, Cord checked his watch. "All right, that's enough bicycling."

As she slowed the pace, her breathing evened out. "You're a hard taskmaster," she groused.

"You said you wanted to learn some self-defense moves. You have to be in shape to do it."

"I thought I was in shape. I use this thing three times a week."

Without his consent, his eyes scanned her body. When he realized what he was doing, he cleared his throat and said, "You need more wind."

"Yeah, well, I want to be able to defend myself, not compete in the Olympics."

"Quiet or I won't teach you."

She got off the bike and stood before him. Her skintight, two-piece red bodysuit was damp under the arms and between her breasts. Standing close, he could smell the sweat she'd worked up. It should have been offensive, but it wasn't.

"I see right through that gruff exterior, McKay. This tough-guy act is just a front. You're going to do everything you can for me, whether you like it or not." She reached out and touched his arm. "I appreciate it."

Her nails were clipped and unpolished. Supple fingers squeezed him gently.

"Don't give me credit for things I haven't done."

She rolled her eyes and plopped her hands on her hips. "You don't fool me."

"All right." He shook his head. "Let's get back to work. The first thing I'm going to teach you is stunning techniques."

Her face lost its impish quality, and he felt bad. But he ignored her reaction and proceeded to outline the rudiments of common-sense self-defense.

"Always aim for the vital areas," he finished. "Ears, eyes, bridge of the mouth and throat." Her face scrunched in concentration. "Pretend you're the attacker. Lunge for me."

When she did, he raised his arm at a right angle. "This is called a side block," he explained, effectively stopping her. "Then you maneuver your body out of the way, like this." He sidestepped her, lifted his other arm and faked a punch, which, if he'd delivered it, would have clipped her in the mouth. Swiftly, he brought his left foot around and caught her behind the leg. She went down easily, though he grasped her arm to break her fall.

Staring up at him, she said, "I want to know how to do that as well as you do."

She was a tough cookie, all right. Every day for the six days he'd been staying here Cord admired her grit and determination to handle the situation well. "Fine. But you have to practice this daily, so it becomes second nature. And you have to stay in top shape."

"I will," she said, reaching out her hand. He tugged her up and they went at it.

Twenty minutes later, he could have wrung her hair out like a wet rag. She was breathing hard and her face was flushed. But she smiled. "I got it," she proclaimed, bouncing her chin and fisting her hands on her hips after she'd effectively taken him down once.

"Good girl."

Bonelessly, she fell to the floor beside him. "I'm whipped."

"You should be. Stretch now, like I showed you when we started." He tilted his head to indicate the mat they'd laid out on the carpet.

Stacey sprawled out on the vinyl, raised her arms over her head and pointed her toes. He swallowed hard, trying to remember how long it was since he'd made love with a woman.

Since he couldn't answer his own question, he knew it had been too long.

Just as he'd been thrown together with Stacey for too long. He was collecting images of her, making a scrapbook in his mind, and taking it out at night when he wrestled with the sheets while she slept only thirty feet away.

Watching her with Megan had been a trip. A twenty-three-year-old unmarried woman should know nothing about kids, but she'd found common ground with his daughter right away. Cord was surprised he hadn't noticed how similar their taste in fashion was. Bright colors and crazy combinations appealed to both of them.

Watching her with Preston Matthews had been a lot less pleasant. They'd been together on two nights this week and at Cord's suggestion, they stayed home. Stacey had cooked dinner for the two of them on Tuesday. On Thursday, they'd watched movies in the den. Both times Cord had sat in the next room, trying to read, willing his mind not to conjure images of Preston opening her blouse, putting his manicured hand inside...

"I'm going to shower," Stacey said, interrupting his thoughts.

"All right, I'll be up in a few minutes." He tried hard not to watch her as she turned and headed up the back staircase. Waiting until she was out of sight, he jumped on the bike. He set the tension at 7.0 and pedaled as if his life depended on it. He worked out for fifteen minutes, like a man crazed, then got off to do his own stretching.

To distract himself, he studied the workout room. About thirty-by-thirty, it had state-of-the-art weight-lifting equipment, a bike, a rower and a Nordic-Track. Nothing but the best for Gifford Webb. Too bad he hadn't been home often enough to use it eighteen years ago.

There were storage closets along a whole wall and Cord made a mental note to ask Webb why only one was kept locked. On the far wall was a row of glass doors opening up to the pool. For a brief moment, he recalled Helene out there in a modest one-piece black swimsuit teaching Stacey to kick her feet in the water. It bothered him that Stacey remembered none of this, only the bad things that came after Helene's death. Maybe he'd question Webb about that, too.

Finally, Cord trudged up the stairs. He was hoping Stacey had finished her shower. They'd done pretty well giving each other the privacy they'd needed, but the physical contact with her tonight really strained his self-discipline.

Since he heard no running water as he entered the sitting room, he figured she was done in the bathroom. He'd just whipped off his T-shirt, when she knocked on his door. Groaning inwardly, he told her to come in.

When he caught sight of her, Cord moaned. Freshly scrubbed, her skin glowed. Her hair was wet and slicked back off her face, emphasizing those chocolate eyes. She wore a bright orange Syracuse football jersey and red silk boxer shorts. "That felt wonderful," she said, smiling a little shyly.

"Good." He sniffed. "You smell like baby powder."

"I know. I love to use it after I bathe."

Scanning him as he'd done her, Stacey's eyes riveted on his sweaty chest. "Um, Cord?" she said at last.

"Yeah." He walked over to the dresser and pulled out clean pants, hoping to distract his libido.

"I, ah, I..."

He turned and focused on her when she hesitated. His jaw tightened as his gaze flicked over her bare legs. She was too short for them to be so long. "What is it, Stacey?" The question was curt.

Slashes of scarlet appeared on her cheeks. Then she lifted that chin. "Just so you know, I washed out my underwear and it's hanging to dry in the bathroom."

His hand fisted in the soft fleece. "Oh, yeah?" He tried to sound nonchalant.

She dug her toes into the carpet. "Our housekeeper does the laundry, but my...underwear has to be hand-washed. I've avoided doing it for six days, because you're sharing the bathroom, but I was running out." Her face got so red he forgot his own discomfort and only wanted to ease hers. God, she was so innocent sometimes. She finished with "So I washed it, and hung it in the bathroom to dry. I didn't want to surprise you."

Briefly he closed his eyes, blocking out the unwanted image. "Okay."

She turned away from him and crossed to the connecting doors.

"Stacey?"

"Hmm?" She didn't face him.

"There are bound to be things like this while I'm staying here. Try not to be embarrassed. I've seen women's underwear before."

"Okay," she muttered and walked out.

He waited as long as he could to take his shower, but eventually he had to face the music. He went into the bathroom and switched on the light. The air was still misty, and clouded the mirror. He rubbed it with a towel, trying not to look around. But he was engulfed in her scents: soap, lemon and baby powder. Glancing in the mirror, his gaze was drawn to the shower bar directly behind him. Through the glass, he saw, hanging to dry, a menagerie of string bikinis that made a man wonder why a woman would bother with them at all. Cord closed his eyes, but the images of zebra stripes, hot-pink with black lace, kelly green and orange polka dots and satiny red panties were branded on his mind.

Finally he turned around. There were bras to match. Before he let his mind play out a fantasy where his mouth caressed everything her underwear did, Cord sighed heavily as he opened the glass door and yanked on the faucet.

As GIFFORD WEBB waited for McKay in the den, he stared out over the swimming pool, softly lit so the surface of the water sparkled like tiny gold sequins. Helene had loved the pool, had spent many lazy days in there with Stacey. He remembered coming home one night from a four-day business trip to find them frolicking in the water, both naked as the day they were born. He could still see the moon casting them in half shadow, half light. He'd stripped down himself, jumped into the water, played a bit, ordered Helene to stay where she was, then led Stacey to her room and put her to bed.

When he'd returned, he'd made love to Helene right there in the pool. All she'd said was *Oh, Gif, please, be here more to do this. I love you...*

"You wanted to see me?"

Abruptly, Gifford turned to find McKay standing in the doorway. "Yes." Moving away from the windows, Gifford strode to the bar. As he poured a drink, he asked, "Want one?"

"No, thanks."

The younger man had folded his arms across his chest and leaned against the doorframe. *Still cocky as ever.*

No, that wasn't fair. To make up for his unkind thoughts, Gifford said, "I wanted to thank you for signing on until the man stalking Stacey can be caught."

"Well, as you said, I owe you."

Gifford felt the hollow jab of guilt. "I was out of line when I said that."

"What do you mean?"

"Let's just say my attitude's changed in eighteen years. I don't think...that is, I know I was away a lot. I know...Helene was lonely..."

"That's not what you told me when you ran me out of town."

"No, it's not. I was out of my mind that night."

Running a hand through his hair, Cord said, "With reason. Look, Webb, I don't see what good this will do either of us. I've lived with Helene's death on my conscience for almost two decades. Nothing can change that.''

"So have I," Gifford said quietly.

"Besides, I don't want to risk Stacey's finding out about my connection with all of you."

Gifford stared past him, seeing all the wrong turns he'd taken. "I've made mistakes with Stacey, too."

Slowly, McKay came farther into the room. Sticking his hands in his pockets, he said, "Do you realize she's done everything possible to be just the opposite of the way Helene was—her clothes, her career, even what she does with her spare time? I'll bet she hasn't picked up a paintbrush in eighteen years."

"I know," Webb said softly.

"Why did you do make her hate her mother? If nothing else, you had to know how much Helene loved Stacey."

"Actually, I didn't do it all. But that doesn't mean it isn't my fault."

"I don't understand."

"Stacey's grandmother had a big hand in it. At first, after Helene...died, I couldn't bear to be in this house, I was so guilty and grief-stricken. I traveled constantly and left Stacey with Ana," he said, referring to his mother. "I never knew how myopic she was about Helene until it was too late. Much of the damage had been done. Stacey's attitude changed completely toward her mother. I'm at fault for not contradicting all the subtle and not so subtle messages Ana gave her."

"Why didn't you?"

"It hurt too much at first to remember the good things. It was easier just to remember Helene as a slut."

He saw McKay wince. "God, man," Cord said. "You can't believe that about her. It was only—"

Gifford held up his hand. "I know what it was. Now. I just couldn't deal with it then. When Stacey got older, I also couldn't bear to have her think badly of me, so I never tried to rectify her misconceptions about her mother."

"Pretty selfish thing to do to your daughter." McKay's eyes flared blue fire.

Gifford's own temper ignited. "Would you let Megan think badly of you if you could help it?"

Cord stared at him, then sighed. "Listen, this isn't what you wanted to see me about, is it?"

Gifford studied the man before him for long moments, then answered, "No, I want your opinion on what's happening with the stalking. The guy hasn't made a move in five days."

"Because I'm here."

"You think the stalker knows?"

"Everybody in Canfield knows."

"Any guesses on who's doing this to us?"

"As we said before," Cord said, "it could be someone with a grudge against you. In that case, I don't have any idea. But..."

Gifford raised an eyebrow in question.

McKay shifted on his feet. "I think it might be someone Stacey knows."

Gripping his glass, Gifford said, "My God, no."

"It's just a hunch. The stalker could have simply followed her, but a lot of people knew she was going to be on College Hill last Friday night."

"I knew. And Judith. Preston. And Lauren." Gifford frowned. "And Ferron."

"That's right."

"You think it's one of them?"

"Could be. What's more, except for Judith, their relationships with Stacey all seem a little odd." McKay told him about his observations of Lauren, Preston and Ferron.

"I think you're wrong. They might have their eccentricities, but they love Stacey. Even Ferron had a thing for her in high school."

"Well," McKay said, an ironic twist to his mouth, "sometimes love destroys. We both know that, don't we, Webb?"

MATCHMAKING

106

"It's quite a family! The feeling could have easily followed us, but a lot of people know she was going to see Colton. His trail ends there tonight."

"I know. Push Fuller. Pressure. Make it worse," Colton frowned. "And I mean—"

"But a moment, too."

Say how. Control that.

"Come on. We need more fingering to find..."

CHAPTER SIX

AS THE MAN leaned against one of the trees in the Webbs' backyard and looked up at Stacey's window, he drew a knife out of his boot. He took off his black glove and brought the blade to his palm. A little pressure and his skin began to ooze. Simultaneously, he felt the sting and the euphoria that came every time he saw blood. His breath sped up and he felt half-aroused. Lifting his palm to his mouth, he closed his eyes and sucked.

The knife was sharp enough. He'd honed it to a fine lethal edge.

He couldn't wait till he could test it on the bitch.

But he *would* wait. He was very good at waiting. As a little boy, he remembered waiting for the strap. He'd figured if he stayed perfectly still, it wouldn't hurt so much. He was wrong, but each time, he'd waited, motionless.

It had been good practice for the waiting now. Sometimes, he was so close...and she never even knew it because he could stay so still. Sometimes, he was close enough so he could see the fear in her eyes.

He wanted to make her afraid. It was good for women to be afraid. Kept them in line. His old man said so. It was one of the few things they'd agreed on.

Yeah, he liked the bitch being afraid. But he'd have to be patient. One of the reasons he'd done nothing in a week was because he wanted them to get comfortable, to get lulled into believing he'd given up because she had some big-time bodyguard watching over her. Fat chance! No, let them get careless, then he'd strike.

Only this time, maybe he'd miss on purpose. It would make trapping her eventually even more fun. He'd scare her once, then nab her the next time.

Raising the blade to his mouth, he ran his tongue across the cool metal. Where would he start on her, when the time finally came?

He glanced back up at the window. The light was out.

He closed his eyes for a minute and savored the thought of Stacey Webb's blood.

It was better than sex.

DAMN, Stacey thought as she inched away from Preston's mouth. He had her pinned to the back of the couch, so she gained little ground. Sighing futilely, she linked her arms around his neck and tried again to participate in the kiss he'd initiated minutes ago. His lips were smooth and flat and dry when they came back to hers. After a moment, she felt his tongue probing and she opened up to him. He invaded her mouth, shoving his tongue in and out. But she felt . . . nothing.

It should be Cord.

No, oh, please, God, don't let me have these thoughts.

But no deity—not even a female one—could erase the idea once it came to consciousness.

Finally, Preston released her mouth to bury his in her neck. She got a whiff of the expensive cologne that he'd doused himself with—Calvin Klein—and remembered how Cord smelled like the woods and the rain. His scent had lingered on her pillow for days after the nightmare.

Preston's breathing picked up as he slid his hand inside the open vee of her tangerine shirt, releasing a few buttons. His fingertips were smooth, his nails buffed. Stacey couldn't help recalling the feel of Cord's calluses on her wrist.

This is blasphemous. Letting one man touch you, and thinking about another.

You're more like your mother than you think.

"No!"

She hadn't realized she'd spoken the word aloud until Preston drew back and stared at her. "No?"

With self-disgust, her jaw dropped and she closed her eyes. "Um, I'm just too tense for this, Preston."

"Well, if you'd let me do it right, I could make you really relax."

She removed his hand from her chest, and pushed a little. Freed, she scrambled off the couch. "Let's not get into that again."

"Maybe I *want* to get into that again."

She rounded on him. He was so smug sitting there in his righteous indignation. "Preston, this has been a bad time for me. I can't seem to let down."

Standing, he slid his hands into his dress pants. "You can never let down, Stacey."

Anger shot through her. "I have never defended my choices to any man I've ever dated, Preston. I'm not going to start now."

She saw a flash of surprise light his eyes. Wariness accompanied it. "I'm not asking for defense. I want a little affection. Is that so bad?"

"You want sex."

"Well, what's wrong with that? I'm a normal, red-blooded thirty-year-old man. Yes, I want sex from you. Anyone in my place would feel the same. Just because you have some hang-up about your mother..."

Stacey stepped back as if he'd slapped her. One night, in order to soothe his ego, she'd told him how her decision to remain a virgin was based on her mother's infidelity. She'd never expected her confession to be thrown in her face.

"Look, I'm sorry I said that, but give me a break, Stacey." He gestured to the door. "You can bet a guy like Cord McKay wouldn't be so patient."

As if a videotape played in her mind, Stacey saw him holding her in the rain as he stroked her hair. She watched herself lying in his arms in the middle of the night... *I'm not putting the moves on you.* She pictured how he'd held her hand in his all the way down College Hill.

Preston was wrong. Cord McKay could be as patient as Job.

Unfortunately, Stacey wasn't quite so sure about her own self-control around him. Would she give him any *need* to be patient?

Frightened by the thought, she looked at her fiancé. "Preston, this is old ground. Let's—"

He rolled his eyes, then swore. "I'm sick of this," he said as he grabbed his sport coat. "Grow up, Stacey," he called over his shoulder as he slammed the den door. A few seconds later she heard him slam the outer one.

Oh, great, just what she needed right now. She sank into the big recliner, knees bent, head resting on her arms. His anger, at a time when she needed understanding, annoyed her. But her thoughts, her feelings about Cord McKay, terrified her.

She had to stop this.

Or break up with Preston.

The insidious thought wound into her mind and could not be banished.

No, I love Preston.

Do you?

"Stacey?"

She uncurled in the seat and looked up to find Cord McKay, as handsome as sin, and just as tempting, in the archway. "Are you all right?"

"I'm fine."

"You look upset. And I heard doors slamming."

She shook her head, not wanting to speak for fear her words would betray her feelings.

He edged farther into the room. Stacey watched as his policeman's eyes took in minute details: when he looked at the couch, he'd see the pillows were askew; when he looked at her, he'd see her lips were swollen. Would he think she and Preston had been making love? Oh, God, the irony was too great.

"Have a fight?" Cord asked.

"He's an ass sometimes."

"You won't get an argument from me."

She grinned, then she laid her head back on the chair.

"Why are men such jerks?" she asked finally.

Cord was silent for a moment. "I'll explain that, Anastasia, if you button up that blouse."

Her eyes flew open and she looked down. Three of the tiny buttons on her shirt were undone, exposing a slice of hot pink satin against her breast. A red flush crept up her chest, looking like a sunburn, as she closed the gap. She gave him an embarrassed grin. "Thanks, Francis."

Taking a seat on the couch opposite her, he linked his hands between his knees. "Want to talk about it?" he asked.

She stared at him for a minute then shook her head. "It's too personal."

"Maybe I can help. A man of my vast experience . . . and age might be able to put things in perspective."

"You're only thirteen years older than I am."

"Older enough."

Her eyes traveled to the doorway. "Preston is asking for things in this relationship I don't want to give."

"You're engaged. What more could he want?"

She smiled at the implied compliment. "Thank you for that. It salves my ego."

"Your ego shouldn't need salving."

She frowned at his reaction. Her feelings for this man had grown over the last few days, right along with the attraction. And watching him now, she sensed he was experiencing some of the same things. It scared the hell out of her. Drawn to his concentrated stare, she fought the bond deepening between them.

"Well, it's really none of my business, I guess," he finally murmured, shrugging his shoulders.

"I wish that were true."

"I don't understand. Is Matthews giving you some grief about me?"

"If it were only that simple."

"Stacey, tell me what's going on. Maybe I can help." When she hesitated, he said, "Hey, I told you my real name. I told you about Megan's mother. I deserve some confidences in return."

Exasperated, she crossed her arms over her chest and hugged herself tightly. What the hell, maybe getting the problem out in the open would diffuse it. "All right. Preston and I are engaged, and now I find—" she hesitated "—I find I'm . . . I'm attracted to *you*. It bothers me." He said nothing, his expression blank. But there was a trace of color on his cheeks that hadn't been there before. "And now I've embarrassed you."

His grin was boyish and uninhibited, and Stacey wondered what a younger, less world-weary Cord had been like. "Embarrassed me? When zebra-striped panties didn't?"

She laughed.

"Seriously. I'm not embarrassed. You've seen the bodyguard movies—read the books. It happens all the time—the young ingenue begins to feel something for the handsome, hard-edged bodyguard."

She laughed again. "I know you're trying to make me feel better." Then she sobered. "But there's something you don't understand."

"I don't?"

"No. I've got a history here that you know nothing about."

"Something with other men?"

"No, something with Helene."

His shoulders tensed, almost imperceptibly. "Your mother."

"I've always prized fidelity because my mother didn't."

"She didn't?"

"No. She was unfaithful to my father, and I've always hated her for it. I vowed never to be like her."

Cord sat against the cushions and stretched his arm out on the back of the couch. "How do you know all this?"

"When I was thirteen, I heard my father and grandmother arguing." She looked around. "Right here in this den, as a matter of fact. He said she was poisoning my mind against Helene and it had to stop. She said Helene was a slut. She said he'd even caught her in the act once. He was a fool to try to pretend she'd been a good person."

"Oh, Stacey, I'm sorry." His look was stricken.

"From then on, it affected my behavior with boys and men." Unable to remain still with the painful memories, Stacey stood and crossed to the windows facing the pool. "Now, to have these feelings... about another man, about you, while I'm engaged, is horrible. It says horrible things about me."

"No! It doesn't."

She turned to face him. "What do you mean?"

"Feelings like this are understandable. Particularly under these circumstances."

"All I can see is that it says I'm like her."

"Maybe. Or maybe it tells you you've been looking at this wrong."

"Wrong?"

He leaned forward again in his seat. "Yeah. Instead of this saying something bad about you, maybe it can help you understand your mother."

"How?"

"By realizing that people—even good, decent people—can't always help how they feel."

"I don't believe that."

"Stacey, take us as an example. It's not unusual for a client to be attracted to her bodyguard. It's part of the human condition. Maybe what your mother did was only human, too. Have you...have you ever heard her side of the whole thing?"

"Well, no. But..."

"Then take this as a lesson in life. Your mother was human. She wasn't perfect and she went a step further than what you find acceptable. Maybe she even had reasons you don't know about. But that doesn't matter. What matters is that you're a good person. Maybe she was, too."

Stacey sank to the chair by the window, gripping the edges until her knuckles were white. "I...I never thought about it that way."

"Maybe it's time you did."

She looked up at him, disbelief, gratitude and something else welling inside her.

Standing, Cord shifted uneasily. "I guess I'll go check to see everything's set for the night."

She nodded, still staring at him.

"You okay?"

"Yes." He crossed to the door. "Cord?"

He glanced back. "Hmm?"

"You said it's common in these situations for a woman to feel this way about her bodyguard?"

"Yeah."

"Does it go the other way? Do bodyguards develop feelings for the women they protect?"

Before he could answer, there was a loud crash in the front of the house. It sounded like glass breaking.

Cord slammed the door shut and dived for the light switch. The room went black. He grabbed Stacey, hurled her to the floor and pulled her behind the couch. "Stay down. And stay quiet."

She could see only a vague outline of his wide shoulders and feel the strength of his hands on her. He drew one away and she realized he was going for his gun.

Stay down. Stay quiet. She bit her lip and laid her face against Cord's back.

She heard the squeak of the den door and sensed every muscle in Cord tense. He turned his body so she was completely behind him. When Stacey realized he'd be the target instead of her, she froze. Somehow, she never thought that protecting her meant he'd sacrifice his *own* life.

The door squeaked more, and opened fully. She saw light pouring in from the foyer. Odd. Why would the stalker turn on a light?

Cord must have come to the same conclusion because he peeked around the end of the couch.

"Stacey? Are you in here? It's so dark in the house, I broke a vase." It was the familiar voice of her father.

She heard Cord expel a long breath. He fell to his knees. She collapsed on top of him, drained from the adrenaline rush.

It was a long time, and too late, before she realized he'd never answered her question.

THE HOT JUNE SUN beat down on the Webbs' pool. The smell of chlorine rose from the water, reminding Cord of summers spent swimming at the public pool with his buddies.

"How do you spell *happy?*" Megan asked Cord, her forehead creased.

"H-A-P-P-Y," he spelled out, fighting a grin. "This wouldn't be for me, would it?"

"I found them, Megan." He heard Stacey's voice from the other side of the pool.

Cord didn't want to look up. He couldn't bear the sight. But soon she blocked his vision. She was wearing a hot pink, one-piece bathing suit that left nothing to the imagination. "What are you doing here?" Stacey said, pretending exasperation. "Get out, this is a surprise."

He tried to scowl. "I'm helping my daughter with her artwork."

"You don't help make your own Father's Day card, silly," she said, waving at him with her hand. "Go sit with Daddy, Lauren and your mother until we're done."

He was about to protest, but changed his mind. He stood and sauntered toward the other table.

"She kick you out?" Webb asked, sipping a glass of lemonade.

Cord nodded. "Something about not helping with my own card." Sinking onto a plush lounge chair, he bit his tongue to keep from saying anything else. This whole scene was absurd. How the hell had he ended up at the Webbs' swimming pool making small talk with a man who hated him?

From behind mirrored sunglasses, he studied Gifford Webb. Decked out in the Ralph Lauren polo shirt and khaki shorts that Stacey had given him for Father's Day, Webb looked considerably younger than his forty-six years. Right now, he was staring at his daughter, and Cord's daughter, with a look so sad that it added another dent to the wall of resentment Cord had erected against this man many years ago. When Cord glanced at Stacey and Megan under the other umbrella, he saw why.

Heads bent, they were carefully working at their task. Even Cord was reminded of Helene and Stacey and the hours those two had spent at this very pool creating masterpieces.

"It was nice of you to invite us, Gifford," Cord's mother, Nora, said, adjusting her white slacks and green blouse.

"And me," Lauren put in self-effacingly. "You're so wonderful to include me. I'm really an outsider."

Webb looked grateful to be drawn away from the tableau he'd been watching. "Nonsense, Nora. Cord couldn't miss Father's Day with Megan because of us. This seemed the most expedient, and the safest, solution." Then he addressed Stacey's friend. "And you're always welcome here, Lauren, no matter what the day."

Cord tore his eyes away from Stacey and Megan and surveyed the backyard. An eight-foot wooden fence enclosed it. Behind that were several maple and a few oak trees. He'd made sure the gates could now be locked from within, making them impenetrable from the outside. Scaling something that high would also be difficult. They were relatively safe. Still, he wore his gun.

Stacey and Megan rose. Stacey reached into a bag and drew out two visors. Cord chuckled as she placed a black sequined one on Megan. It matched the black-and-white-checked bathing suit she had on. Stacey plopped one with purple sequins on her own head and said something to Megan, which earned Stacey a vigorous hug. Cord's insides tightened. Then they trekked hand in hand across the flagstone patio.

"Happy Father's Day, Daddy," Megan said, toppling into his lap and bestowing a card and package on him.

"Thanks, pumpkin." He nuzzled his face in her hair, which was frizzy and wild all around her head.

"Stacey helped me with the card."

Glancing down at the artwork, he saw the under-statement of Megan's words. The background was in-deed filled in by Megan, but silhouetted against her childish scrawls was an outline of his face, unmistak-able with its bumpy nose and strong jaw. Next to it was a smaller profile of Megan's pug-nose and fluffy bangs.

"She draws good," Megan said.

"Yeah. Real good." *Just like her mother.*

"Open the gift." Cord looked up at the husky tone from Stacey. Her face was animated, and lit from within. He could see she was enjoying this.

Without commenting, he tore at the haphazardly wrapped package. Inside was a wild-print oversize shirt. It was the last thing Cord would have pur-chased for himself, but it suited Megan's taste per-fectly. And Stacey's.

"Put it on, Daddy."

Cord hesitated. His eyes flew to Gifford, who frowned.

"Come on, McKay. We've seen bare chests," Sta-cey teased.

"It's okay for Daddy to go without a shirt," Me-gan put in. "But not us girls."

Stacey chuckled. "Yes, I know. Well, Cord?"

He stood abruptly. "I was going to change into my suit, anyway. I'll put on both."

Stacey glanced at his chest, clothed with a loose sport shirt, and back to his eyes. He could tell she'd suddenly remembered that he wore a gun. And this wasn't just a simple get-together. He was here for a reason.

He had an overwhelming urge to hold her to him, press those trembling lips to his chest and tell her everything was going to be all right. Again. Instead of succumbing, he opted for distracting her. "While I do that, why don't you show Megan that fancy braid I don't know how to do. Especially if we're going swimming."

When he returned five minutes later, Stacey had brushed out Megan's hair, separated it into strands and was deftly weaving it into a French braid. Gifford hunched over in his chair, speaking to Megan. His mother and Lauren sipped lemonade quietly, and Lauren's eyes were fastened to Gifford as he spoke to the little girl.

"And then she said that she was too old for lullabies and made me sing a Beatles song to her," Gifford said.

All five people laughed at what was obviously a story about Stacey's youth.

Cord was about ten feet away when Stacey looked over at Gifford. Suddenly, her jaw gaped and her face went ashen. She dropped the thick strands of Megan's hair and fell back in her seat. It looked almost as if she'd had some kind of physical attack. Or something had hit her from behind.

Cord fumbled for the gun he'd stuck in his duffel bag and leaped across the short distance that separated them. Gifford glanced up as Cord came crashing into a lawn chair. By the time he reached them, Cord had already scanned the area and was convinced that no one was in sight, but that didn't preclude the possibility of someone's being out there with a long-range weapon.

Grabbing Megan and yanking her behind him, he said, "Stacey? Are you hurt anywhere?"

She shook her head. She seemed dazed...but not hurt. Close examination revealed she was breathing fast and sweat beaded on her lip.

Gifford slid off the chair, sank to his knees and grabbed his daughter's hands. "Honey, what is it?"

She blinked, stared at her father, then at Megan huddling behind Cord's legs. "I had a memory..."

"A memory?"

"I guess like a flashback."

Breathing normally now that he knew Stacey wasn't injured, Cord sank to a chair and pulled Megan onto his lap. Reaching around, he tucked the gun into his waistband. Megan jammed two fingers into her mouth and sucked vigorously.

"I don't understand," Gifford said, keeping Stacey's hands in a death grip.

Stacey closed her eyes as if to deal with a deep searing pain. When she opened them again, they were bleak. "It was about Helene, Daddy."

Gifford slumped over but didn't let go of his daughter.

"It was so real. When you were talking to Megan, I had this...vision of you leaning over me, teasing me about something while...she braided my hair. Right here on this patio."

Gifford blanched.

"Did that ever *happen?*" she asked.

Gifford glanced at Cord.

"Daddy?"

Standing, Gifford shoved unsteady hands into his pockets. "I suppose it could have, honey, although I don't remember the exact incident."

"Did she . . . did she used to do my hair?"

Gifford's smile was so poignant, Cord felt guilt ricochet through him. "She loved doing your hair. You wore it long until you were about six. She used to braid it—" he glanced at Megan "—like you did Megan's. Then you'd try to braid hers and you'd both end up giggling, usually on the ground."

"I never knew." Stacey's voice was clogged with suppressed tears.

Cord tried to remain impassive, but it was hard when Webb looked at him again. He recalled his words to Webb.

Do you realize how she's done everything possible to be just the opposite of Helene... Why did you make Stacey hate her mother? If nothing else, you had to know how much Helene loved Stacey... Pretty selfish thing to do to your daughter.

As if Webb remembered it, too, he nodded and turned to Stacey. "Honey, you had a lot of good times with your mother before she died. Would you like me to tell you about some of them?"

"My mother died, too," Megan said, drawing everyone's attention.

"We know, love." Cord's voice was soft.

"I feel bad about it. Do you, Stacey?" Megan asked.

Stacey looked at her father, then back to Megan. "Truthfully, honey, I never thought so. But I don't know anymore."

CHAPTER SEVEN

"SON OF A BITCH!" The blood oozed from Cord's face, tinting the shaving cream a light pink. He was having a hard time concentrating on even the simplest task.

Stacey...Stacey...Stacey. He could think of nothing else. For the last two weeks, all his mind seemed capable of doing was replaying images of the woman. He was obsessed.

Which was why he'd planned to bring a date tonight.

Nasty thing to do to her on her birthday.

It's for her own good.

Quickly Cord rinsed his face, then reached for the small towel. When he brought it to his nose, he inhaled Stacey's scent. She must have used it earlier when she'd showered and dressed for the evening.

And what a night it would be. Cord had absolutely refused to allow a birthday celebration at a local restaurant. Everyone—except Matthews—had understood. Apparently, he'd planned some big shindig at Canfield Country Club. Instead, they were having a catered dinner at the Webb home. Stacey hadn't seemed to mind the change in plans, but her fiancé had been miffed.

There was a knock on the bathroom door. "Cord, I left my ring in there. Are you decent?"

"No."

There was silence.

Quickly, he pulled on the cutoffs he'd shucked earlier and yanked open the door.

An impish smile tugged at the corners of her mouth. "Don't worry, tough guy, I wasn't trying to catch a glimpse of you naked."

"No sass, lady."

Stacey ducked into the bathroom, which was easily the size of Megan's bedroom, but seemed minuscule whenever they occupied it simultaneously. Retrieving her ring, she slipped it on, then faced him. Before he realized what she was doing, she reached for a tissue, then blotted the blood on his face. The smell of her lotion, powder and shampoo wafted up, teasing him. His bare chest heaved and he was terrified she'd see the effects of her nearness.

"You cut yourself. What were you thinking about?"

"My date."

Stacey's hand froze. "You have a date tonight?"

"Yeah, didn't I tell you?"

"No, you didn't."

"Oh, well, your father said to go ahead and ask someone."

Stacey swallowed hard. "You never told me you were dating anyone."

Cord stepped back, trying hard to ignore the hurt in her voice. "I didn't realize I had to clear my social calendar with you."

"Of course you don't. I didn't mean that. So, who is this mystery woman?"

"Eileen Martin."

"Daddy's lawyer?"

"Well, she works for Rossetta and Rossetta."

Leaning back on the sink, Stacey crossed her arms over her chest. "How long have you been seeing her?"

"Two years, on and off."

"How on and off?"

"Stacey, this isn't really any of your business." He picked up his watch from the vanity. "Look, it's getting late."

She bit her lip and said nothing for several long seconds. "All right." Pushing away from the sink, she stepped toward the door.

"Stacey?" She turned. "Thanks for asking Megan tonight."

Her smile was tender. "Megan and I are buddies."

"Soul mates, you mean." For the first time, he noticed her outfit. "At least I thought you were. What's with the Victorian dress? You only wear that stuff to work."

Stacey tugged at the high collar of the classic white sheath she wore. "Preston likes this dress. I thought I'd wear it for him."

Cord's stomach muscles clenched. "Soothing ruffled feathers?"

"Something like that. Anyway, I'll fit in better with Eileen." Then she asked, "How's Megan getting here?"

"Eileen's picking her up." He stared past Stacey's shoulder. "They're close."

Stacey stepped back, as if he'd delivered a blow, then left the bathroom without another word.

He slammed his hand on the vanity. He was doing this for her own good. His reaction to her was getting out of hand, and he had to do something quick before he did something stupid. Like kiss the hurt from her face. Like ease the tension from her shoulders with a long slow massage. Like make her moan and call his name as he buried himself deep inside her.

Oh, yeah, right, McKay. And just imagine the repercussions of that little fantasy when she finds out you bedded her mother, too.

"EVERYTHING LOOKS GREAT, Daddy." Stacey tried to infuse some enthusiasm into her voice. She'd been looking forward to the small, intimate gathering—until about an hour ago.

"Sorry about canceling the bash at the country club."

Stacey shook her head. "Don't be. You know that's not my style. Preston was more upset about it than I was."

Her father peered at her closely. "Things aren't good between you two, are they?"

"No. He isn't dealing with all this very well. And he doesn't like Cord very much."

"McKay's a hard man, Stacey."

"Do you like him, Dad?"

"I appreciate his helping us."

"But?"

"I respect his skill." He glanced over to where Cord sat with his daughter on his lap, the lush Eileen Martin at his elbow. "But like him? No, I don't."

Stacey watched Eileen lean over, her hand on Cord's knee, and whisper something in his ear. He laughed and she blushed. "Well, Eileen Martin clearly likes him. I wouldn't have thought she was his type."

Her father's jaw locked.

"Daddy? What's wrong?"

He turned to her, but before he could answer, Lauren and Mark Dunn wandered over.

"Happy Birthday, Stacey," Lauren said brightly, kissing her friend on the cheek.

"Thanks. Hi, Mark."

"Hi. Happy Birthday." Thank God Mark didn't try to kiss her, too. She really disliked the man because he treated Lauren so badly.

As they chatted, Stacey studied Mark, wondering for the hundredth time what her friend found appealing about the guy. His face was shadowed—he was obviously trying to grow a beard. Dressed in black, he was about Cord's size, but his bulk seemed threatening to Stacey. Probably because she strongly suspected he'd used it on Lauren.

"The place looks great, Gifford. Did you decorate it?" Lauren asked.

"Yes."

"All your favorite colors, Stacey," her friend commented wistfully.

Stacey felt a sharp pang of sympathy for Lauren, whose father had never done anything for her except teach her that men like Mark Dunn were attractive.

Preston joined the group, snaking an arm around Stacey's waist. "Hi, everyone. Doesn't the birthday girl look great?"

Stacey's eyes strayed to Megan. Now, *there* was a great outfit. A fuchsia sundress over a lime green tank top and sneakers. The colors contrasted sharply with Eileen Martin's burgundy suit. She and Megan couldn't be all *that* close.

From across the room Stacey saw Cord focus on Preston's embracing arm, then she caught Cord's eye. His gaze burned hers briefly. When he looked away, he lifted his hand and rested it on the couch behind his date. His fingers toyed with her thick auburn hair.

Stacey reached up to push her own mop out of her eyes.

"You need a haircut, babe," Preston said affectionately. "I don't think I've ever seen your hair this long."

"I know. I'm weeks overdue. Things have just been so hectic. And frankly, I haven't wanted to ask Cord to sit in a beauty parlor for an hour after work."

Preston tensed. "He's getting paid enough to sit in a damned *sauna* for an hour, if you want him to."

A fantasy, starring Cord's sweat-soaked, all-male flesh, swamped Stacey.

"I like Stacey's hair longer." Gifford reached out and ruffled her locks. "It reminds me of when she was little. It was always a riot of curls around her face and shoulders then. It looks good, honey."

Stacey's gaze drifted to Eileen Martin's long auburn hair.

Maybe Stacey wouldn't cut hers.

WHEN CORD SAW the table set for dinner, he groaned. He'd been hoping for a buffet. An almost-five-year-old didn't need a formal, sit-down meal at nine o'clock at night. He'd have to spend most of his time watching that she didn't soil the crisp linen tablecloth or break the Steuben crystal that graced each place setting.

Stacey sat down at the middle of the table, so Cord chose a seat at the far end. He pulled a chair out for Eileen, then one for Megan, who shook her head. "I want to sit next to Stacey."

"No, honey, I need you near me. Stacey's got—"

Mischief lit the birthday girl's face. "I've got a place reserved for Ms. Megan McKay right here," Stacey said, pointing to her left.

Cord's heart flip-flopped when he saw a grin split Megan's face. She squirmed away from him, yanked the tablecloth in the process and barely avoided taking several pieces of sterling silver with her.

Sighing, Cord sank into his chair. Eileen leaned into him. Her perfume was summer-night sultry, but it didn't turn him on. Not in the slightest. Funny how baby powder seemed to do the trick these days.

"She's fine, Cord. Relax." Under the table, Eileen stroked his thigh. "I don't suppose I'm going to get a chance to do that for you tonight?"

"What?"

"Relax you." Eileen's green eyes sparkled with sexual promise.

Cord tried to participate. Maybe that was it, he just wasn't trying. He leaned closer to her. "Would you like that, Eileen?"

Her face flushed becomingly. "You know I would."

Cord laughed, and even to his own ears, the sound was low and sexy. When he looked up, he saw Stacey staring at them. Jealous sparks flamed in her big brown eyes. Cord felt interested in sex, all right. But with the wrong woman. Probably the one woman in the world he could never have. He reached for the glass of red wine by his plate and took two long gulps. The drink didn't help. Instead, it intensified the heat inside him, fueling it, swirling red-hot desire into his loins. He wished he could take Eileen up on her offer, but he knew he wouldn't. He couldn't make love to one woman when he wanted another.

Halfway through dinner, disaster struck. Megan was pushing the glazed duck around her plate as if it was a toy instead of food. Cord was just about to tell her to eat her vegetables, when her fork slipped. Duck à l'orange slid off the plate. Hiking up onto her knees, Megan reached over to get it. Simultaneously, Stacey lifted her wineglass from the table. Right arm bumped left arm and the Beaujolais splashed down the front of Preston's favorite white dress.

Megan gasped, and her tearful eyes sought her father. As he jerked back his chair and rounded the table, he saw Stacey stretch out her hand to Megan's neck and squeeze it gently. Cord just reached them, when Preston said, "Dammit, Stacey, the wine is all over you. I told you a kid shouldn't be at a dinner like this."

Anger licked at Cord as he yanked back Megan's chair, dislodging Stacey's hand. He said nothing as he scooped up his daughter, drew her into his chest and strode out of the dining room. He found his way to the back of the house and onto the dimly lit patio. Sinking into a lounge chair, he cuddled his softly weeping child in his lap.

Gently he crooned nonsense words to her for a few minutes. When she quieted, he said, "Did I ever tell you about the time I was a waiter at a restaurant?" Megan shook her head. "I was serving at a wedding, and poured coffee down the front of the bride's white dress."

Megan looked up at him with owl eyes.

"It's true, honey. I felt bad like you do now. But accidents happen."

"What did the bride say?" he heard from behind him.

Megan and he both pivoted in the chaise to see Stacey at the French doors. The moon cast her in half light, but Cord could make out the red stain radiating from the center of her dress.

"She was very nice about it," Cord said. "I offered to pay for the cleaning bill, but she wouldn't let me."

"Can we get Stacey's dress fixed, Daddy?" Megan asked.

Stacey crossed the patio and sat down on the edge of their chair. She was so close, Cord could see she'd bitten off the small amount of lipstick she'd applied earlier.

"Meggie? Don't offer to do that, okay?" Stacey said.

"Why?"

"Because I really hate this dress. I only wore it for Preston." She winked. "Now that's it's ruined, I never have to wear it again."

Megan looked over at Stacey hopefully, but her little body remained tense.

"Now, if it had been my peacock blue sequined dress, I might be mad. Have you ever seen that one?"

Megan shook her head.

Stacey stood. "Want to come look at it? I have to change, anyway. Maybe I'll put that one on. It's my favorite." She looked at Cord. "I should have worn my favorite dress, anyway, since it's my birthday."

"You won't get an argument from me," Cord said hoarsely.

Stacey stood, picked up Megan from the chair and headed for the house.

"Stace?" Cord called to her.

The two turned to look at him. The moon shimmered around their heads, casting them both in a soft halo.

"Thanks."

GLUMLY, Stacey stared at the adjoining door to Cord's room. When she'd finished getting ready for bed, she'd noticed a sliver of light from underneath his door and couldn't resist the lure. Decent enough in baseball pajamas, she raised her hand to knock, then hesitated. What was she doing here?

She'd seen Cord kiss Eileen Martin good-night. After everyone had left, Stacey had gone up to her room, and without turning on any lights, had been about to close the blinds on the window that faced the front of the house, when she'd heard Eileen's sensual laugh waft up from the driveway below. Entranced, Stacey had looked down to see Cord secure an already-sleeping Megan in the back of Eileen's car, shut the door and turn to the mature, smart, sophisticated woman. Eileen had lost no time in circling her arms around Cord's neck, pulling his head down and covering his mouth with hers. Then, Cord had taken over. With his whole body. Stacey had watched him fit the other woman to him, banding his arms around her. Though she'd felt like a voyeur, she couldn't look away. The kiss had gone on for a long time...

Stacey knocked on the door.

"Come in." His tone was the one men used when you interrupted them watching a baseball game. Well, too bad. She wasn't any too pleased about the events of the evening, either.

When she opened the door, he was sitting on his bed reading, dressed in low-slung fleece shorts and dark wire-rimmed glasses. And nothing else. Her mouth went dry but she managed to say, "I just want to say good-night."

His jaw tight, Cord stared at her, then set the book down on the mattress. "Did you have a nice birthday?"

"It was okay." She crossed fully into the room. "Can I sit down for a minute?"

He nodded.

She sank onto the bed, a safe distance from him.

"Did Megan ruin it for you?"

"No, of course not. Preston did."

Cord sat up straight. "Stacey, how did you ever end up with him? He doesn't seem like your type."

He was, until now. "He fit right into my plans."

"Plans?"

"Yeah. A carefully ordered life with no surprises and few risks has always been a priority for me."

"Why?"

She sighed. "Oh, Cord it's such a cliché."

"What is?"

"It's because of Helene. She was reckless and ruined a lot of lives in the process. I decided if I was careful, and safe, I wouldn't end up like she did."

"And Preston?"

"Is careful and safe. Unfortunately, he's also stubborn and inflexible. I was furious at his crack about Megan. I'll never forgive him for that."

"Did you fight before he left? I thought I heard raised voices in the den."

"Yes, and it was another beauty."

"Sorry."

Picking at the threads of the quilt, Stacey asked, "What about you? Did you have a good time?"

"Yep."

"Did Eileen?"

"I don't want to discuss Eileen," he said tightly.

"Why? You know all about Preston."

"It's not the same thing."

"I saw you kiss her."

"Spying on us, little girl?"

"I'm not a little girl, Cord. You can pretend that I am, all you want, but it won't change things."

When he just glared at her, she asked, "What's the matter, did I hit a nerve?"

"What do you mean?"

"Why don't you want to talk about the women in your life? Do you have some deep dark secret in your past?" When he didn't answer, but his face paled, she blurted out, "Are you sleeping with Eileen Martin?"

"That's none of your concern."

A needle of pain pricked her heart. "Oh, that's right, I forgot. I just have an adolescent crush on my bodyguard. His sex life isn't any of my business."

"You got it."

"Well, I want to know, anyway."

"Why?"

So I can torture myself with images of her having you. When she realized that was exactly what she'd do, Stacey stood abruptly. "Oh, never mind. This is a stupid conversation."

"I agree. And from now on, I'd appreciate it if you kept your cute little nose out of my personal life."

"Fine, McKay. And you can stay my bodyguard, but you can stay *out* of my private life, too."

"Suits me."

Furious at the tears that threatened, Stacey whirled and stomped to her own room. She yanked back the covers, and climbed in bed.

Her companion, jealousy, was cold comfort.

THEY WERE STILL snapping at each other eighteen hours later. Cord sat in the reception area outside her office ready to spit nails. She'd been in a mood all morning and he knew why. The same reason he'd bitten her head off when she wouldn't practice some self-defense moves with him before work...

"Why are you dressed for the office already? It's only seven o'clock."

"I have a heavy schedule today. I want to go in early."

"What about our morning workout?"

"I don't want to practice today."

"Well, tough, you don't have any choice."

"Yes, I do."

"Don't act like a spoiled brat, Stacey."

She crossed her arms over her chest. "Don't treat me like a child just because I do or say something you don't like. You tried that last night and it didn't work."

"Is that what this is all about? Last night?"

Turning from him, she'd walked to the door, then glanced over her shoulder. "This is all about the fact that I have a lot of work to do today. And since you're employed by my father, you'd better be ready to leave in fifteen minutes. I'll be having coffee in the kitchen."

At noon, in the CGW building, Cord was still flaming at her treatment of him. Rising, he walked to the door of her office. He leaned back against the jamb and crossed his arms over his chest, watching her. She was all trussed up today in a navy blue suit with a row of military-style buttons and red trim around the hem and sleeves of her jacket. Still, it couldn't disguise the fullness of her breasts. He wondered for the thousandth time what they would feel like in his hands.

"What do you want?" Stacey's voice was February-afternoon cold.

"I'm hungry."

"So, go eat."

"Come with me. I'd like to get out of here for a while."

"I don't want any food."

"Come with me, anyway."

"No."

"Stacey, stop acting like—"

Unexpectedly she rose. "Don't start that again, Cord." Brown eyes shot fire at him.

He glared at her, then turned and left, muttering under his breath.

She had every right to be angry at him. He'd tried to send her a message by bringing Eileen to dinner, as if Stacey were some adolescent girl he could manipulate. Then, he'd spoken to her as if she were a child when they'd talked afterward.

But God, he'd had no choice. When she'd been across the room with Matthews before dinner, and the man had touched her, Cord had wanted to jerk her out of her fiancé's embrace, throw her over his shoulder and stalk from the room.

And in his thirty-six years, he couldn't ever remember feeling like that about a woman.

She'd only intensified how he felt by the way she'd handled Megan. When Stacey had come out on the patio, she'd erased all of Megan's youthful anxiety, and cheered up his daughter in a way he hadn't been able to do. He'd wanted to sink to his knees and thank her.

But when she'd returned to the party in the blue sequins, he knew he was doomed. The dress hugged every female curve, scooped low in the back and skimmed her knees. He'd gotten so hard he thought he might embarrass himself...

Plopping down in front of the phone at an empty desk, Cord pulled out the directory, and looked up·the number of Canfield's one pizza parlor.

Maybe food would soothe his overactive libido.

But he doubted it.

LATER THAT AFTERNOON, Cord prowled around the office making sure everything was still secure.

After that, he got out his laptop and worked on the case. He had software from his days on the police force that helped solve cases like this—predicting next moves, drawing up psychological profiles, even guessing suspects from information entered on who the victim knew. Cord was updating the statistics, when Stacey strode out of her office. "I have a meeting upstairs with the financial staff."

"It wasn't on the daily agenda you gave me."

She faced him squarely. "No? Must be I had other things on my mind and forgot to fill you in. Oh, and I made an appointment after work to get my hair cut." She jabbed at the elevator button.

Coming up behind her, he said, "Why the hell did you do that?"

Dark, sensitive eyes glanced at him before they turned ice cold. "Make the appointment?"

"Yeah. To cut this?" He reached out and captured a lock in his fingers before he realized what he was doing. Her hair was as soft as velvet, its reddish high-lights more vivid now that it had grown some.

"It's a mess. I never wear my hair this long."

"I like it."

One of the elevators arrived so Stacey stepped onto it. "Your point?"

He followed but thought best not to respond. When the doors closed, Cord noticed the interior of the elevator was half torn apart. The drywall had been removed, and insulation showed in between the beams set about twelve inches apart. Even the ceiling had been ripped out and replaced by the newly required trapdoor. "I wonder when they did this," he mused aloud.

She tapped her foot. "Must be today bec—" Suddenly, the entire car jolted and stopped. Unbalanced, Stacey tumbled back against the wall, banging her skull on an exposed beam. "Damn," she said, raising her hand to rub the spot.

"Let me see."

She shook her head. "It's okay."

Ignoring her, he tugged her close and threaded his hands through the heavy brown mass. Curls surrounded his fingers, and for a minute he luxuriated in their silkiness. Then he felt for the bump. "You've got a little goose egg." His voice was husky, as if they'd just kissed.

He *might* have kissed her if the elevator hadn't jolted again and resumed its motion. He stepped away from her, trying to contain the furnace blast of heat that suffused him.

Disgusted by his reaction, he studied the elevator. "Don't take this one again. I don't like the feel of it."

"Yes, sir," she said with sarcasm that could have cut through granite.

They rode the rest of the way in silence.

AT SIX O'CLOCK, he was still pacing. He'd spent most of the day out of her sight, but close enough to protect her. He went to her office again. "Stacey, I have to talk to the guard downstairs before we leave for the night. If you want to get to that hair appointment on time, we'd better go now."

She glanced at her watch, then looked up at him. Dark circles smudged the skin under her eyes, and fatigue lines bracketed her mouth. She'd been working hard all day, and probably hadn't gotten much more sleep than he had last night.

"I can't go yet," she told him. "I'm waiting for a long-distance call from our office in Washington State. There's only a four-hour window when I can talk to them because of the time difference."

"Sorry, Stacey, you have to come with me. I've really got to check out something with Hank," he said, referring to the security guard downstairs.

Clearly exasperated, she blew the bangs out of her eyes. "Can't you do that without me? I'll come right down—" Just then, the phone rang. "Yes?" she said after she picked up the receiver. She slapped her hand over the mouthpiece. "It's Washington. I'll be down in ten minutes. Then we can leave for my hair appointment."

He shook his head.

"Cord, please. I can't take another round with you today." From the lines of stress in her face, and her too-bright eyes, he believed her.

"All right. But if you're not down in ten minutes, I'm coming to get you."

She didn't answer and he left.

TEN MINUTES LATER, he said to Hank, "Call her, would you?"

The gray-haired security man smiled. "She sure is a handful. I wouldn't want your job."

Cord smiled back, but it died when Hank's wrinkled forehead creased even more. "No answer."

Fear sliced through Cord. He strode to the elevators and pushed the button. Then he glanced up. *Three* was lit for both cars. And neither was moving. He jabbed the buttons mercilessly. Still no movement.

His heart thumping, Cord raced for the stairs. He yanked on the heavy metal door. It wouldn't budge.

Hank came up behind him. "What is it?"

"This door is locked."

"Nah, it's been sticking lately. But the repairmen came today. Let me give it a try." He pulled on the door.

Though older than Cord, Hank had bulk and muscle. Still, the door didn't open. "That's strange," he said. "I thought it was fixed."

"Hank, was the elevator repaired today, too?"

"Yeah, by the same company. But they were called off the job before they could finish."

"Listen carefully. I think Stacey's stuck on that elevator. How else can we get up there?"

The older man scowled. "There's only the stairs and the elevators. Ain't no other way up. Not unless you sprout wings."

THE MINUTE the elevator stopped at the third floor, the interior lights went out. Stacey huddled back into the corner and gripped the handrail. Pitch blackness surrounded her. With every ounce of strength she had, she forced herself to bite back a scream. Or a whimper. Instead, she breathed in deeply as Cord had taught her to do in their daily exercises.

If you're really scared, take a deep breath until you've got your wits about you. If no one is threatening you, think of something pleasant.

She conjured up the image of Megan trying on all Stacey's necklaces last night. When Stacey's breathing was normal again, she raised her hands to the wall and felt her way along it. The paper covering the insulation was rough, and the Fiberglas poked through in places, scratching her hands. She sneezed twice, but kept moving. She found the control panel with her fingers, but couldn't see it. She tried to visualize where the emergency button was. She pictured the rows of buttons that went to the floors of the building. She remembered seeing the red Emergency button about six inches below. Groping, she found it and pressed. It rang like a school bell, but to her, the echoing sound was like chimes from the angels. Now someone would know she was stuck.

Cord will know, anyway, you jerk. He'll come. Just wait it out. She sank to the floor. What was happening? Was the elevator just stuck, or . . . was the stalker involved?

Don't jump to conclusions. This elevator was under repair. It was just stuck. If only she'd listened to Cord and not used it.

Please, God, let it be just stuck.

She tried to picture the inside of the elevator again. Maybe there was some other way to start it, or—oh, God, yes, there might be a phone. She felt her way back to the controls once more. Down about a foot— sure enough, there was a small compartment. She opened the door and grasped a phone. She picked up the receiver. It was dead. Her heart rate tripled.

Sliding back to the floor, she rested her head on her knees. She had to make plans. If the stalker had done this, what would he do now that he had her stuck on the third floor? Or was she between floors? If she was on the third floor, would he open the doors and grab her? What would she do if he did? What weapons did she have?

There was a can of Mace in her purse. Cord had insisted she carry it. On hands and knees, snagging her panty hose and abrading her palms on the skidproof flooring, she searched for her purse. She found it in a corner against the wall. Frantically, she opened the zipper and fished around inside until she found the small cylinder. Closing her hand around it, she sank onto the floor and prayed.

Suddenly, she felt the entire car shimmy. There was a loud thump on the roof of the elevator. She looked up. Though she couldn't see anything, she pictured the ceiling of the elevator and the mandatory trapdoor that had been installed. Oh, no, someone was coming through it.

When a sharp sliver of light pierced the darkness, she whispered, *I love you, Cord.*

And waited for her attacker.

From the well-lit elevator shaft, a figure leaped into the car and poised above her. She raised her can of Mace. He blocked out the light so she could only see his silhouette. But God, she'd know those shoulders anywhere...

"Cord."

He sank to his knees and she dropped the Mace and crawled into his arms.

She buried her face in his neck. His hands gripped her waist, then one banded around her. Another locked on her neck so tight it hurt. She could hear his heart was thumping in his chest and felt a shiver go through him.

"I was so scared," she mumbled into his skin.

"I was, too."

"I'm sorry I was such a bitch today."

"I'm sorry I was such a bastard."

"I was jealous. From last night."

He gripped her tighter. "I was, too."

Stacey's heart skidded to a halt with Cord's first, real admission that he cared for her. "Take me home," she whispered, "and stay with me."

"You can count on it."

CHAPTER EIGHT

WHEN THE NIGHTMARE came six hours later, Cord was holding her. She jerked awake in a sweat, startling him out of sleep, too. His strong arms encircled her—and she knew he hadn't let go of her all night. He wore sweatpants and she had on long red cotton pajamas. Both had changed when they'd gotten home after the elevator incident, and she'd asked him to stay with her until she fell asleep. With a light left on in the corner of the room, they'd settled on top of the covers, and slept soundly.

He rubbed her back and kissed the top of her head, securing it under his chin, close to his chest. "Another dream?"

"Y-yes."

"Do you remember any of it?"

"Uh-huh."

"Tell me."

She shook her head.

"Stacey, maybe it will help."

There was a long silence. Then she said, "It was about my mother."

Cord stiffened. Stacey felt it all through him.

"I was at the cemetery. I was really little, and I was crying."

"It's probably what happened when she died, sweetheart."

Burying her face in his skin, breathing in the maleness, she said, "I guess. It seems that lately—since the stalking stuff—I've started to remember all sorts of things about Helene. Things that happened when I was around Megan's age."

"You were around Megan's age when Helene died, weren't you? Maybe that's why."

"Well, something's got these memories coming back like an old film clip."

If possible, Cord's muscles tightened even more. Stacey said, "Cord, does this bother you so much because of your father?"

He didn't answer right away, but finally asked, "What do you mean?"

"Well, every time we talk about Helene, you freeze up. I thought maybe it reminded you of your relationship with your dad."

"Maybe it does. I don't like to talk about him."

"Like you said, it might help to tell someone."

"Maybe."

"Tell *me*."

"I don't want to change the subject from your nightmare. I think you should get it all out."

"I will, if you tell me about your father."

"Okay." His chest heaved under her cheek. "It's the classic cobbler-whose-kids-had-no-shoes story."

"How?"

"He was the best cop Canfield ever saw. Worked miracles with juvenile offenders. But he was never home, never had time for me. When he *was* there, he was unbending. Cops and teachers are usually stricter with their own children because of their experience with kids in trouble. But my knowing that now doesn't help.''

"Is that why you left Canfield when you were eighteen?"

His hand stopped making lazy circles on her back. "Partly."

"And it's why you didn't want to leave Megan and take this job protecting me, isn't it?"

"Yes."

"But you did."

"For you." His voice was gravelly.

"Maybe your father had some of that same need to protect people."

"Over and over again?"

"No, probably not. But maybe there were extenuating circumstances for him, too, that you don't know about. Maybe you should give him the benefit of the doubt. Like you told me to do for Helene."

Cord's pause was meaningful. "How'd you get so smart for somebody so young?" he asked.

"I'm not that young, Cord."

Slowly, she lifted his hand from around her waist and brought it to her breast. "I'm a full-grown woman."

His fingers flexed on her flesh, without his conscious consent, she guessed. Their weight and pressure against her created a buzz of sexual excitement. She felt his heat through her pajamas.

"Stacey…" The warning in his voice was diluted by its unmistakable huskiness.

She pulled back, but pressed his hand closer to her. He didn't remove it. She looked up at his stubbled jaw, then at his mouth.

"Don't look at me that way."

Her lips curved. "Why?"

"You know why. I'm trying to be noble here."

"Screw nobility."

"Stacey..."

"Kiss me, Cord."

"No. This isn't appropriate behavior for your bodyguard. It's dangerous."

"Put your mouth on mine."

"No. You're just reacting out of stress."

"I want to taste your tongue."

"You're too young. I'm too jaded."

"Please, Cord." She inched her lower body close to his. When she felt his erection press against her, she smiled seductively. "You want to."

His eyes closed briefly. "I never said I didn't want to."

Stacey reached up and encircled his neck with her hand. "I want to, too. I want to do things with you I've never wanted to do with any man before."

He groaned. A deep, male, primal groan.

Then he lowered his head.

The kiss was not tender. Nor was it tentative. He took her mouth with a greed that bespoke weeks of wanting. He pressed hard against her lips, then bathed them with his tongue. When she opened them to him, he slid it inside. Simultaneously, he laid her back onto the pillow, angled his body over her and pressed her into the mattress. All the while, his hand kneaded her breast. His tongue mated with hers and swept the inside of her mouth until he pulled back. His arm braced beside her, he looked down into her eyes. "You are the most precious thing I've ever touched in my life." His hand moved to work loose the three big buttons on her pajama top. Bared to him, the sight of her made his eyes glitter. "And the loveliest." He returned his hand to her bare and aching breast, grazing the nipple with his calluses, then rolling it between his thumb and finger. It hardened instantly and sent a rush of feminine response through her. Her moan echoed an invitation in the still semidarkness.

Lowering his head again, he brought his mouth to hers. His kiss was rapacious. He devoured her lips, bit them with gentle aggression, soothed them with his tongue. He kissed the corners of her mouth, worked his way to her jaw, then to the sensitive skin at her neck. She moaned again. "Ah, Stace, don't make those sounds. They inflame me. I'm so hard I'm ready to burst."

"Make love to me," she murmured.

The bald invitation sobered Cord. Already, he was on the brink of losing control. Taking a deep, desperate breath, he drew back from her. Her chest was heaving as if she couldn't get enough air, he noticed as he buttoned up her pajamas. Her lips were swollen from his passion; he smoothed his thumb over them. His beard had raised tiny red pinpricks on her cheek. She looked wanton and ready and more seductive than a harem girl. He wasn't sure he could back away.

Except that she was Helene's daughter. He hadn't backed away from the mother eighteen years ago, and it had ruined lives. He couldn't ruin any more by seducing Stacey.

"I can't make love to you, Stace."

"Why?"

"For all the reasons I've already given you."

"They aren't good enough."

No, but the real one is. He should just tell her and get it over with. Now was the time, given how vulnerable he felt toward her, how his willpower was ready to snap like a frayed rope drawn too tightly. But the truth was, he was afraid she'd kick him out of her life for good, and he couldn't risk that now. He couldn't risk her safety in any way. So he opted for the most credible reason he could think of, hating how it would hurt her.

Reaching down, he grabbed her left hand. He tugged it up, then flicked her wrist so her eyes came flush with her engagement ring. "You belong to someone else."

Color suffused her face. But it was the tears brimming—and what they meant—that nearly undid him. Infidelity of any kind was abhorrent to her. Cord knew how she felt and he'd taken full advantage of her vulnerability. He despised his action but anything was better than making love to her and dealing with that hurt when she found out about him and Helene.

"I'm going to get up now, and go to my own room," he said. "We can't do this again, Stacey. Do you understand?" God, he sounded so arrogant—so rational, so in control. In reality, he was a breath away from ripping off her pajamas and burying himself inside her, regardless of the consequences. The kiss had released the desire that had been banked inside him far too long.

"I understand," she said gravely.

"Good."

PEDALING FAST, Stacey breathed in deeply, trying to outrace the images that chased her like the ancient Furies.

You're just like Helene, they told her. *You would have let him make love to you. You're engaged to someone else.*

She pedaled faster. The blood rushed to her face and her calf muscles stung. She wiped the dripping sweat from her forehead but kept going.

"Training for the decathlon?" she heard from the double doors which led out to the pool.

"Hi, Daddy."

"Hi." Gifford crossed into the room and Stacey slowed down the bike. "Cord's out on the patio. He just filled me in on all the details from last night."

Not all the details, I'm sure.

"I'm sorry I was out of town. You must have been terrified."

Stacey nodded, then felt the moisture gather in her eyes. She stopped pedaling and exhaled sharply, trying to regain some control.

"Come here, honey, let me give you a hug," Gifford said.

In seconds, she was in the arms of her father—arms that had seen her through closet monsters and measles, boys and braces. "I'm so tired of all this, Daddy, I can hardly think straight."

"I know."

"Are the police going to do anything about last night?"

He hesitated, which meant no. "Well, Cord raised all kinds of hell with Valentino, but they checked out the elevator today, and they say it showed no signs of tampering. It was under repair, and just stuck. Same thing for the stairway door."

Stacey drew back and looked at her father. "What happened with the stairway?"

"Didn't Cord tell you?"

"Ah...no. We didn't talk much afterward, and I was busy all day at work."

"Apparently, the ground-floor door was stuck along with the elevators."

"Then how did Cord get to me?"

"He took the service elevator that goes directly to the top-floor executive offices, then went down the stairs to the third floor. Then he came through the trapdoor in the ceiling, since the elevator was between floors."

Stacey started to shiver, remembering her fear when she'd seen the door open above her. "How can the police think this is a coincidence after everything else that's happened to me?"

"I don't know, honey. It seems preplanned to me, too."

Drawing away from her father and placing a quick peck on his cheek, Stacey flopped onto the couch. "It's all too much. The stalking. The problems with Preston. Helene."

Gifford cocked his head. "Helene?"

She stared at her father. "I'm being bombarded with memories, Daddy."

"Like at the pool on Father's Day?"

"Yes."

"Honey, I meant what I said about talking about her. Maybe that would help."

"Maybe."

Gifford's eyes strayed to the wall of storage closets. "I have a better idea. Come on—I want to show you some things."

He crossed to the other side of the room and retrieved a key hidden in a potted plant. After he'd unlocked and opened the door of one storage closet, he switched on a light in the five-by-six-foot area. Inside, Stacey saw boxes piled to the ceiling, and stretched canvases stacked along the wall. She recognized them as the work she'd done in high school.

"You kept my paintings?"

Gifford turned to her. "Of course, every single one of them."

Stacey pulled out a canvas. When she turned it over, a geyser of emotion swept through her. The distinct odor of oils and turpentine recalled hours spent in the art room at school and in the spare room upstairs that she'd used as a studio. When she looked at the painting, she saw the swirling blues, greens and yellows that had dominated her work. She remembered her teachers in high school had praised her technique and encouraged her to keep painting.

Her father watched as she flipped through the canvases. "That was my favorite," he said when she got to an outdoor scene of a babbling brook and surrounding trees.

She smiled wistfully. "It won first place in the Scholastic Art Show. I remember how proud you were."

"It hung in the library for a year until you made me take it down."

She shook her head at her youthful rebellion.

"Why did you do that, Stacey? What's the real reason you quit art school?"

How could she tell him that when she was a freshman in college, she'd found out her mother had been an artist? Her father's eyes were always so sad when he talked about Helene, Stacey hated to bring up her name. Although she'd always wondered why he'd been more sad than angry, since Helene had betrayed him so badly.

"Lots of reasons," she hedged. Then she pointed to some cartons. "What's in those boxes?"

Gifford studied her for a minute, then turned around. "They're things of your mother's that I didn't give away or destroy." He looked at her again. "Maybe I knew deep in my heart that this day would come."

"What do you mean?"

Sighing, he ran a hand through his hair and sank onto one of the boxes. "Honey, you've grown up with a skewed view of your mother. She wasn't what Ana led you to believe. What I allowed her to tell you."

The familiar rage welled in Stacey. "She was unfaithful to you, wasn't she?"

"Yes, she was. But I don't think you have a clear picture of that, either."

"In what way?"

"Stacey, I was gone a lot. More than a lot. I traveled several nights a week and entertained customers when I was in town. Your mother got lonely."

"That's no excuse."

"No, but she was only human."

As clearly as if he was standing next to her, not out on the patio, Stacey heard Cord say, *Your mother was just human. Maybe she even had reasons you don't know about. But that doesn't matter. What matters is that you're a good person. Maybe she was, too.*

"Why are you telling me this, Daddy? It must kill you to talk about it."

"Because it's not fair that you think badly of her any longer. She loved you very much, Stacey."

At her questioning look, Gifford shook his head and turned back to the boxes. He riffled through a couple, then said, "Here it is." Picking up a large crate, he set it on top of the others and withdrew a sketchbook. From Stacey's vantage point, she could see several others. Her skin tingled and a strange sensation trickled through her. Then she remembered . . . Helene sticking a book like this in her bag. *Come on, love, I want to draw you out by the pool.*

"They're hers," Stacey whispered.

Her father's eyes were so filled with regret, Stacey wanted to grab the book and throw it away. Almost as much as she wanted to see what was inside. He handed it to her. She ran her fingers over the familiar red surface then lifted the cover.

The first charcoal sketch was of an infant. In the corner it said, *One day old.* The child nestled in a blanket and slept soundly. Tiny fingernails had been carefully drawn, and wisps of hair peeked out from a hospital cap.

She turned the page. *One week old.* The baby had grown. Awake now, huge eyes stared out at the world. Two strong masculine hands held the little bundle. Stacey knew those hands well.

Page after page of her infancy followed. From one to the next, she grew, her hair got longer, her features more distinct. She was a happy child. Her first smile was captured. One grinning mouth had two little teeth poking out.

The book ended with her birthday. A cake with one candle sat in front of her. Frosting covered her face, hands and clothes. She was laughing and Stacey could almost hear the tinkle of childish giggling.

The images began to waver with her tears, so she looked up. "They're all of me."

Her father nodded, his own eyes moist. Then he picked up four more sketchbooks. "She did one each year. Until she died."

Stacey closed her eyes to keep back the tears, but they leaked out, anyway. She swiped at them, then took the books from her father. Sliding to the floor, her back to the wall, she turned the pages.

It took a long time, but Gifford sat where he was, on the crate, watching his daughter become acquainted with the childhood he had stolen from her. It was almost more than he could bear.

Stacey looked exhausted when she finished. "I never knew."

"She loved you very much," he repeated.

Raising soulful eyes to him, she said, "Why, Daddy? Why did you let me think . . . let me grow up believing she never loved us?"

His shoulders slumped like an old man's. "It was never my intention to do that, honey, but things got out of hand with your grandmother. Before I knew it, she'd filled your mind with poison about Helene. But I take full responsibility. I was too cowardly to let you know the truth."

"Cowardly? Why?"

"Because the truth would have shown you how unhappy I'd made your mother. If I'd been home more . . . if I'd listened more to what she was telling me, she'd be alive today."

His daughter came off the floor to stand before him. He didn't want to look at her, knowing he'd see well-deserved blame and accusation in her eyes. When he managed the courage to face her, his heart almost stopped. Instead of justifiable rage, he saw forgiveness. God, she was more like her mother than he'd realized.

She put her arms around him. "Oh, Daddy."

They held each other and grieved for the woman who had loved them both.

"Stacey, there's something else. Another part of this. I'm beginning to see I . . . I haven't viewed you as adult all these years, that I've tried to keep you a child."

She pulled away to look at him. Wiping her eyes, she said, "Maybe I've encouraged that, Daddy. I've noticed I behave differently around you, I act more like a kid. I'd like that to change."

"So would I." Gifford smiled sadly, thinking of what a beautiful woman she'd become, both inside and out.

Stacey smiled, too. Then she waved her hand at the other boxes. "Well, what's in the rest of those?"

Shaking his head, Gifford turned to confront the myriad memories he hadn't faced in years. "Some personal things that belonged to Helene. Jewelry, a few pieces of clothing, some books. Lots of pictures. Truthfully, I don't remember what's in all of them."

Stacey smiled at him again—weakly, this time—and he wondered what it felt like to know your hero had feet of clay. But he was glad this was all out in the open.

All but McKay. He prayed to God she never found out about that. She'd never forgive either one of them.

His daughter dug into a box. She ferreted through some evening bags and shawls of Helene's, then she pulled out another sketchbook. Gifford didn't think he'd ever seen it.

"Another one?" she asked, her mouth turned up slightly.

"I guess. I don't remember that one, but it was a long time ago."

Stacey casually leafed open the book. Her forehead creased and she bit her lip. When she turned the page and her hand trembled, Gifford asked, "Stacey, what is it?"

She raised such incredibly sad eyes to him that he was alarmed. "Stacey?"

"Oh, Daddy." She held out the sketchbook. He took it and stared down at the open picture.

On the eight-by-ten page was a full-blown charcoal sketch of him, twenty-three years ago. He posed beneath a tree in his father's backyard, gripping an overhead branch. His grin was cocky as he winked at the artist. He and Helene had both been Stacey's age, on the brink of starting a life together. He looked happier than he ever remembered being.

He flipped the page. There he was in his tux. Eyes sparkling, trim, fit, his wedding ring gleamed on his finger.

Another page revealed him in a business suit, his hair shorter, more the executive now. It was the beginning of his career, the beginning of the change in him. Successive pages showed that transformation through Helene's eyes...he looked older, more sophisticated...hurried...then tired. Once or twice, he was relaxed, holding Stacey or in the pool. When he came to a sketch of him in bed, obviously after they'd just made love—he was naked from the waist up, his lap covered with a sheet—Gifford had to close the book.

The lump in his throat threatened to overcome him. He wanted to scream, to cry, to smash the nearest breakable object. Years ago, he'd stopped feeling that searing, sickening pain at Helene's accident—at the futility and uselessness of her death. But now he felt the grief so deep, it leveled him. He'd had so much, and thrown it all away for success that now meant so little to him, it made a mockery of his life. The tears he'd held at bay, to be strong for his daughter, escaped. He clutched at his heart, hoping to stop the agony.

"Daddy?"

Stacey's image blurred before him; trying to focus on the only good thing he had left in his life, he finally said, "This was...unexpected."

Her voice raw, she said, "You'd never seen the sketches?"

"No, I packed up stuff I didn't even look at. God knows why."

"From what I saw in the pictures, I can tell she must have really loved you."

"And you, honey."

Stacey smiled and hugged him again.

Behind them, Gifford heard, "What's going on in here?" The voice of another person Helene had loved. Cord McKay.

THE SITUATION between Cord and Stacey simmered for four days, almost coming to a boiling point several times. It reached meltdown one night when Cord insisted they work on some new self-defense techniques. It was now well into July—Cord had been living at the Webbs' for almost a month. Every day, they'd practiced the three or four maneuvers Cord had taught her, but he seemed determined to add more.

Tonight he was pushing her to the limit. She was exhausted from not sleeping well; worried about the stalker, she felt vulnerable and alone; with the new knowledge about her mother, she felt confused; and tormenting her was the memory of Cord's kiss and caresses in her bed that night, how he'd responded to her—and how he'd rejected her. But finally, it was the knowledge that she was in love with him, not Preston, that dug deepest into her soul. Regardless of what happened between her and Cord, she'd have to end her engagement.

"Come on, Stacey. You're not concentrating." Cord's annoyed tone grated on her.

"I am too."

"Oh, sure, I could have raped or killed you three times already."

She glared at him. "Right about now, I don't really care."

Like lightning, just as quick and deadly, he grabbed her wrist and squeezed tightly. "Don't *ever* say anything like that again."

Tears stung the backs of her eyes, but she'd be damned if she'd cry in front of him again. She just nodded.

"Now, be assertive," he said.

All right, McKay. You want assertive. I'll give you assertive.

"Let's try it again. I'm coming up from behind. I get you in a bear hug. What's the first thing you do?"

Stacey swung her hips out of the way and brought her fist back. He'd said to go for the testicles. She went for them mercilessly.

He was quick, she'd give him that. Darting out of the way just in time, he cursed fluently.

"Well, you said to go for it. Of course, I wouldn't want to ruin you for Eileen."

"Shut up."

"Excuse me?"

"I said shut up, or you'll be sorry where your smart mouth gets you."

"I'm never sorry for what I sa—"

A quick twist of his leg landed her flat on her back. Glowering up at him, she decided, *This is war.*

Lithely she sprang to her feet. "Let's try that again. And don't let up on me."

"Don't worry, babe, I have no intention of making this easy for you."

Another grab from behind. Another swivel of her hips. He parried her groin attack, so Stacey quickly whipped her foot around his leg. His arms flew out to balance himself and she took advantage of the vulnerable exposure of his chest to jab her elbow into his ribs. He doubled over and fell to the floor.

"Is that assertive enough? Am I paying close enough attention?" She wiped the sweat out of her eyes and stuck her hands on her hips.

He nodded, but before she could step back, he sneaked his hand around an ankle, toppling her down next to him.

"Major lesson in self-defense, Stacey. Never get cocky about your victories."

"Go to hell, McKay."

She tried to rise but Cord rolled over, pinning her beneath him. Her chest heaved as she bucked futilely.

"What are you so angry about?" he asked. "Is it because I didn't make love to you four days ago?"

No, this is because I've fallen in love with you, you jerk. Had her hands been free, she would have slugged him. He was so dense. "All right, I admit I wanted to make love with you," she said. "I may be many things, but I don't lie to myself. Unlike you."

"What the hell does that mean?"

"You wanted to just as much as I did." She lifted her chin. "I could tell." She arched her hips against his. "Just like I can tell now."

Easing back up on his elbows, he started to pull away. "That's it, McKay," she said. "Run away. That's your M.O., isn't it—flee from the conflict. You've spent your whole life avoiding involvement, running away. Why? What happened to you in the past?"

His face went ashen. More sweat beaded on his upper lip. "I gave you my reasons. Besides, you're engaged."

Not for long. What would he do when he no longer had that safety net?

The thought made her lips curl. He frowned, as if he'd read her mind.

"Let me up, would you, caveman? You've proved your superior strength, and your superior willpower."

For now.

ROLLING OVER on his narrow twin bed, the man slid his arms underneath his head, and stared up at the ceiling. The stains on the plaster of his rented room reminded him of the seedy house on Erie Avenue where he'd grown up. He'd spent many nights in a bed just like this, listening to the muffled screams of his mother, and then later, after she'd left, to those of his father's "friends." Goddamned whores were all alike. Women made you beat the hell out of them, then wanted you to hump them till they couldn't even walk.

The image reminded him of Stacey Webb. He laughed aloud. Her pals thought they were so clever, figuring out how to get to her even though he'd managed to disable the elevator and block the door. But he'd *planned* it that way. He wanted McKay to rescue her. And he wanted to be there when it happened, to see how scared she was, to watch those lush lips tremble with fear. Of *him*. He'd had to go out of his way to accomplish that one. If the secretary in the repair shop hadn't been such a hot number, he never would've been able to pull it off. Yeah, his father had been right—all cats are gray in the dark.

He wondered if Stacey Webb would be any different—feel any different when he touched her, tasted her, rammed himself inside her. The thought made him hard.

He sprung out of bed and walked over to the poster on the wall. He'd had the photo of her enlarged as big as he could get it, then carefully cut out the other half of the picture. She was alone on his wall, all by herself in the shiny blue dress that clung to her ass like a man's hand.

Reaching into his boot, he yanked out the knife. Methodically he dragged the blade across her face. Then, beginning at her throat, he carved up the photograph.

CHAPTER NINE

"HI, love. I'm so glad you called." Preston lounged in the doorway of his chic condominium in Pillar's Post, one of the many small villages surrounding Canfield. He peered over her shoulder to the parking lot. "Well, look at that. If it isn't Clint Eastwood, Kevin Costner and Bruce Willis all rolled into one."

Frowning, Stacey nodded. "I asked him to stay in the truck. I wanted some privacy."

Preston's eyes locked with hers. His leer made her shiver. And not from desire. "Smart girl. Come in."

Stacey stepped over the threshold and moved past him; he closed the door and grasped her shoulders before she could turn around. One hand slid to span her waist and the other angled toward her breast. She squirmed away, unable to bear his touch after...

"Preston, we have to talk."

He stiffened. "I want to touch first. I've been out of town for a whole week. I've missed you. I need what little you'll give me tonight, Stacey."

A hammer of guilt pounded inside her. It jarred her conscience, spurring the inevitable comparison to Helene. She pivoted to face him. "There won't be any more touching, Preston."

"What is it now? More limitations? I have to tell you, I'm getting really sick of this." He strode to the black lacquer cabinet in the center of the huge, cathedral-ceilinged great room and poured himself a drink. Scotch in hand, he sat down on the white leather sofa, sprawled confidently and said, "All right. Hit me with this one."

He was making it easy. In answer, Stacey slipped off his ring, crossed the room and stretched out her hand. "I can't keep this, Preston. I'm breaking our engagement."

His classic jaw gaped. "What?"

"I can't marry you."

"I . . . I never expected this."

"I'm sorry."

Robotically he reached out and took the ring. He fingered it for a minute then looked up at her. "Stacey, you've been under a lot of pressure these last few months. This isn't a good time to make such a big decision."

Jamming her hands into the pockets of her oversize red silk shirt, she sighed. "It's not because of the stalking. Or maybe it is, indirectly. In any case, I've come to realize how different we are, how we don't even like the same things. I can't commit myself to a lifetime of living up to your expectations."

"You've never had a problem with my expectations before."

"I know. But I've changed." Unwillingly, she looked toward the door. "Things don't seem the way they used to anymore. I . . . have a different perspective on life now."

Preston was too smart to miss a subtlety. Ironically, it was one of the things she'd truly liked about him. "This wouldn't have anything to do with McKay, would it?"

In spite of her attempt to stifle the response, Stacey felt herself blush. "I don't want to talk about Cord. I just want to be fair to you."

Preston slammed his drink down on the table. Glass meeting glass echoed like a gunshot. Then he bolted off the couch. "Fair? *Fair?* You've got to be kidding. You haven't been fair to me since the first time you refused to go to bed with me. Dammit, Stacey. I haven't touched another woman in months, even though you've played the ice princess."

In months. They'd been seriously dating for over a year. The knowledge made her mission a little easier.

He paced. "I can't believe you'd dump me for a washed-up cop who never even made it to college."

If Stacey ever doubted her resolve, this strengthened it in a heartbeat. "I won't listen to more insults about my bodyguard."

Eyes narrowed, Preston asked, "And how close to his body have you gotten? Has he been sampling what's mine all these weeks?"

"I'm leaving. Goodbye, Preston. I hope you find someone who makes you happy."

Insolent shoulders shrugged. "Don't worry, doll. I'll be just fine."

"I'm sure that's true. I'm sorry if I hurt you."

"Don't flatter yourself. I'm just surprised you're letting go of such a good catch."

Without responding, Stacey turned and headed for the door. She didn't look back as she exited and hurried to the truck where Cord waited for her. Though she was certain that breaking up with Preston was the right thing to do, she was shaking from the unpleasant scene when she slid into the passenger seat.

Cord asked, "You okay?"

She nodded.

"Want to tell me about it?"

She gave him a sideways glance.

"All right, all right, I know we agreed to no personal stuff between us."

"Actually, I'd like to talk to Lauren. Would you take me to her house?"

For a split second, he turned wounded eyes on her; then the look was gone. "Sure. You made it clear that since Daddy's paying the bill, my time is yours."

"Can it, McKay. I'm not in the mood."

"Yes, ma'am."

They drove to Lauren's in silence. She lived in a small Cape Cod on the south side of Canfield—a house her parents had left her. Grateful to see lights on inside, Stacey yanked open the truck door. Cord did the same on his side.

"What are you doing?" she asked, her voice razor-sharp.

"It's dark here, and not as close to the street as Matthews's place. I'm escorting you to the door." He held up his hand when she opened her mouth to protest. "Don't bother. You can freeze me out all you want, but as long as I'm on the case, I make the safety decisions."

Turning her back without answering, Stacey bit her lip to keep from snapping at him. They climbed the lower flight of steps, then the upper one.

Stacey pressed the doorbell, then they waited. She rang it again, then again. Glancing at the street, she said, "Her car is here. Do you think she went out with someone?"

"Yeah, maybe Prince Charming." Cord shared her dislike of Mark Dunn.

Stacey banged on the door. "Lauren, it's me, Stacey."

Just when she was about to give up, the front door creaked. Through its slit, Stacey saw the Japanese-print kimono she'd given Lauren for her birthday. It was dark in the entryway. "Lauren, it's me."

In a hoarse voice, Lauren said, "I know. Go away, Stacey. I'm busy."

Unobtrusively, Cord eased the door open with his foot. He peered inside, having a better angle than Stacey. He said, "Lauren, how about letting us come in?"

Stacey's head snapped to Cord. His tone was so gentle, so soothing, it alerted her instantly.

"Lauren?" he continued in the same coaxing voice, "let us in. I can help."

Her friend choked back a sob. "Nobody can help," she said, leaning her head on the door. "Just go away. Please, Stacey, just go." It was then that Stacey got a glimpse of the red welt on her friend's shoulder where the robe had pulled away.

Cord inched closer to the door. "Is he still here, Lauren?"

"No."

"All right. Will you call us if you need us?"

"Yes."

With a look of painful resignation, Lauren closed and locked the door. Raising both fists, Stacey pounded for almost a minute, then stopped and slumped against the wood.

Cord touched her arm. "There's nothing you can do."

"I can't just leave her here."

"I gather this has been going on for some time. Haven't you already tried to talk to her about it?"

"Of course I have."

"And?"

"It hasn't helped."

"You can't *force* abused women to change, Stace."

"I know." Tears leaked from her eyes as she descended the steps, leaving her childhood friend to deal with her personal demons, in her own private hell.

CORD TRIED not to think about Lauren Sellers on the drive back to the Webbs' house. He understood the battered woman's syndrome, but it didn't stop the bile that rose in his throat at the thought of Lauren's situation. To distract himself, he thought about Megan. God, he missed her. Talking to her three times a day wasn't enough. To ease that pain he let his mind wander to what was going on between Stacey and Matthews.

When she'd asked him to take her to the swank condominium tonight, then wait in the truck, taunting visions of her smooth skin, her full breasts under

Matthews's hands nearly drove him wild. She'd returned too fast for any real damage to be done—except maybe a quickie. Of course, Stacey didn't seem to be the type for a fast tumble. He'd bet she liked her sex long and slow. He knew just how he'd—dammit, McKay, you're behaving like an adolescent boy. He willed his mind blank for the rest of the drive.

When they got home, Stacey was silent as they walked into the deserted foyer, then to the den. Her father had business out of town for two days and was staying over in Atlanta for the weekend. Cord squelched the knowledge that he and Stacey were alone in the house for four full days. And three long nights.

As soon as they reached the den, Stacey faced him squarely. "I want to talk to you."

Something about her tone set off his trouble detector.

"I . . . ah . . . have some work to do. Let's wait until tomorrow." *After I've marshaled my defenses a little more.*

"Not on your life, buddy."

Had she read his mind? Cowardice told him to run for his life. Something inexplicable and irresistible drew him to her.

When he came fully into the room, she said bluntly, "Look." She held up her left hand.

He saw nothing. Nothing. *Nothing!*

"Stacey? What have you done?"

Her angled chin was all the confirmation he needed. "I've broken my engagement with Preston."

Elation fluttered wildly in his heart before he could quell it. "Why?" he croaked.

"That's a stupid question." She came toward him, her hips swaying gracefully in the red silk walking shorts.

"Answer it, anyway."

Her hands reached him first, glided up his chest, nestled in the hair visible under three open buttons of his sport shirt. His heart jump-started.

"I couldn't stay engaged to one man when I'm in love with another."

Cord was sure he was going into cardiac arrest when she spoke those precious words.

But they're words you have no right to hear, McKay.

Damn! What was he thinking?

He grasped her clever hands, which had wandered to his neck. Wanting with all his heart and battered soul to leave them where they were, to take what she so innocently offered to the man who had almost ruined her life, he pulled them from his thrumming body. Stepping back, he said, "Stacey, sweetheart, you don't know what you're doing. Listen, you'll make up with Matthews. It's just the circumstances...the forced separation, probably the abstinence that's causing this breach. Once you've resumed your normal relationship, things will be better."

Could her big brown eyes possibly get more innocent? "What do you mean?"

Oh, God, she was going to make him spell it out. "You know what I mean. Your sexual relationship." The phrase grated on his nerve endings like knuckles on a cheese shredder. "Men get testy when

they're...deprived...of what they normally have.''
He pulled away completely and ran an exasperated
hand through his hair. ''Dammit, Stacey. You can't be
this dense. Once you've resumed your normal sexual
relationship, Matthews will settle down again.''

He never expected the laughter. It bubbled up out
of her, soft and amused and again...innocent.
''There's nothing to wait for.''

''What do you mean?''

''Now who's being dense?''

''Stacey, what are you saying?''

''Preston and I have never made love, Cord. I've
never been with a man. And right now, I'm very, very
glad. You'll be my first.''

Absolute joy and undiluted terror hammerlocked
his heart. *''What?''*

Giving him a sultry laugh, she inched closer and
began to unbutton her shirt. ''I'm sure this is a surprise, but I thought the news would please you.
Knowing no man has ever had me before. Knowing
you'll be the only one. Don't you like that idea, Francis?''

Blood pooled in his groin, telling *him,* at least, how
much he liked it. Every primitive instinct he owned
reared inside him at her words, at her invitation, at the
fact that he could possess her as no man ever had before. He was a breath away from accepting her offer,
when the fluttering of the curtains at the window di-
verted his attention. The window where he'd stood
when this woman's father had told him eighteen years
ago exactly what kind of man he was. Cord had
changed since then, but if he took Helene's daughter

up on her offer, all that would be lost. He couldn't bear to be again what he was eighteen years ago, so he scrambled for some words that would release him from the velvet bonds of her confession. He sought something kind to say.

"Listen to me, Anastasia," he finally said as gently as he could. "You're caught up in the situation. What seems romantic to you now will pale once this nightmare is over. You'd regret giving me this precious gift."

Her smile was a legacy from Jezebel. "Never." Close now, she fitted herself to him. "I love you, Cord."

The words were manna from heaven, feeding his troubled soul. But he had to refuse the feast, had to walk away from the banquet. Worse, to get his point across, he'd have to be cruel. And cutting. Though every fiber of his being protested, he said, "No, little girl, you don't love me. You'll see that soon enough. Meanwhile, I guess I'm just gonna have to tell you. You're not my type."

For as long as Cord lived, he'd never forget the look on Stacey's face. Etched on her features was hurt so deep, he knew instinctively she'd never forgive him. She looked as if she was about to be physically ill. He was on the verge of reaching for her, and taking back every blasphemous word, when she jerked away from him and tore out of the room. Eventually, he heard her bedroom door slam.

Cord couldn't breathe. He felt as sickened as she looked. He strode out to the patio. Sinking onto a chair, he buried his face in his hands.

He didn't know how much later it was—ten minutes or sixty—when he was roused from his self-flagellation by a rustle at the doorway to the pool area.

Stacey stood silhouetted by the inside light, dressed in cutoffs and an oversize shirt, keys jangling in her hand. Like a man condemned, he forced himself to look at her face. Her flawless skin was mottled; red splotches marred her cheeks. But it was her eyes that leveled him. They were crimson-rimmed from crying; worse, the look in them caught him behind the knees. There was no accusation, no rage, no resentment. He could have handled those, he would have preferred those. But her always-animated eyes had turned muddy with sadness—a bleak, old, weary grief that he couldn't bear to look at.

"Are you all right?" Was that ancient, gravelly sound his *voice?*

She bit her lip, but angled her chin. From underneath the broken exterior, her grit surfaced. "No, I'm not all right. What I need right now is to be alone. I...I've got to get out of here." Her gaze whipped around the deck area, then landed on him with an almost audible thud. "I've got to get away from you for a little while."

His body tightened. As insults went, it was mild. But it cut deep. "No."

Squaring her shoulders, she matched his implacable stare. "You don't understand. I've got to be alone for a while. I need to...get back to myself...and I can't do that while you're around."

"Then do it in your room. Or downstairs. I'll stay away from you, but you're not going anywhere."

He could see her stretch to keep the icy calm that had come over her. Then she said, "I'll be careful. I'll lock the doors to the car. I'll stay on town roads—I'll just drive up and down Market Street if I have to."

"I said no."

"Cord, you don't understand."

"No. I'm sorry, Stacey. You can't."

The icy calm melted. Fiery fury replaced it, her eyes darkening to burning charcoal. "I'm not a child you can order about. If I was, I'd have stormed out without telling you." She raised her chin. "I could have done that, and you wouldn't have been able to catch me." She punctuated her comment with a look that said, "You jerk" and finished, "No matter how hard you try, you can't make me into something I'm not. I'm handling this maturely. I'm telling you what I need. Right now, I have to get away from you." Her glare slapped him in the face. "I *am* leaving."

Pivoting, she went back inside, crossed the den, then disappeared. It took him a few seconds to react. By the time he got to the front door, she had it open.

He slammed it shut with a force born of frustration, anger and desire. He let the anger override the other painful emotions. "I said, you're not going anywhere."

She reached for the door handle again, but her efforts were futile. Physically, at least, he was much stronger than she was. She turned and tried to side-step him, but he blocked her way with his body. Finally, she raised blistering eyes at him and snapped, "I'm leaving, Cord. If you want to stop me, you'll have to do it bodily."

He was pretty sure she didn't mean it as a challenge. But he didn't particularly care. At the moment, his sole concern was keeping her safe. So he bent over, hooked his hands behind her knees and tossed her over his shoulder. Then he headed up the staircase.

"Let me go..." She started to kick, so he grabbed her feet. She pounded his back and his shoulder, which began to ache with her weight and her pummeling.

"Cord, let me go. You can't do this to me!"

"Oh yeah?" he asked, hiking up the steps. "Watch me."

Reaching the top, he crossed the twenty-foot hallway in record time. He kicked open the door to the sitting room, stalked in, dropped her onto the couch, then went back to the door to lock it. When he did, she scrambled off the sofa and bounded for the bathroom. He heard her lock the door from inside. No doubt she meant to exit through her adjoining bedroom. "Forget it, babe." He lifted his foot and put it through the hollow-core door. It splintered, and he finished the job by kicking the lock open. On the other side of the bathroom, her mouth agape, Stacey froze. For a moment. Then she raced to her room.

He tackled her on the bed. Their chests met with counterpoint gulps of breath as he pinned her beneath him. Her eyes sparked fire. "You wouldn't dare keep me here by force."

"Oh, I'd dare, all right." Then, gazing down at her, close enough to see the anger but also the trace of fear in those beautiful eyes he loved, the rage drained out of him as quickly as it had come. His voice gentled as he said, "But what I couldn't do is hurt you."

She stared at him for long seconds. "You hurt me every time you reject me, Cord. Every time you tell me I'm too young, I don't know my own mind, I'm not your type, that you don't return my feelings. Especially since I sense it's a lie. I wish—" tears began to roll down her cheeks "—I wish you'd just tell me how you really feel."

It was all too much. The old guilt he'd lived with for eighteen years coalesced with the new guilt he felt for unwittingly hurting her. In a reckless, split-second decision, he tossed both out of his mind. Without analyzing it, for once without censoring his thoughts or feelings for her, he gave in to the need he'd stifled for weeks. "All right, Stacey. You win."

POISED ABOVE HER, Cord stared into Stacey's brimming eyes and willed himself to slow down. He opened his mouth to tease her, to coax, but the words wouldn't come. He took a deep breath, trying to contain the passion that had seethed inside him since the moment she'd confessed she'd never been with another man.

Never.

The knowledge forced him to think clearly; he pulled back. Just for a minute. With as much tenderness as he could summon, he pressed her into the mattress, framed her face with his hands and whispered, "Stace." His voice was raspy with the depth of his emotions.

"What?"

"I'll only ask this once. You've never made love before. Are you sure you want to? With me?"

Her smile seemed to come from her soul. "I'm sure."

"All right, then." Drawing away from her, he hauled himself from the bed and went into his room. He returned with an unopened box of condoms.

The look she gave him when she recognized what he held was accusatory. "You're . . . prepared?"

He put the box on the nightstand and covered her again with his weight. "They were in my shaving kit, sweetheart." He kissed the tip of her nose. They've been there a long time. I hope they're still good."

Another smile spread across her face. Cord lowered his lips to hers; as soon as he tasted her, the urgency returned. His need for her clawed inside him, demanding to be appeased.

Innocently, willingly, she opened her mouth to him and he invaded it. She was so sweet it jolted him. Releasing her mouth, he tracked kisses to her neck, ravenous for the taste of her skin. His nose brushed her hair and the scents of baby powder and lemon shampoo enveloped him.

With an unsteady hand, he sought the buttons of her shirt. Fumbling like a schoolboy, he quelled the urge to rip open the silky material. When he finally had the garment undone, he found her tucked into a red satin bra scalloped with lace. He flicked the clasp.

"You are so lovely. I want to devour you."

"I want that, too."

His hand closed over a swollen breast. He groaned at how good she felt, how right. He'd dreamed so often of doing this again. Now it was real. Desire over-rode everything else as he took her nipple in his mouth and suckled greedily.

Driven by the need to feel her naked beneath him, he shifted to the side and pulled off her bra and shirt in one swoop. His hands explored her body, outlining each rib, curving inward with the slope of her waist. At her hips, he dragged down her shorts and panties to-gether and pulled them off. She shivered. He smiled and cupped her.

Closing her eyes, she arched into his palm. He moved it in rhythmic circles until her breath sped up and her face flushed. When she opened her eyes, she touched his chest. "Take this off," she said, yanking at his shirt. "I want to see you."

Buttons flew to the floor as he ripped them open. When his hand came in contact with cold steel, Cord swore. "I forgot," he said, tearing at the buckle of the shoulder holster and whipping off the gun. It was a stark reminder of the danger they faced.

Deliberately, he discarded both the weapon and the reality of their circumstances. He knew that what he was doing was unprofessional, was wrong. For so many reasons. But it was too late for self-recrimination. He'd concentrate on making her first sexual experience good and loving.

Stacey watched the doubt harden Cord's jaw and darken his eyes to navy. She clutched at his shoul-ders, afraid he'd changed his mind. Dragging him closer, she kissed him with fear and urgency and the most acute need she'd ever felt. He consumed her mouth, her neck, his hands roughly caressing all the skin he could reach. She felt chilled and scorched at the same time. When he came to the juncture of her thighs, she parted them for him. He palmed her, then inserted a finger.

"Oh, Stace," he said. "You're so ready. So wet."

"Cord, I want you. Please."

But he continued the movement until she had to close her eyes. Gasping for breath, she fell back into the mattress. He pulled off the rest of his clothes, then fumbled for the box on the dresser. Through half-closed lids, she watched him tear the packet with his teeth, then quickly sheathe himself.

Intrigued, Stacey reached out to touch his solid length. It was warm and pulsing. She studied his face as her fingers closed around him. His throat moved as he swallowed hard. And he withdrew her hand.

Grasping her thigh, he turned her to her side, facing him. Then he angled his body and scissored his legs with hers. "This will be better, love," he said, his voice a shaky whisper. "I can control the angle and touch you more." He took a pillow and slid it beneath her head. "Besides, I get to watch you."

Again, Stacey arched but he didn't enter her; instead, he stayed poised at her opening. "There's one thing you need to know before we do this."

"What?" she managed to say.

"I love you, Anastasia."

Stacey's heart skidded to a halt. Tears welled in her eyes, but she blinked them back. "I love you, too, Francis."

His eyes locked on hers in a sacred bond as he inched into her. "Does it hurt?" He grimaced. "I'm trying to go slow, but..."

"It feels wonderful." She thrust her hips forward.

He groaned as he plunged into her, then stilled, holding himself rigidly for a few seconds. When he began to move, he took long, smooth strokes, grazing her inside. Her whole body tightened. She trembled and moaned. Her vision blurred. Circles of pleasure swirled within her, radiating from the center of her body to all her extremities. It built and built until it burst upon her; hundreds of pinpricks of pleasure shot through her. She called his name over and over.

She was still gasping for breath when she felt him grab her hips. His fingers dug into her flesh as his thrusts came harder and quicker; in seconds he stiffened. "Oh, Stace...Stace," he called out, then pushed and pushed and finally emptied himself in her.

Spent, he collapsed against the pillow and cuddled her to him. Tucking her head against his chest, he held her tightly and kissed her hair. She could hear the escalated beat of his heart pounding in his chest. Lovingly, she laid a hand over it, smiling against his sweat-soaked skin, inhaling his unique scent.

She had him now. Finally. He was hers. And she knew deep in her heart that nothing could ever wrench them apart.

Not after this.

CHAPTER TEN

AT 7:00 A.M., deliciously sore and gladly exhausted, Stacey tried to disentangle herself from her spoonlike position with Cord, to shower and get ready for work. Though how she was going to concentrate all day, and not attack him, was in question.

But Cord seemed to have other ideas. The arm thrown across her chest vised around her and she was immobilized. "You're not going anywhere, Anastasia."

Sighing, fitting herself to him, she closed her eyes and inhaled the scents that surrounded her. His sweat and hers. The distinct and aphrodisiac smell of sex; the earthy odors sneaking in from the open windows and skylights.

Her mind drifted to the night before. They'd slept briefly, then he went downstairs to lock up and set the alarms. When he returned with a cold tray of food, and she fed it to him, he tried to resist her but lost the first skirmish with his willpower. Shoving aside the food, he'd pulled her on top of him and shown her how being in control could be pleasurable for her.

Then they went to sleep for the night—or so she thought. It was still dark out when she felt his light kisses on her back. Her skin tingled and she allowed the ministration as long as she could. Easing her over, he pressed her into the pillows and gave her a taste of the missionary position. When they'd awakened at dawn, only half of the condoms were left in the box...

Cord flipped over on his stomach, tightened the arm bracing her and reached for the phone. On her back now, she watched the play of his muscles as he dialed from the awkward angle.

"Give me the fifth-floor finance division." His gravelly voice conjured the erotic words he'd spoken each time he'd come inside her last night. He handed her the phone.

"What?" she asked him.

"It's your secretary. Tell her you're not coming to work today."

His peremptory words were softened by the sexual glimmer in his eyes, making them a crystalline blue.

"Why?"

"I want these next few days with you, Stace. Just you and me. No stalker, no father, no ex-fiancé. And no past."

It seemed he added the last almost unconsciously. "Cord?"

The question was lost as her secretary asked for instructions to cover Stacey's unexpected need to be out of the office.

When she finished, Cord took the phone from her, reached over, unplugged it and wrapped her in his arms once more. God, she needed him. Wanted him. Wanted to spend her whole life with him. Would he make any comments about the future? Did he connect love with commitment? There was still so much she didn't know about him. But he was right. She wouldn't bog down these four days with worry.

"What are you thinking about?" he asked, nuzzling her ear.

"Making love."

He chuckled. "You're a natural." His features softened. "I can't believe I was the first guy."

"Are you glad?" She tried to quell the note of insecurity that crept into her voice.

Gently he turned her to fully face him. "Are you kidding? The thought of Matthews's hands on you has driven me nuts for weeks. Truly, Stace, it's the most precious gift I've ever been given." He paused, searching her face. "Tell me why you waited."

"I've hinted at it before."

He frowned. "I don't understand."

"It's because of my mother's infidelity." She sighed. "But now, I think you may have been right. I may have misjudged her. In the storage room the other day...those were sketchbooks we were looking at. After seeing how she drew my father...she must have loved him very much."

Cord's expression turned granite. "Your mother loved *you* as much," he finally said.

"Why would you say that?"

"I...ah, I saw the sketches she did of you."

Frowning, Stacey shook her head. "You came into the storage room after we put the sketchbooks away. How did you see them?"

Cord swallowed hard. "Why are we talking about this? Didn't I say I wanted nothing to intrude on these four days? This is our fantasy weekend together."

Stacey blushed.

"What?"

"I've *had* fantasies of you," she said.

He gave her a wolfish grin. "I've had them of you, too."

She eased up on her elbow. "I want to know your fantasies, Cord."

"Never ask a man that."

"I want to fulfill them. I want to be everything you want in a woman." *So you'll never want another.*

His sometimes icy blue eyes flamed with burning interest. And desire. "You are."

EARLY FRIDAY EVENING Cord lounged across from Stacey on a chaise by the pool. "Stace?"

"Hmm?" She looked up from her sketchbook and scanned his long lean frame, clad only in black swim trunks.

"Are you going to stay at Canfield Glass forever?"

Her eyes narrowed on him. "How do you do that?"

"Do what?"

"Know what I'm thinking?"

"Osmosis."

"Oh, clever, McKay. We haven't been that close."

"Are you kidding? I'm almost out of rubbers."

She could feel the heat rise to her cheeks. "Well, I liked the other ways, too, where you don't need them."

"Have you no shame, woman?"

"None, where you're concerned."

That brought a slight trace of color on his cheekbones. Combined with the sunburn he'd gotten from the few hours they'd spent frolicking in the pool, it looked good on him. As a matter of fact, Cord had never looked as good as he did now. There was something about him today, an absence of tension. She hadn't realized how coiled he'd been, until he *un*-coiled. Sketching him, she noticed even more how relaxed he was.

"Anyway, I can't see you punching numbers the rest of your life," he continued.

"I do more than that."

"You don't use your real talent."

She watched him closely. "I'll make you a deal. I'll discuss that, if you'll answer a question for me."

He stiffened. "Depends on the question."

"What do you plan to do with your life?"

Dark sadness glimmered in his eyes. He leaned back, and said, "I'm not sure. After I had to give up police work..."

"You miss it so much it hurts, don't you?"

"How could *you* know that?"

"Just some things you've said. I gather even coming back to Canfield was difficult."

"It was."

"Tell me why."

"I haven't ever told anyone about this." She remained silent as he looked out at the sunset. "First of all, the nature of the work was so different. In Canfield, we get one or two cases of homicide every few years. In New York murders are commonplace."

"What else?"

"The calls for service are more frequent there, too. When I first came here, I thought I'd go stir-crazy on duty with nothing to do. But you know what got to me the most?''

"What?"

"Police work is more personal here. An officer knows the people who are hurt, who do foolish or terrible things. In the big city, it's all anonymous. That's easier somehow." He shook his head. "But I'd do it all over again for Meggie."

Stacey scowled.

"What is it?" Cord asked.

"You miss her, don't you?"

"More than I could ever imagine."

"I'm sorry it's too dangerous to see her more often. But we'll get to see her in two weeks, on her birthday, won't we?"

"Uh-huh. Hard to believe she'll be five."

"Old enough for pierced ears, I think."

He arched a dark blond eyebrow. "Do I detect a conspiracy here?"

"No conspiracy. Anyway, answer my question about what you're going to do."

"I don't know. I kind of like this bodyguard stuff. Particularly when I've got such a nice body to guard."

"Forget it, McKay. You're not guarding other bodies, if I have any say."

His face shuttered more quickly than a camera lens. The gesture told her very clearly she would have no say. They would have no future. And she was too afraid of hearing him confirm this to confront him about it. Instead, she went on, "To answer *your* question, I don't know about the Glassworks job." She peered at the image of him she'd created. God, the sketch broadcast her feelings like a news clip. All the love she felt, all the hope for keeping him in her life, was scrawled across the paper. "Maybe I'll think about doing something more creative."

"Good. You're wasting your talent at CGW."

"You wouldn't happen to want me away from Preston, would you, Cord?"

He spread his legs so his feet touched down on either side of the chaise. "Come here, and I'll show you what I want."

She stood, crossed the few feet to him and knelt between his legs. "How long before it's dark?" she asked.

"Why?"

"Because you know that pool fantasy you told me about?"

He swallowed hard and nodded.

"It's time to make it come true."

"WHERE ARE WE GOING? You said we could stay here all weekend." Stacey tugged on a pink cotton dress and slipped into sandals as Cord shrugged into a shirt early Saturday morning.

"We can. But if I don't go to the drugstore, we'll be playing chess for the next two days."

She smiled, then her face sobered. It was something she'd been doing a lot. Laughing one minute, somber the next. Rightfully so, given his mixed feelings about their relationship.

"I don't care if I get pregnant," she said unexpectedly. "I'd love to have your baby."

Cord struggled to remain impassive at her statement. He prayed that she didn't detect the momentary leap of hope he felt in his soul when he pictured her now-flat belly swollen with his child. "Stace, don't joke."

"I'm not joking."

"Then don't be foolish."

"Don't start on my being too young, McKay."

"All right, just get dressed. Besides the drugstore, I have to stop at my house . . . to pick up some things I need."

She studied him for a minute, but obviously decided to drop the subject. "Will I get to see Meggie? That would be worth leaving here. Almost."

"No, my mother took her to my aunt's in Elmore for the weekend. We also have to pick up the new bathroom door I ordered. I have to stain it and hang it before your father gets home."

Impish delight turned up the corners of her mouth. "That should teach you to control your caveman instincts."

He grabbed her arm and pulled her to him, mimicking a roughness she'd know was feigned. "You should be glad about those instincts. We wouldn't be together if it wasn't for those instincts."

She raised her chin, her eyes clear and determined. "We were meant to be together. I feel it in my soul."

She couldn't have been more wrong. But he said nothing, kissing her briefly instead.

They ran their errands and were back home in an hour. It was late afternoon by the time Cord had stained the door and hung it. Of course, Stacey had done her best to distract him, floating on her back in the pool clad in a shameless bikini that he told her he was going to burn after this weekend. The whole task had taken twice as long because she'd managed to entice him to stop when he was replacing the door, leave it partly unhinged and make love to her right on the bathroom floor.

There was no doubt she had him behaving in uncharacteristic ways, especially now. *God, what a lovesick sap you are, McKay,* he thought later as he reread the note he'd written, sealed it in an envelope, scrawled her name on the front, and stuck it under her bedroom door. He berated himself all the way downstairs, and as he picked up the phone to call in favors several people around town owed him.

At nine o'clock, he paced the pool area. Late August twilight cloaked the patio, and the crickets had started their nightly serenade. He ran his hand inside the starched collar of his pristine white shirt, and loosened the Windsor knot of his tie, thankful he didn't have to suffer this kind of torture every day.

But it was worth every twinge when Stacey appeared in the archway of the French doors. Her eyes swept the scene, but when they landed on him, they stuck . . . and glowed. "Wow!" she whispered.

"Wow, yourself. You look exquisite."

Her jaw gaped. She managed to strut to him, though, making his mouth go dry. "I've never seen you like this," she said.

"I know." He felt his heart stutter. "You like it?"

"Are you kidding? You fill out a pair of jeans like no man I've ever seen before, but what your shoulders do to that wool is lethal. Nice suit, McKay. Come from New York?''

''Yep. My one and only splurge on fancy clothes.''

''It was worth every penny. Do you know what the gray does to your eyes?''

He grinned as she ran her hand across a lapel, then straightened the knot of his silk tie. He kissed her nose, ran his palm down the back of her sequined dress and cupped her bottom. He leaned over and whispered in her ear, ''The night of your birthday...? When you wore this...? I wanted to break Matthews's arm when he touched you. I wanted so badly to have my hands on you when you were in this dress.''

Her smile was sinful. ''Is that why your note told me to wear it?''

He nodded.

''Then touch all you like.'' She pitched that purring voice lower. ''I don't have any underwear on beneath it.''

''Witch! Keep that up, and I'm going to lose sight of the purpose of this evening.''

''Which is?''

''Well, it certainly *isn't* to take you on the slate pavement—which is where we're headed if you don't watch that sassy mouth of yours.''

She pouted as if she'd taken lessons from Marilyn Monroe. ''You don't like my mouth?''

In answer, he kissed it hard. Then he let go of her while he still could, and strode into the house, switched on a soft, romantic rock CD and returned to the table he'd set up in the corner. She was already there, inspecting what he'd put out. Lifting the Dom Perignon from its bucket, he poured champagne into two Steuben crystal goblets. Facing her, he handed her a glass.

"What are we celebrating?"

He traced her jaw with his free hand. "I'm not much with words, Stace, so I thought I'd show you how I felt..." His throat clogged. Emotion welled up inside him, hard to control, since he'd spent a lifetime avoiding this kind of intense feeling.

She must have caught his state of mind. "You've told me you love me, Cord. I believe you."

He shook his head. "I've got to be sure you know how much I care." Lifting a strand of curly hair and fingering its silkiness, he said, "You mean so much to me. You are so precious, so special..."

Her eyes grew wide, but she didn't speak.

"I don't deserve you, Stace. But you've got to know, to understand, that I've never, ever felt this way about a woman before." He smiled ruefully. "I want to show you all this tonight. I want to spoil you rotten, to court you, to give you all the romance I won't—" He cut off the negative reference to the future. He wouldn't think about another man having her someday. He wouldn't think about another man romancing her like this. He wouldn't think about her committing herself for life to some other guy. He shifted the mood, and smiled, though his heart felt crushed by the knowledge that all those things would happen. "I want to do something for you, *with* you, besides jump you on the bathroom floor."

Tears had formed in her luscious brown eyes, but she smiled. "The bathroom floor will never be the same to me. I've loved every single thing you've done to me in the last three days." She looked around. "And I love this." She looped an arm around his neck and clinked glasses with him. "I love you, Cord McKay. In an Armani suit, in faded jeans and as bare as the day you were born. Nothing will ever change that."

He knew the one thing that would. When he told her about Helene ... His heart stopped beating for a second. He hadn't realized he'd decided to do it. But the overflowing love he felt for her right now, the bubbling, effusive depth of feeling he'd developed for this lovely young woman, hit him with the accuracy of an arrow hitting a bull's-eye, forcing him to admit that he *had* to be honest with her. It was a sham to their feelings, an insult to his love for her and her love for him, to keep this obscene secret any longer.

But he didn't have to tell her tonight. Not tonight, he thought as he took her glass, set both down and drew her into his arms. Tonight, they'd dance under the moonlight, eat the lobster and white asparagus he'd ordered from the most expensive restaurant in Canfield and make love.

Sunday would be soon enough for the confession that would end it all.

AT NOON the next day—their intimate weekend drawing to a close—Stacey sat at the kitchen table dressed in Cord's shirt, sketching him again, while he fixed bacon and eggs.

As she lovingly drew the long lines of his back, she said casually, "What happens now, Cord?"

"We catch the stalker."

"Yes, I know that. But what happens between us?"

He gripped the spatula with a force that would bend steel. Turning to face her, his hair rakishly disheveled, jeans riding low on his hips, there was a sadness in his face that tore at her heart. "We have to talk."

"Yes. Let's talk about the future."

He crossed his arms over his chest. "We have no future. After we catch the stalker, I'm out of your life."

She wanted to scream, to shake him. Instead she forced herself to say calmly, "Do you think I'm going to let you go that easily?"

He made his way across the tile and crouched in front of her. "Stace, you've got your whole life ahead of you. You're young and beautiful and you'll make someone a wonderful partner someday. But it won't be me."

"Why?"

"Because I've done things in my past that would taint you."

"I don't care what you've done. You were a policeman and you had to do things to protect others, to survive. Like a soldier in war. Those things make you a hero, not a monster."

"I'm no hero, Stacey."

"You're no monster, either. I love you."

"I love you, too. God forgive me."

"But you'll let me go."

"Yes."

Anger flared, quick and potent. "Can you really live your life knowing I'll be doing the things we did together this weekend with another man?"

He white-knuckled the edge of her chair. "That's a low blow."

"I don't care. I'll fight as dirty as I have to to keep you."

"If I thought there was any chance, sweetheart, I'd take it. But there's none."

"Don't you think I'd be a good mother to Meggie?"

He thought about it too long.

"And don't lie this time, like you did when you said I wasn't your type."

The bleakest eyes she'd ever seen stared out at her. "You'd be a wonderful mother to Meggie."

She smiled weakly. "Thank you for that."

He reached up and pulled her down so his forehead could meet hers. "Just do me one favor. No matter what happens, promise me you'll always believe I love you."

She held him tightly. "I promise."

A gasp came from the doorway. Both Stacey and Cord looked up. Gifford Webb stood in the entrance like an avenging angel. His eyes bored into them, filled with surprise, anger...and a look of betrayal. The first two emotions Stacey understood, but not the last.

DÉJÀ VU, so intense and piercing, swept through Gifford as he watched his daughter in the arms of the man who had almost ruined their lives. Stunned, he grasped the doorframe, unable to comment.

McKay moved first; he rose and stepped back from Stacey. Gifford saw she was dressed in McKay's shirt. His eyes flew from his daughter to McKay, who stepped in front of her to shield her from Gifford. The action betrayed their guilt, but also Cord McKay's spontaneous reaction to protect Stacey. Gifford wanted to wail at the irony of it.

Misinterpreting the charged atmosphere, Stacey stood and sidled up next to McKay. "Daddy, we didn't expect you until tonight."

"So I gather. I took an earlier flight."

"Oh."

"Stacey, I want to talk to McKay alone."

Fire darted from her brown eyes, so like his own. But apparently, she was more like her mother than he could have ever predicted. "Absolutely not. I refuse to be treated like a child in this."

"It's okay, Stace. I think it's for the best," McKay said.

"No." She ran a shaky hand through her hair. "Look, Dad, I know this is a shock, but I'm twenty-four years old. What did you expect, that I'd live like a nun?"

McKay shot her a look that Gifford didn't understand.

"It's not that, honey."

"I know it must be hard to be faced with the fact that your daughter's a sexual being, but—"

"It's not that at all."

Cord said, "It's a problem for your father because I'm supposed to be protecting you, not..." He shifted uncomfortably.

"Making love to me. We might as well call it what it is," Stacey said, exasperation lacing every word.

"And this is inappropriate behavior for a body-guard," Cord finished.

"Who's being paid by me."

"Dad, you make this sound so seedy."

If you only knew, Gifford thought.

With her characteristic stubbornness, Stacey raised her chin. "It's not seedy. It's beautiful and wonderful and I love him."

No, oh please, God, no.

Just then, the phone rang. Gifford welcomed the interruption to collect himself. Stacey walked to it, barely decent in the long shirt that skimmed her thighs. "Hello. Oh, Lauren."

McKay swung his head around. "You need to talk to her."

Stacey glanced from him to Gifford. "All right. I'll take it in the den. Hang up for me."

Unwilling to let McKay do that domestic task, Gifford crossed to the phone, watched Stacey leave, then both he and McKay waited until Stacey picked it up in the other room.

When he hung up, silence descended on them like a death knell. Gifford wanted to smash everything in sight. "The last time... I found you here, I went into a rage. When I got rid of you, I told Helene to get out."

McKay's jaw hardened. "I figured it was some-thing like that."

"She was hysterical when she left. She cracked up the car... It wasn't until after the police came, and I identified the body, that I found out exactly what had happened that afternoon.''

Cord rammed his hands into his pockets, and begrudgingly Gifford admitted that this had to be excruciating for him, too.

''How did you find out?'' the younger man asked.

Gifford paced. ''She left a letter. She must have written it when she went up to pack.'' Tears stung his eyes. ''It certainly didn't excuse what you two did, but it put everything in a different light. I could have forgiven her, especially since I recognize how much I was to blame.'' He turned to face the other man. ''But it was too late.''

Unwillingly, Gifford acknowledged the moisture in McKay's eyes.

''I might even be able to forgive you, McKay, but I could never forget. I could never allow you and my daughter to—''

''It doesn't matter. I can never forgive myself.'' McKay's voice was hoarse, and Gifford felt an unwanted pang of sympathy for the man. McKay had only been eighteen.

''A relationship with Helene's daughter is out of the question,'' Gifford told him.

McKay winced. ''I know.''

''How did this happen, then?''

''I take full responsibility for it.''

''Was it just a convenient lay for you?''

''No!'' The vehemence in McKay's tone was convincing. ''No, never.'' Then he face Gifford squarely. ''I love Stacey.''

Gifford hadn't expected that. He sank onto a bar stool. "And she thinks she's in love with you."

"She says she is."

"So, she's going to get hurt."

"Yes. As I said, it's my fault for letting it go this far. Would you like to find another bodyguard?"

Gifford looked over McKay's shoulder and saw Stacey come to the doorway. "No, I won't let you do that," she said firmly. "But there's no time to argue this out. Lauren's in the emergency room at the hospital. We've got to go there right way. She asked especially for you to come, Dad."

CHAPTER ELEVEN

"ARE YOU COMFORTABLE?" Stacey asked as she settled Lauren into the sofa bed that Cord had occupied for the last few weeks.

Lauren nodded, and Stacey guessed that she was embarrassed about lying to her best friend about her "accident."

"Can I do anything for you?"

"Just sit with me for a while."

Sighing, Stacey sank onto the mattress.

"I'm sorry," Lauren said. "I know Cord was using this room, and you felt safer with him so close."

"It's not that." She looked around, noting that Cord had taken all his gear with him to the spare room near her father's suite. "Things have gotten complicated."

"I don't understand."

"That's okay. Now's not the time to get into it. Lauren, tell me what really happened?"

Lauren's eyes filled. "I told you. I fell down the stairs." She fingered the cast on her left arm. "I broke it because I was clumsy."

In a Herculean attempt to control her anger, Stacey said quietly, "I know Mark did this to you."

Lauren shook her head. "No, he didn't. Don't worry, I'll be gone tomorrow night and you and your father won't have to take care of me anymore."

"Don't be silly. You're going to need help for a while. You'll stay here."

"You don't need this. Not with what you're going through."

"Shh...it's all right." Stacey wished the sedative they'd given Lauren would start taking effect. Her friend was getting agitated.

As if on cue, Lauren yawned. "I need to—"

"You need to get some rest."

Finally, Lauren's eyes closed. "All right, but I'll go tomorrow."

"We'll talk about it then."

Once Lauren was asleep, Stacey went in search of Cord. The room he'd taken was right next to her father's and she found him, curiously, standing at the master suite's doorway. Following his gaze, Stacey took in her father's king-size bed, heavy wooden dressers and the fieldstone fireplace in the corner.

"Cord."

He jumped, then turned around. His face was white. "I didn't hear you."

"You were a million miles away."

"Years away," he said, and glanced back at the room.

"Cord, we've got to talk."

"All right." His voice was raspy, and unbelievably sad. He followed her into the room where he'd put his belongings. "How is she?" he asked.

"Physically, she's fine, except, of course, that her arm is fractured in two places. Emotionally, she's wasted. She still insists she fell down the stairs, when I know damn well that animal did it."

"Abuse is a complicated thing."

"You've had experience with this?"

"Some. Before I got into special protection."

Stacey cocked her head. "There's so much I don't know about you."

The color that had returned to his face leeched out.

"Cord?"

"Sit down, Stace. We need to talk about something."

"Yes, about us. Lauren's staying here doesn't change things between us."

"No, but your father's...awareness of the situation does."

"Daddy will get used to the idea of our being together."

"Never."

"Well, maybe not under his roof. When this is all over, I'll move out if I have to."

Wearily, Cord dropped to an easy chair. Stacey followed him, and curled in his lap. His arms went around her. "Sweetheart, this isn't the answer."

She kissed his neck. "I told you I was going to fight dirty."

"Let's just lay off the whole discussion now, all right? After seeing Lauren hurt so badly, we need to talk about the stalker."

"What's the connection?"

"I haven't told you this before, but I think the stalker might be someone you know."

She drew back and met his gaze. *"What?"*

"I've thought all along that he knew too much about your whereabouts."

"Who do you suspect?"

"Everyone. Including Mark Dunn."

Stacey felt her stomach roil. "Oh, my God." Cord pulled her tight. She let him hold her close for a moment, then pulled away again. "Why haven't you told me this before?"

"I'm not sure. I guess I wanted more proof."

"I don't like being kept in the dark about my own safety."

She felt him stiffen. "I'm doing what I think is best."

"Well, as usual, we have very different views on that. I'm going to say this only once. I don't *ever* want you to lie to me. And not telling me something is as bad as lying. I find lies by omission very hard to forgive."

Cord swallowed, but didn't respond. Stacey was shocked. Usually, he met her head-on in their disagreements.

His guilty look unnerved her, and she wondered what hid behind those bleak blue eyes.

STACEY LOOKED UP from her sketchbook at Cord, who stood in the doorway of her room. He leaned against the jamb, watching her carefully. "You've got to get out of here for a while," he said.

"I've been to work every day."

"I know. But between taking care of Lauren for the past week, and our...separation...you look like you could use some fun."

"Do I get to choose what it is?"

"Absolutely not. But what I have in mind will please you almost as much."

"Impossible, but tell me your plan, anyway."

"Let's go buy Megan a birthday present."

"All right, McKay. You came pretty close."

"How about some pierced earrings?"

"You're kidding?"

"Nope, between the two of you, you wore me down. But only one in each ear. She's too young for the menagerie you put in yours."

Stacey eased back on the chair. "You seemed pretty taken with my ears last weekend. How quickly you forget in three days."

His mouth went dry. "I haven't forgotten anything." *Including the fact that I have yet to tell you about Helene.* But, damn, things had been so hectic with Gifford's return and Lauren's "accident" that he hadn't had a chance. "Come on, I'll even spring for ice cream."

"Only if it's chocolate chip mint."

Cord turned away so she wouldn't see his reaction to the taunt. They'd done delicious things with Stacey's favorite dessert during their marathon of lovemaking.

They hit the downtown mall at about 7:00 p.m. Cord followed Stacey to a store called We're All Ears, where they purchased tiny gold hoops and round posts and a gift certificate. They were headed for the ice-cream shop, when they passed a huge department store that advertised matching outfits for adults and kids. A lavender lace minidress snagged Stacey's attention. "Wait, Cord, look."

He looked, and pictured Stacey's long legs displayed in the revealing garment. Her words Sunday morning haunted him, *Can you really live your life knowing I'll be doing the things we did together this weekend with another man?*

"It's too short."

"Oh, don't be a stick-in-the-mud. I want to try it on. Besides, Megan would love the miniature one."

Cord agreed only because, suddenly, he was struck by the realization that he'd probably never get to do this with her again. Never shop for a dress with her. Never pick out something for Megan with her. Never pretend he had a right to be with her.

And when he told her about Helene, she'd never look at him again with that sexy, teasing glint in her eyes.

"All right."

It took them forever to find the right department in the huge store. The mall was new, complete with megastores like this one, and an enclosed parking garage where they had left the truck. As Stacey flicked through the racks, Cord waited patiently, savoring the moments with her.

When she found the two dresses, he eyed hers disapprovingly. "Like I said, it's too short. And it will be too tight. Let's go."

"No way. I like the way you look when you think about me in this dress. Let's find the fitting room."

The nearest one was several feet away. Cord followed her to it, and stood outside waiting. Sure enough, when she came out, her appearance pole-axed him. The dress was too short. Too tight. And so sexy it made him hurt.

"Forget it."

She giggled. "After seeing your face, an act of God couldn't keep me from buying this." She disappeared into the fitting room.

He smiled as he waited for her to change.

Leaning against the wall, he was distracted by a salesclerk coming toward him. She was a little on the plump side, her hefty bosom heaving as she came up to him. "Do you know any first aid? There's a child two departments over who's having some kind of attack. She's only five. I've called 911, but we're afraid . . ."

All thought fled as Cord pictured Megan in a similar situation. Operating on well-honed police instincts, he followed the woman through the store. He was ten feet away from a crowd of people obviously gathered around the child, when he realized he hadn't told Stacey to stay put. He stopped abruptly. Turning to the clearly breathless clerk, he said, "Go back to the fitting room. Find Stacey Webb—about five-three, one hundred fifteen pounds, dark hair and eyes. Tell her what happened, and bring her over here."

The woman started to speak, when a loud piercing wail rent the air. Cord dashed toward it, separating the flock of onlookers. On the floor, a child Megan's size convulsed. Her head was thrown back and her tiny body shook in grotesque contortions. "I'm a police

officer," Cord said firmly. "I know what to do."
Kneeling, he took over.

The child was calm in ten minutes. Cord looked up
to see ambulance attendants coming toward him with
the same salesclerk who'd drafted him to help. Stacey
was not with her. Alarm prickled his spine. He jumped
up as the medics bent to take care of the child.

Roughly he grabbed the woman's arms. "Where's
Stacey?"

The florid-faced clerk puffed for breath. "I had to
meet the ambulance people at the door so they'd know
where to go. I'm sorry, I couldn't go get your girlfriend."

His heart thudding in his chest, Cord dashed away
from the woman and raced through the two interven-
ing departments. He reached the fitting rooms, a
deadly foreboding pulsing through him. He headed
straight into the cubicles. Wildly whipping aside each
curtain, he searched for Stacey.

She was gone.

Calling upon all his training, he willed himself to
stay calm. She could be paying for the dresses. No
cashier was open near them, so he methodically
checked the closest one, then the next. Damn, this
store was big. After four stations, and no one had seen
her, he began to panic.

Stacey had disappeared from right under his nose.

HESITANTLY, Stacey opened the door to the parking
garage. She'd made the decision to go to the truck
when she'd exited the fitting room and Cord had not
been there. Assaulted by an uneasy feeling, she'd

briefly searched the area, then stashed the dresses in a
nearby rack. Cord had told her once, when he'd first
begun to guard her, that if they were ever out and got
separated, to go straight to the car and lock herself
inside. On the few occasions that they'd gone anywhere, he'd made sure she noted the location when
they parked.

Unfortunately, this time they'd had to park in the
multi-level garage. She'd debated the wisdom of returning to the car alone, but she couldn't think of another way to find Cord. And they *had* agreed on this
plan.

Twilight streamed in from the open sides, but it was
still dark and shadowed. The muggy night accented
the smell of oil sitting in pools on the concrete under
the cars. A slight breeze raised goose bumps on her
arms; her footfalls on the ramp to level seven echoed
through the still, silent area. She bit her lip. It would
be okay. She was scared, but Cord would already be
at the truck, or he'd come soon.

A horn honked two levels below; she started vio-
lently. Then she laughed nervously at how jumpy she
was. *Calm down, Stacey. You have no reason to think
anyone's here.* All she had to do was hurry to the
truck, get inside with the spare keys Cord had given
her and lock the doors. In minutes, she reached the
vehicle and grasped the handle.

A hand slapped across her face.

Stacey froze when she felt the prick of a knife at her
neck.

Oh, God, it was the stalker.

"Gotcha," he said hoarsely. His voice was gravelly. Was he disguising it? She tried to remain calm, to observe the details which might reveal his identity. But she started to shake when he moved his hand from her mouth down to her breast.

"Hmm, they feel as soft as they look." He lowered the knife to her other breast and laid the flat part of it against her. "Gonna cut ya here first, whore, then lots of other places."

Oh, God, please, help me.

But in a crystal-clear moment, Stacey realized it wasn't up to God. It was up to her.

Stay calm, and don't panic, Cord would say.

She forced herself to think.

Don't aggravate him, he'd tell her.

She slumped against him.

"No struggle, girlie? Aw, where's the fun in that?"

He wedged the knife between the bodice of her dress and her chest and jerked his arm. The buttons flew onto the pavement. He returned the blade to her skin. It was cold. Slicing the wispy lace of her bra, he nicked her in the process. She didn't look down. She knew she'd panic at the sight of her own blood.

Wait for an opening.

A motorcycle backfired somewhere in the garage. The man jerked around, maintaining his hold on her waist, but swinging away the hand that held the knife.

Pulling back, she jabbed her elbow into his ski-masked face. His teeth cracked and he let go of her waist. She ran, cursing the sandals she'd chosen over sneakers. She headed out blindly. He tackled her before she'd covered a few feet. She fell to the concrete with a thud, arms flying up to protect herself. He tried to cover her, but she caught him in the groin with her knee. He groaned like a wounded animal, letting go of her enough so that she could scramble away. She struggled to her feet and ran again. The exit sign was up ahead. She was almost to the ramp, when he grabbed her from behind. The force of his weight pitched her forward and she banged her head against the rusted iron railing.

"Damn bitch," he snapped. "I'll cut you up right here."

A meaty arm encircled her neck and clinched. She couldn't breathe. In a last-ditch effort to save herself, she reached up with her right hand and dug her nails into his face, through the ski mask.

Suddenly, the door above them swung open and Cord barreled through. The last thing Stacey saw was him leaping over the railing right on top of the two of them. Then there was only blackness.

THE EMERGENCY WARD was deserted as Cord sat by Stacey's bed. She'd regained consciousness in the ambulance and had weaved in and out of it since their arrival an hour ago. Her father sat on the other side of the bed in sober-faced silence.

"If you want, I'll call the Anderson people again," Cord told him.

"Why would I want that?" Hands steepled, Webb stared over at him.

"I bungled it tonight."

"You saved her life. At a cost to you," he added, nodding at the sling around Cord's neck and arm.

"I'm all right. It's sore as hell, but it'll get better."
When Gifford was silent, Cord confessed quietly, "I
lost her."

"How did that happen?"

Briefly, Cord explained the emergency in the store.

"You had to help," Webb said.

"I should have alerted Stacey. I wasn't thinking."

"Hindsight is always twenty-twenty."

"I thought you'd be flaming."

"Cord," Gifford said hoarsely, and Cord realized
that was the first time Gifford had called him anything but McKay. "You've protected Stacey well and
saved her life at least twice. I'm grateful. I'm not
about to criticize the job you're doing."

"Well, I don't feel the same way."

"I think we're always harder on ourselves."

"Cord?" Stacey's voice was weak. "Are you all
right?"

"I'm fine, sweetheart."

She looked at his sling. "Your shoulder?"

"It's okay. How are *you?*"

"My head hurts."

"I'll bet it does."

"Daddy?"

"Hi, honey." Webb came to the edge of his chair.
Cord watched the man dam up his emotions.

"Don't be mad at Cord. I couldn't find him, so
I—"

"I'm not mad at anyone."

Her face tensed. "Who...who was it?"

Gifford glanced at Cord.

"Please...don't keep anything from me."

"We still don't know, Stace," Cord said.

"You didn't beat him to a pulp?"

"Ah, no. He caught me in the shoulder with a boot. By the time I'd recovered enough to reach for my gun, he'd gone."

"We still don't know who he is?"

"Nope."

Stacey bit her lip. "He was the same size as Mark Dunn."

"Yes, I know." Cord heard the strain in his voice.

This time, Stacey shivered. "Where's Lauren?"

"Judith is with her." Gifford turned to Cord. "What do we do now?"

"We push the police to put more effort into this case. Then, we wait, again." He paused, then added, "If you're sure that's what you want."

Gifford glanced from his daughter back to Cord. "I want you with us. Stacey needs you."

STACEY STARED at her mother's coffin.

It should've been pink, Mommy's favorite color, or green like her eyes. Why was it that ugly black? She'd touched the box in the big red building with the funny name—some kind of home—and it was cold and hard.

Her father said the coffin was dark to show respect, but Mommy wouldn't have wanted that. Stacey knew. Like she knew other things about Mommy. When she was sad. When she cried for no reason.

Reaching down, her father smoothed his hand over her hair. It made her feel bad because Mommy always did that when Stacey couldn't go to sleep. Her father told her she'd never see Mommy again, that she

*was in heaven. But she knew better. Mommy had told
her she'd be back. Just before she left. She hadn't
come back yet, but she would. Mommy always did
what she said she would.*

*"Come on, honey," her father said, tugging on her
hand.*

"No, we can't leave Mommy."

"Honey, we have to leave Mommy."

"Please, please. Mommy...Mommy...don't leave."

Her father squatted and scooped her up.

*She buried her face in his neck as they walked to the
road that was covered with stones. She yelped when
her dad squeezed her too tight. "Daddy!"*

*But he didn't let go. She looked up and saw her fa-
ther staring at someone.*

*The boy/man that used to come and see Mommy
was standing on the other side of the road. She called
him that because once, when she asked Mommy if he
was a boy or a man, Mommy said he was a boy in a
man's body. Whatever that meant.*

*"Stay here," her father said, handing her to her
grandmother. His voice sounded like it did when he
got mad at Mommy. "Ana, watch her," he told
Grandma.*

Then he walked real mad-like to the boy/man.

But before he got there, the boy/man was gone.

STACEY AWOKE in a sweat from the most realistic
dream she'd ever had. Her chest heaving, she scanned
her surroundings to make sure she knew where she
was. Her bedroom was dimly lit, and she was alone.
Lauren was asleep in the sitting room and Cord was

bunked down at the other end of the house. Limply, she fell back against the pillows.

The dream was still with her and Cord had been in it. He was the boy/man on the road. But it had been so real . . .

"Stupid," she said aloud. Everyone knew that dreams were like edited movies, often combining various parts of a person's life. Her unconscious had put her childhood nightmare together with the man she loved. Still, it disturbed her.

Rolling over, she tried to quell the sense of unease the nightmare had left her with. For twenty-two minutes she eyed the progression of the numbers on the red digital clock. Unable to endure one more flip, she threw back the covers and climbed out of bed. Her satiny pink chemise and tap pants were damp from sweat; she shivered despite the balmy summer night. Stopping to get a matching robe—Lauren had given her the ensemble for her birthday—she padded out of the room and down the hall to Cord's door. Since he'd moved out of her suite, he'd insisted both her bedroom door and his remain open during the night. She peered in.

The moon cast crisscross patterns on his back. Half of his face was buried in the pillow that he gripped with his big, strong hand. His breathing was deep and even—until she stepped into the room and walked to him.

Without warning, he bolted from the bed and grabbed her. She was on the mattress, pinned beneath him, before she could take another breath. Not that she minded.

He did. "Dammit, Stacey, what are you doing?" His breathing was rapid, his eyes wide and alert.

"I needed to see you."

His touch on her gentled. Lifting a hand to her hair, he brushed some strands off her face. "Don't do this."

"Do what?"

"Tempt me." His hand strayed to the open vee of her robe. "Make me want you so bad I ache. I can't sleep. When I finally manage to doze off, I dream about you. It's bad enough. Please don't make it worse."

"I didn't come to tease. I came because I had another nightmare."

Easing off her, he laid his head on the pillow and pulled her close. "Like the last one?"

"Worse. I remember it all. The funny thing is, it wasn't really a dream. It was another flashback. Except you were in it."

She felt his heart thudding in his chest.

Stacey wondered why. "I know how things filter into dreams... What's going on in real life intrudes on your unconscious. But it was eerie."

Cord still didn't say anything.

"Are you all right?" she asked.

"Yeah. Tell—" he cleared his throat "—tell me about it."

"I was at my mother's funeral. Crying for her not to leave me. That's all I usually remember, and not even that until lately. Anyway, my father is carrying me, and then he stops and looks out over the cemetery. That's where you came in this time. He's looking at you." She buried her face in his chest, letting the hair tickle her nose. "It's dumb. Must be because I miss you so much."

"I miss you, too."

"I don't want to spend my life missing you, Cord. I love you."

"I love you, too, baby."

"But you'll let me go."

"I have no choice."

She leaned up on her elbow. "Why? Tell me why you have no choice. And don't lie to me about it being our age difference, my youth, my lack of worldliness."

"No, I won't lie."

"Then tell me, Cord."

His sigh was heavy. "All right. I'll tell you tomorrow. There's something I have to do first."

CORD KNOCKED on the library door the next morning before they all left for work.

"Come in." The older man stood when Cord entered. "Is something wrong? Stacey?"

"Stacey is fine, at least physically. It's her emotions that concern me."

"Sit down," Gifford said, indicating a chair as he took one himself. "What's going on?"

"She had a dream about Helene's burial. Only it was more of a flashback." Gifford's forehead creased as Cord spoke. "And I was in it."

"No!" Slapping his hand down on the desk, he repeated, "No!"

"It's true. Apparently, she recalls the whole incident at the cemetery, except that she thinks my being in the dream is just her unconscious playing tricks, juxtaposing the present and the past.''

"So she doesn't know the truth?"

"No," he said. "Not yet."

"What do you mean?"

"Obviously Stacey has remembered things about Helene consciously because of my presence here. Now it's happening unconsciously. Each time she has this dream, she remembers more and more. Gifford, she's too bright not to piece it all together. She's going to guess—or remember."

"How can this have happened?"

"Because you let me back into your lives."

"What do we do now?"

"We have to tell her the truth."

"No! Absolutely not!"

"Then you're risking her physical safety as well as her emotional state."

"How?"

"I'm afraid if she finds out about me and Helene indirectly, she'll be so angry with both of us that she won't let me protect her. I don't want to risk that."

"Do you know what we're risking the other way?"

"I know what *I'm* risking. She'll kick me out of her life. You'll still have her."

"And you're willing to give her up?"

"To keep her safe, I'd do anything. Even have her hate me."

"I don't want to do this, Cord."

"By God, neither do I. But, as you said before, sometimes we don't have a choice."

CHAPTER TWELVE

As THEY CROSSED TOWN and headed for Cord's house, Stacey smiled to herself in the dim light of the truck cab. The breeze rustled her hair, and his, while the scents of late-summer enveloped them.

"Your mother and Megan are still at your aunt's?"

"Yeah. They'll be home Sunday." He reached over and squeezed her hand. "My house is a good place to talk. We won't be interrupted."

And we can make love in your bed afterward, Stacey thought but didn't articulate. He'd just knit those dark blond eyebrows together, and the sad look in his eyes would turn bleaker. But Stacey wasn't worried. She entwined her fingers with his, feeling their callused tips, rough on the back of her hand.

She knew tonight was some kind of crossroads for him. Cord was finally going to tell her what he'd been holding back all these months. And she was so sure they could get past whatever it was, she'd stashed some condoms in her purse—to celebrate afterward. And maybe, when she proved she could forgive him anything...she spun a delicious fantasy of being his wife and a mother to Megan.

When they pulled into the driveway, he shut off the engine but didn't open the door. In the sudden silence, he turned to her. "Stace, you've got to promise me two things before we go inside."

She sensed his somberness. "Anything."

"That after we have this conversation, you won't do anything to jeopardize your safety."

His comment irritated her, but she ignored it. "I won't, Cord." This time, she squeezed *his* arm, the soft cotton sliding beneath her palm. "What's the second thing?"

"That you'll try to believe I love you, I've always loved you." She thought his eyes glistened.

A cold premonition swept through her, but she suppressed it. "I believe it now, and I'll believe it later. But I want you to remember something."

"What?"

"There's nothing you could say, nothing you could tell me, that would change how I feel about you."

Roughly, he grasped her neck, yanked her close and gave her a hard, possessive kiss. Without speaking, he opened the truck door. She climbed out her side, circled the front, took his hand and held it tightly until they were inside. He flicked on a muted light in the corner of the living room and sank onto the couch. Following him, she bent over and lightly kissed his cheek. The smell of the woodsy after-shave she'd come to associate with him soothed her. Plunking down beside him, she turned to face him fully. "Okay, shoot. What's this deep dark secret that's going to keep us apart?"

He reached out and caught a few strands of her hair in his fingers, lightly rubbing them. The slight tug made her lean toward him. "Do you remember when the issue first came up about me being your body-guard?"

"Yes, you resisted the idea. You said you weren't suitable."

His laugh was raw. "I wasn't. I'm not."

"Why?"

"Because I have a connection with your family that you don't know about."

Stacey recalled her early impressions that he knew her father...

"Cord, I know you didn't want to do this. Because of your daughter especially. But I sense there's another reason. Does my father know you from somewhere?"

"No, your father doesn't know me at all."

She said aloud, "I asked you if you knew my father, that very first day."

"I did know him." He drew in a deep breath. "And I knew your mother."

Another conversation came into focus. *Helene?* he'd asked. *My mother,* she'd answered. Stacey clasped her hands in her lap. "But you acted like you didn't even know my mother's name when I told you about the dreams."

"That's right—I was acting."

Stacey shifted restlessly on the sofa. She scrutinized his face, noting the high color in his cheeks and the lines bracketing his unsmiling mouth. He'd lied to her. Tension, and a niggling hurt, came with that knowledge. "How did you know her? Them?"

"When I was in high school, I worked as a bag boy at the Foodmart. I also delivered groceries. Sometimes to your house. That's how I met your parents. The summer after I graduated, your father hired me to do yard work, take care of the pool, stuff like that. As he got busier and busier, I took on more responsibility around your place.''

"Our house? You spent time at our house?"

"Yes."

"Then you knew me? When I was . . . what, five?"

"Yes."

The dream came out of nowhere, like a monster in a grade B movie. *The boy/man at the cemetery.* That had really happened. A sixth sense of foreboding curled through her. The slight breeze from the open window chilled her arms and legs, bare under the short T-shirt dress she wore. She rubbed her limbs, but couldn't get warm.

He continued, "That summer, I spent a lot of time at your house. Things at home for me were bad—my father and I fought all the time, and it was getting horrible for my mother." His jaw clenched, the way it did every time he discussed his father. "They'd argue about me, then she'd cry, later, when he left to go to the station."

"So you spent time at my house?"

"Yes. Your mother was a warm, understanding person. She sensed early on things weren't going well for me. Little by little, over a glass of lemonade or some cookies, she drew it out of me. She was sympathetic, insightful."

Stacey sat back and cocked her head, sending waves of too-long hair into her eyes. She finger-combed it back. "Cord, I don't understand why you kept this

from me. It sounds like you knew my mother well, like
you knew a side of her I'd never remembered. Why on
earth wouldn't you tell me this, especially since you
understood how confused I was about her?''

Cord stood and crossed to the window. Pulling back
the sheers, he stared out. His shoulders were rigid, his
whole body poised, as if expecting a blow. She could
just make out the bulge of his gun in its leather holster. Stacey waited.

When he turned around, that strained, haunted look
was on his face again. "I didn't tell you because
something happened between . . . between Helene and
me that I never wanted you to know about.''

Icy dread slapped Stacey in the face. "What?"

Cord cleared his throat. "That summer, at the end
of August, my father and I had a terrible battle. All
along, I'd resisted the idea of going to college, though
I'd applied and gotten accepted at a few. He told me
to shape up and get those school forms in, or to get out
of his house. My mother intervened, as usual, and told
him she'd leave with me if he forced the issue.''

"What does this have to do with *my* mother?"

"When I came to work that afternoon, I was overwrought. Your mother picked up on my state of mind
right away. You were out for the day with your grandmother, and Helene spent hours talking to me about
my options. That was the kind of person she was.
Unselfish, caring.''

"What happened?"

"Your father came home about six. I was cleaning
the pool, and I heard them arguing from their bedroom above the patio about a trip he had to take. He

was packing and your mother begged him not to go.
Apparently, this was an ongoing bone of contention
between them. He raised his voice and told her to stop
nagging him. Her response was quiet, subdued, like
always. Then he said . . ."

Cord stopped and folded his arms over his chest.
The skin stretched tight across his cheekbones.

"He said what? Tell me, Cord."

"He said if she didn't stop nagging him, he might
just decide not to come back."

"Oh, my God."

"Stace, he was different then. Work was everything to him. He was young and ambitious and foolish. Don't judge him too harshly."

Something clicked for Stacey. "Cord, this was the
day she died, wasn't it?"

"Yes."

"She and Daddy had a terrible fight the day she
died?"

"Yes."

"And?"

"He left. She stayed in their room. At first it was
quiet, but then I could hear her sobbing. I couldn't
stand it, Stacey. She'd been so kind to me. I couldn't
keep cleaning the pool while she cried in her bedroom."

Another image of Cord, standing before the master suite, just three days ago, flashed through her
mind. He'd jumped when she came up behind her,
then turned around. His face had been white . . .

"I didn't hear you."

"You were a million miles away."

"Years away," he'd said, and glanced back at the room.

As she looked at him now, she saw that same sadness suffusing his features. She said, "So what did you do?"

"I went upstairs to find her."

"What did you do?" The pitch of her voice rose a notch.

He didn't answer.

"What happened?"

"I held her. She cried for a long time in my arms."

Stacey swallowed hard. He'd held her mother. On her parents' bed. "And? Did my father come home and find you? Is that what happened? And he got the wrong idea?"

The look on Cord's face knotted her stomach. "Your father *did* come back. But he got the right idea."

Every nerve in Stacey's body tingled. Her skin got clammy and her mouth went dry. She inched back on the sofa. "The right idea? Surely you don't mean . . . you and my mother didn't . . ."

In a flash, so quickly that it caught her off guard, Cord flew across the room, knelt before her and took her hands in his. He rubbed them, almost unconsciously. "Yes, Stacey, we did. But it wasn't what it seems. It was for comfort. For solace. Both our worlds had fallen apart. We . . . needed each other. It was only once, between two desperate people."

Her chest tightened as she peered into the face of the man she loved.

Of the man who had slept with her mother.

"Y-you slept with my *mother?* You made love with my *mother?*"

Again his eyes glistened. "Yes, Stacey, I did."

She felt the bile rise in her throat. She clamped down on the images that assaulted her—images of Cord, with her mother. Her stomach churning, she bit her lip until it hurt. "No! No! I won't believe this. It can't be true."

"It is."

"No, please, say it isn't true."

"I'm sorry, Stace."

"Oh, God, it's so... obscene."

"Sweetheart, it wasn't like that."

Something clutched her insides. She felt dizzy and spots swam before her eyes. She asked, "Were you in love with her?"

"I loved her. As a friend. As a person who cared about me, helped me at a time when I had nothing else. And she loved me the same way."

"But you had sex with her?" The images came again. This time more vivid, more real.

"It's complicated... it was born out of desperation, not passion."

Stacey withdrew her hands from his and sank into the cushions, taking in deep, steadying breaths. *I need to handle this like an adult,* she told herself. *I need to handle this well.*

But her mother? And Cord? His words came back to her. *Your mother was only human...* after she told him about overhearing her grandmother and her father arguing.

She raised her hands to her mouth as she felt the tears fill her eyes. The jumbled pieces fused together in her mind, completing the macabre puzzle. "You were the one. You were the one my father found her with."

Cord pulled her hands from her mouth and held them in his again. "I was the *only* one your mother ever did this with. Afterward, she told me it had never happened before, had never even *occurred* to her to do something like this. That she loved Gifford so much. I know that was true."

He seemed to think his words would make it easier. Stacey wished it had been a hundred other men—just not the one man in this world she loved. Oh, God, he'd touched her mother the way he'd touched her. The awful images kept coming and she couldn't stop them.

Control it, Stacey. Be mature about this.

But she couldn't. Searching his moist blue eyes for something that would make the truth less painful, she asked, "How...how could you let anything happen between us? You knew right from the beginning what your history was with my family. But you let it happen between us. You *let* it. How could you do that?"

"I was wrong."

His image wavered through her tears. Her relationship with Cord suddenly seemed sordid. What had been the most beautiful experience of her life had turned seedy. "Unless—oh, God, tell me it isn't true. It wasn't some kinky thing for you, was it? Screw the mother, then the daughter? To make some grotesque comparison."

"No! Stacey, no, please. It was never that."

She shrank from him, pulled away her hands and closed her eyes to shut him out.

"Stace, please, think back on our time together. I couldn't have faked that. It was all real. I love you."

More images cascaded over her...his first kiss...the gentle yet sexy tug of his mouth on her breast...how he'd touched her in places she didn't even know men and women touched.

"Stacey—you said...you promised...please, tell me you believe my love was real."

She studied his face, searching for the man who had been her tender lover. "I want to believe it, I said I would...it's just that...."

And then she began to weep. Unable to stop the flow, not even wanting to, she let the tears come. He sat back on the couch, drew her to him and held her. "Go ahead, sweetheart, let it out. It's worth crying over."

She did. And she let Cord—the man who had caused the pain—hold her the entire time. With no pride, she gripped his shirt and allowed comfort to come from the man who had torn her world apart with just a few words.

When she finally quieted, Cord felt the tension in her body ease slightly. He scrambled for words to diminish her pain, to dilute the agony that would come when she had time to internalize all this. "There's something more you should know, Stace. The reason your father came back that day was to work things out with Helene. He'd canceled his trip. He'd come to tell her he was sorry."

"And he found you."

Cord nodded, conjuring the stricken face of Gifford Webb when he'd walked into the bedroom. It was a vision Cord would never forget as long as he lived. And now, the same look of disbelief and hurt was etched on Stacey's lovely face.

She drew away from him, and he guessed the reminder of her father's pain made her unable to touch the man who'd caused it. She stood shakily, moved to the chair, leaned against it and wrapped her arms around her waist. "What did my father do?"

"He exploded. I don't know exactly what he said to your mother, because I got dressed and went downstairs." Cord watched her face as he told her the rest, the sadness in those chestnut eyes searing his soul. "He came down a few minutes later. We talked and I left."

"You got *dressed?* Oh, God." She closed her eyes briefly, then asked, "Did you see her again?"

Cord shook his head. "She died that night. You'll need to ask your father about what happened between them. He'll want to tell you that part. Just know that he was young, and shocked, and anything he did was out of anger, justifiable anger..."

"Now it all makes sense...those horrible dreams were a flashback to what really happened." She stared over his shoulder as she recited a litany of memories. "Ana brought me back, and my mother had her bags packed. She and my father were fighting. He told her to get out. I begged her not to go. But he made her leave." Stacey's hoarse voice stung his conscience. "Then she cracked up the car." She turned to face

Cord, her breath hitching, her eyes wide and disbelieving. "My father was responsible for her death."

Rising from the couch, Cord crossed to her. He grasped her arms and forced her to look at him. "It was a knee-jerk reaction. He was in shock. He didn't know the situation. Look at it from his viewpoint. Stacey, don't judge him too harshly."

"Too harshly?" She threw off his touch and stepped back from him. "And that wasn't all he did, was it? He knew when he hired you to be my bodyguard...my...my father was a *part* of this...this charade."

"Stacey, listen, neither one of us wanted me back in your lives. But we were trying to protect you."

"Protect me?" The added blow of her father's deceit, of his betrayal, broke the last of her restraint. She began to pace. "*Protect me?* Do you realize what you two let happen? *You* made love to me when you knew you'd slept with my mother. And *my father*...he knew, too. He saw us together in the kitchen that morning and he still never told me the truth."

"Stacey, that was the hardest thing he ever did."

She continued pacing, as if she hadn't heard Cord. Her hurt and anger seemed to escalate with each step. "He let you back into our lives. He let you be around me..."

"Please. Give your father a chance to explain."

Stopping suddenly, she rounded on him. "No. I don't want any explanation from him. And I don't want any more from *you.*"

"Stacey, listen—"

"No. I'm done listening. I want to go...anywhere." She looked around, almost wildly. "Just get me out of here. Away from you. Away from this whole ugly mess."

FROM THE DOORWAY of his library, Gifford watched Stacey and Cord walk into the foyer. He stood perfectly still, trying to calm his churning stomach. Their stiff carriage and drawn faces testified to the emotional ravishment that had taken its toll on both of them. Stacey was several feet ahead of Cord, silently proclaiming her feelings.

Not noticing Gifford, Cord caught up to Stacey by the staircase and grabbed her arm. She shrugged off his hand, but faced him from the first step. "What?" she asked.

"Just remember your promise. Don't do anything foolish, to endanger yourself."

His daughter's usually mischievous face scowled. "You still don't get it, do you? I'm not some child that's going to risk her safety because she's upset."

Gifford shifted uneasily, and the action snagged Stacey's attention. She pierced him with stricken eyes. Her gaze locked with his for a minute, then she turned to Cord. "Because my mother—because of what both of you did—I grew up without my mother, and, contrary to what both of you may think, I've learned to depend on myself more than most women. I won't give the stalker an opportunity to get at me just because the two of you aren't the men I thought you were."

Gifford wasn't surprised at her words, but he hadn't let himself speculate how much it would hurt. Bracing his arm on the doorway, he jammed one hand into his pocket and fisted it. "I'm sorry, honey."

"Yeah, Dad, so am I." She stared at him as if he was a stranger, turned and took the stairs two at a time.

His heart racing, Gifford called after her, "Stacey—can we talk about this?"

She stopped halfway up and faced him. "Not right now. I'm feeling too raw." Even from a distance, he could see her lips quiver and her eyes fill. His daughter was on the brink of losing control, and he couldn't help her this time. Would she ever allow him close again? She pivoted, and hiked up the rest of the steps. The closing of her door echoed ominously through the foyer.

Gifford looked to Cord, who'd sagged against the banister. "Will you come in and tell me what happened, McKay?"

Nodding, Cord followed him into the library. Gifford noticed the slight tremble in his own hands as he poured generous amounts of Scotch for both of them. He gave one glass to Cord, who took it, sank onto a wing chair and gulped the liquor.

"What happened?"

Quickly, as if each word caused him pain, Cord told Gifford what he'd said to Stacey, and her reaction. "She's hurt, and disgusted." He ran a shaky hand through his hair. "I didn't expect the last. I...I didn't know that she'd feel so...repulsed by me, by the thought of her and me together." Gifford saw moisture gather in the younger man's eyes. "I can take everything else. I expected her to hate me, to end our relationship, but this... I'm not sure I can handle *this.*" He set down his drink, leaned over and buried his face in his hands.

Gifford watched Cord McKay with a deep sense of guilt. He'd blamed and punished the boy years ago, and now he was watching the man suffer because Gifford had insisted Cord put his life on the line for Stacey. Crossing to him, Gifford placed a fatherly hand on his shoulder. "I'm sorry, Cord. For now, and for eighteen years ago." He squeezed gently. "We've both wronged Stacey, but your actions were unselfish. You tried to avoid getting involved with us. I pushed it... because I was afraid for her life. But I should have found an alternative. I should have foreseen this happening. I was wrong. Again."

Cord's shoulders shook, and Gifford kept his hand where it was, trying to comfort the younger man. He closed his eyes to block out the evidence of the pain he'd caused.

TWO HOURS LATER, Gifford went in search of Stacey. He and Cord had talked for a while after Cord had composed himself. Then Cord had gone to take a shower and was in the spare room. Gifford waited as long as he could, but finally gave in to the need to see his daughter. When she wasn't in her bedroom, he searched the house. He found her in the workout room, pedaling the exercise bicycle fast enough to fly. "Can we talk, Stacey?"

She kept pedaling. "I don't think it's a good time to do that." Her words were low and throaty. She'd obviously been crying.

"Would you just listen to me then?"

She nodded but didn't get off the bike. He came into the room and stood before her. Her flushed face accented her drawn lips and hollow eyes. Their rich brown was ringed with red, and her eyelids were puffy.

"I want you to know that I take full responsibility for your mother's death."

Stacey stiffened and stopped pedaling. Her knuckles whitened on the handlebars.

"I was wrong in two ways," he went on. "I left her alone too much, and I was insensitive to her needs." He swallowed hard, the confession as painful as picking glass slivers out of skin. "She tried to tell me, but I was too ambitious and too foolish."

Stacey continued to stare at him. Her eyes narrowed as if she were seeing him for the first time. In a way, she was. As she'd said earlier, he wasn't the man she thought he was. The awareness cut deep.

"After I found them together, I kicked her out, without letting her explain." He coughed. "But she did explain . . . she left me a note . . . telling me how it really was between her and McKay."

Stacey's eyes darkened; she frowned as she absorbed the new piece of information.

"But it was too late by then," Gifford said. "I didn't get a second chance. She'd smashed up the car. . . . She *died* because of my self-righteous indignation."

Gifford watched his daughter's face crumple, watched her will back tears.

"I blamed Cord before, but I won't do it again. *I* was the adult in this situation. So was Helene. McKay was just a kid. When I think of how I forced him out of town, away from his family..."

"You *what?*"

"Didn't he tell you?"

Stacey shook her head.

Ah, he'd misjudged the man so badly. "I told him to leave Canfield or I'd ruin his family. What I did was inexcusable...I know it just adds another layer to my selfishness. But you have to know the extent of my sins."

Stacey got off the bike and wiped the sweat from her face. "Why didn't Cord tell me this?"

"I think we've both underestimated his nobility."

She shook her head, every muscle exposed in her spandex suit tightening. "No...no. He let me fall in love with him, knowing the connection he had with Helene. *You* did the same thing. Why?"

Staring at Stacey, Gifford answered the only way he could. Honestly. "I would have done anything to keep you safe. Your life is more important to me than your love. I know you hate me now because of what I did to your mother. But the stalking...I was trying to protect you. That's why I brought Cord back into our lives. It may have been an error in judgment, but at least tell me you understand why I did it."

Stacey didn't say anything for a minute, staring silently at him. Then she said, "I'm feeling a lot of conflicting emotions right now." She bit her lip and looked at him the way she used to when she was a child and afraid of the night. "But I don't hate you, Dad. I never could."

Closing his eyes, he silently thanked God for generosity he didn't deserve. Then, in a miraculous show of selflessness, his daughter gave him exactly what he needed. She stepped forward and hugged him.

Just like her mother. Helene would have been so proud of her.

LIKE A ZOMBIE, Stacey climbed the back staircase, passed slowly down the hall and through the door to her room. The workout hadn't helped—it had just made her more edgy, sent more adrenaline pumping through her. Scanning the familiar decor, Stacey shook her head. Whereas before, this room had echoed the intimacy of her lovemaking with Cord, now regret and emptiness bounced in vibrant rhythms around her.

Before the reminder could smother her, Lauren came from the sitting room where she'd been resting.

"There you are," Lauren said in her soft alto voice. "I've been looking all over for you. I thought I heard you come in earlier."

Stacey felt the tears rise again as she looked at her best friend.

"Stacey? What's wrong?"

Reining in her emotions, Stacey sank onto the long green chaise that was adjacent to the front windows. "Cord knew my mother, Lauren." She laughed, but even to her own ears the sound was shrill. "In the biblical sense."

"What are you talking about?" Lauren came and sat at the end of the chaise, her cast bumping gently against Stacey's leg. Her eyes were wide with concern.

"He worked here when he was eighteen. He was the one my father found with my mother the night she died."

"*What?*" Lauren's usually pale complexion mottled.

"He slept with my mother."

"Oh, my God, poor Gifford."

A chill skittered through Stacey as she stared at her friend. She knew Lauren loved her father, had always seen him as a surrogate parent, but she'd expected her friend's sympathy to be for her.

As if she'd read Stacey's mind, Lauren reached out and took her hand. "And poor you. Oh, Stacey, I'm sorry."

"Yeah, me, too. It's so unreal." Stacey lay back against the pillows. "I'm sorry, too."

"What did your father say?"

Briefly, Stacey recounted the story.

Lauren's grip tightened on Stacey's hand. "How could she have done that to him? Betrayed him like that? He's so kind, so giving, so virile. She must have been a horrible woman."

"No, the ironic thing is, all this has given me a completely different view of Helene. She was pretty innocent."

"You can't mean you blame your father."

Shaking her head, Stacey felt the curls Cord loved flop into her face. "I don't *blame* anyone."

Lauren's stiff posture relaxed. "What *are* you feeling?"

"About Daddy?" Lauren nodded. "I'm furious with him for not telling me about Cord's connection with my mother right away. And I'm still in shock over what happened between Cord and my mother."

"Stacey, from what you just told me, the facts remain the same. Your mother cheated on your father."

Sucking in a deep breath, Stacey said, "But, Lauren, I grew up thinking she was a slut. In reality, she was a lonely young woman—not even thirty—who turned to another man for comfort. It happened only once. That changes things."

"Do you think it was easy for your father?"

"Of course not. But even he admits he was wrong. He made mistakes." She paused for a moment, then said, "You know what the saddest thing about this is?"

"What?"

"They really loved each other. They could have worked this out. He could have forgiven her, and they could have had a happy life together."

Lauren frowned. Then she stood and crossed to the windows, and peered out thoughtfully. "It wasn't meant to be, Stacey. Some things—they just happen outside of your control." She turned and looked at her friend. "Are you going to punish your father for what happened to Helene?"

"No. He's punished himself enough already. I don't know, though, what our relationship can be like now."

"Why?"

"Because he lied to me. I'm not sure I can forget that."

"What about Cord?"

Stacey felt pain in every part of her body. "He's out of my life after the stalker is caught. I could never trust him again."

"Because he slept with your mother."

"It's more than that. It's so awful—I can hardly even think about it—that he was close to her that way. But the worst part is that knowing his connection to my mother, he still made love to me—he still let me fall in love with him. He should have told me everything before this happened between us."

"I wonder why he didn't."

"It doesn't matter. Both he and Daddy treated me like a child, and let me down." She stared over at her friend. "You know, Lauren, you're the only person, in my whole life, who has never let me down."

She saw Lauren gulp, overcome with emotion. "Stacey, I—"

"No, don't say anything. Just always be here for me. I don't know what I'd do, now, if I lost that."

CHAPTER THIRTEEN

THE MAN PLUCKED a toothpick from its holder as the hostess for the Center Street Coffee Shop took his money. Sticking it in his mouth, he glanced over her shoulder. Through the large, plate-glass window, he saw Cord McKay slouched against the building directly across the street. Even from a distance, he could see McKay's stiff shoulders and the disgruntled tilt of his chin.

So, there's trouble in paradise. Good. Horny men are easily distracted.

"Thank you, sir. Come back again." The petite woman with the mousy brown hair gave him an insipid smile.

He nodded. *Sir. I like that. Maybe I'll have Stacey Webb call me that. On her knees.*

Exiting the shop, he crossed the street against the light, dodging the cars. He resisted flipping the finger to the creeps who blared their horns. It was important not to give away too much.

Just a few stores down, he stopped. "McKay, I didn't see you there."

McKay's stare was cold, and in spite of himself, he shivered. This was no man to fool with.

"Yeah, well, you better watch that jaywalking. The cops could get you."

Both of them laughed at the joke, although it was a strained sound, especially from McKay.

Damn you, you bastard, for making me nervous. She'll pay for your arrogance. And somehow, I'll let you know that.

"So, what are you doin' here?" He folded his arms over his dark shirt, and willed himself to relax.

Jamming his hands into his pockets, McKay jerked his head to the shop behind him. "Stacey's in there."

He peered up at the sign. Margaret's Hair Studio. "She gettin' her hair cut?"

A curt nod told him of McKay's displeasure. *Interesting.*

"I kinda like it long, don't you?" he said smoothly. He'd had visions of yanking it back. Hard. "But she's always worn it short. That why she's cuttin' it?"

The other man shrugged. "Beats me." McKay studied his face, as if he was looking for something. "Cut yourself shaving?" he asked, his eyes focusing on the small bandage that covered what was left of Stacey Webb's scratches, when she'd clawed him through the ski mask.

"Naw. Scraped my cheek on some bushes I was trimmin'."

McKay nodded.

Getting suspicious, McKay? Do you know?

"Having a bite to eat?" McKay indicated the coffee shop.

He nodded. "Yeah. I've gotta be to work at ten."

"On the late shift this week?"

Why the questions? What are you looking for? "Yep. We're shorthanded, as usual." *Do you think it's me? Are you checking out my schedule?*

The possibility made the blood course through him. The adrenaline came fast and furious as he thought about it. He'd always liked a good game of cat and mouse.

Just then, the door opened. McKay turned to watch Stacey exit from the building. His jaw dropped. "Aw, Stacey," he said, his eyes glued to her hair.

For a minute, her face paled. Then, she sucked in a breath and looked down her nose at him. "I take it you don't like my new haircut."

"Geez, did you have to get it cut so short?" McKay said.

She lifted her chin. "Yes, I did."

Then she turned to him. She smiled, though it was weak, and didn't reach her eyes. "Hi."

"Hi." He pretended to inspect her hair. "I like it, Stacey." Actually, it looked like hell. It was about two inches all over, and it had been sprayed so it spiked up in the front in that fancy hairdo he'd seen in magazines. What was the word they'd used in those old movies? When they punished women for adultery? *Shorn,* it looked shorn. *Fitting,* he thought. Now she'd look the part when he gave her the punishment she deserved.

When he thought of how she'd escaped him five days ago, the rage threatened to erupt right here on Center Street. But he'd lost his chance because he'd gotten angry then. So he had to control himself now. He wouldn't make the same mistake twice. This time, he was staying calm and cool. He'd comforted himself all week with visions of her on her knees, her hands tied behind her back as he sliced her. She'd be crying, and begging. Ah, he loved it when women begged. He was really looking forward to Stacey Webb's pleas. It made everything so much sweeter. And it would be soon. Very soon. The thought gave him a hard-on.

"Hey, are you okay?" McKay asked.

He turned to look at the lovesick sap. "Huh?"

"Stacey asked you what you were doing here. You didn't answer. Are you all right?"

"I'm good." *Oh, I'm really good.* He glanced down at his boot, his fingers itching to caress the sleek metal hidden there. *I'm very good.*

And it wouldn't be too long before Stacey Webb found out.

GIFFORD INSISTED they celebrate Megan's birthday at his home. It was early August, and Cord was sitting on the pool deck when Nora and his daughter arrived. Megan catapulted onto his lap and hugged him fiercely. Over her shoulders, Cord watched Stacey walk through the French doors. Megan tracked his gaze, then clambered down and made a running leap into Stacey's arms. "Stacey, what happened to your hair?"

Yeah, what happened?

But Cord knew. Just as he knew why she'd stopped sketching. As he watched the woman he loved scoop up his daughter and nuzzle her neck, his whole body tightened. He remembered what her mouth felt like in the crook of his own neck; he remembered how she'd sucked him there, leaving red marks that testified to their lovemaking.

He hadn't touched her in five days, and he was going through withdrawal. Every muscle tensed when she came near. His skin itched when she accidentally brushed against him. His heart pumped faster each time he smelled her baby-powder scent.

Megan turned in Stacey's arms to look at him. "Daddy, do you like Stacey's hair?"

"It's okay," he said, keeping his voice as neutral as possible. Actually, it looked a hell of a lot better today than last night when she'd gotten it butchered. Washed and dried, it fell in waves all around her head. Though still too short for his taste, it looked feminine and silky, instead of slick and sophisticated.

"Can I get mine cut like yours?" Megan asked.

Stacey gripped Megan tightly, her face pinched. "No, honey, don't do that."

"Why?"

"Yeah, Stacey, why?" Cord said.

Biting her lip, she said, "Because I like braiding your hair."

A searing cold gripped Cord. What would Megan do when Stacey was out of their lives? He hadn't planned on his daughter getting so attached to her. Damn, another mistake.

Gifford and Lauren emerged from the house carrying several brightly wrapped packages.

Her little arms gripping Stacey's neck, Megan looked over her shoulder. "What are those?"

"Those? Oh, I don't know. Dad?" Stacey said to Gifford. "What are those?"

Gifford added his packages to the pile of presents stacked on and around a glass umbrella table. "I'm not sure. Is today somebody's birthday?"

Megan's eyes grew into big blue pools. "It's mine. But I already had my party today, and got lots of presents. Am I getting more?"

"You sure are," Gifford said, gazing tenderly at the child.

"Daddy couldn't be at my party," Megan told them, her face scrunching into a frown.

For the first time in a week, Stacey looked at Cord with warmth. "I know, Megan. I'm sorry."

Cord stood and crossed the short distance to them. Megan turned and reached out to him. As he took the little girl from Stacey, his arm accidentally brushed Stacey's breast. She sucked in her breath and he stiffened.

Cord cleared his throat. "Well," he said, then kissed the top of Megan's head. "This way, you get to have two parties."

Nora McKay came up behind them. "Your daddy spoils you, peanut."

"*He* told me that's what daddies are for," Megan said, pointing to Gifford.

The stricken look on Gifford's face told Cord that he and Stacey were still having a rough time. They'd been dancing around each other all week, trying to forge a new relationship. It was painful to watch.

But at least Gifford had a chance with Stacey.

Cord had none.

Gifford broke the tension. "Hot dogs are ready. The cake is here. Let's eat first."

Megan smiled. "Hot dogs are my favorite."

"I know." Gifford winked at the little girl. "They were Stacey's favorite, too."

Pain darkened Stacey's eyes to the color of midnight, but she captured her father's gaze. "I remember how you used to cut them up for me in strips so I wouldn't choke."

"I was terrified that something would happen to you," Gifford said, then blanched. "Too terrified, I guess."

Reaching out, Stacey squeezed his arm. "No, Dad. It's a good memory. I have lots of them."

Cord turned away. It was too hard to see Stacey's generosity, when he knew he'd never be the recipient of it again.

After hot dogs, Megan opted for the presents. "I'll save Daddy's for last," she said, her eyes twinkling.

"Daddy's?" He smacked his forehead with his palm. "Was I supposed to get you a present?"

Megan ran to him, threw her arms around his neck and hugged him. Behind the child, he saw moisture gather in Stacey's eyes. He held her gaze. If she was going to kick them out of her life, let her see what she was losing. If nothing else, he knew he was a good father.

The presents took a while. A huge stuffed giraffe from Lauren, who, as always, sat on the sidelines and said little. A package of beads from Nora for Megan to make her own necklaces.

The birthday girl picked up Gifford's package next and ripped it open. Stacey's smile faded as she saw the art supplies—charcoal, crayons, paints, chalk, ink, markers, and reams of different size and shape paper. "The big one goes with it," Gifford told her. Megan hurtled to the stand-up gift and tore off the paper: it was an easel, taller than she was.

Her eyes round saucers, Megan said, "Wow. Thank you, Mr. Webb." Impulsively, Megan gave him a hug. Gifford held her tightly. Cord watched Stacey's eyes shine at her father. He had to look away again. He shifted his gaze and caught Lauren staring at the tableau: her eyes were narrowed as she gripped the edge of the lawn chair with her uncasted hand.

"Open mine next," he heard Stacey say. He looked back to see his daughter tear off the paper on a huge box, carefully wrapped in pink and silver foil. Slowly, Megan lifted the gift out. A watermelon-colored rain slicker. Then a deep purple bodysuit. A neon yellow miniskirt. Cord watched, a lump in his throat, as Megan fussed over each article of clothing.

But there was no lavender minidress among them.

Megan went to Stacey and gave her a big, sloppy kiss; Stacey's eyes closed as she whispered something to Megan. In his gut, Cord knew they were the three words she'd never say to him again. Kicking him in the groin couldn't have hurt more.

Megan finally got around to opening the first of his presents. Excited, she fumbled with the paper as she unwrapped the pair of earrings. She flung herself at Cord and locked her arms around his neck.

Returning the hug, he said, "There's still a big one for you to open, honey."

Megan disentangled herself and returned to the gifts. She squealed with delight as she ripped off enough paper to see the shiny pink bike with small training wheels on the back. "Daddy, you got me a two-wheeler."

"Well, it's not quite a two-wheeler yet."

"It will be, soon. Stacey said she'd help me learn. Didn't you, Stacey?"

But she won't be around to do it. Her stricken look told Cord she was thinking the same thing.

After cake and ice cream, Gifford stood and looked at his watch. "Well, I hate to leave this gathering, but I've got to catch my plane." He turned to Stacey. "I could still cancel this trip...if you think..."

Stacey smiled at him. "No, Dad, go."

Gifford's face fell.

Stacey rose and slipped an arm around his waist. "But I'll help you with your stuff."

Lauren came off the chair. "Do you still have time to drop me off, Gifford?"

"Sure, Lauren, if you're sure you want to go home."

Stacey protested. "Lauren, I don't think..."

"Stacey, we've been through this," Lauren said. "I can't stay here forever. I need to start taking care of myself. My arm is much better." She turned to Gifford and beamed him a smile. "I'll be right down."

The rest of the party broke up about nine. By then, Megan was practically asleep in Cord's arms. Stacey walked with them to the car, where Nora was waiting.

Just as he was about to put Megan in the back, she reached out her arms to Stacey. Stacey took the little girl, and cuddled her.

"Wanna know what I wished when I blew out my candles?" Megan said sleepily.

Stacey smiled. "Sure."

"For you to be my mother."

Cord, Nora and Stacey froze. Discreetly, Nora circled the car and got behind the wheel. Stacey hugged Megan, kissed her hair and handed her to Cord. Guiltily, he took his child, but couldn't meet Stacey's eyes.

In a pregnant silence, Cord and Stacey watched Nora and Megan drive away. Unable to bear the constricting band of tension around her heart, Stacey turned to the house and walked through the front door. Behind her, Cord clicked the locks and set the alarm. Having already secured the back of the house, he quietly followed her up the stairs.

She entered her room and so did he. Without speaking, he checked all the windows and disappeared into the sitting room. She heard the rattle of the back door as he checked that, too. Always the bodyguard. He was so good at his work. Almost as good as he was at lovemaking. *Stop it, Stacey. Don't think about him that way.*

Her thoughts flew to Megan. That hurt almost as much. God, she loved the little girl. To have lost them both was intolerable. She crossed to the mirror and looked at herself. The woman who stared back at her was a stranger. She liked the soft curls—but not as much as the longer style she'd told Margaret to clip off. Because Cord liked it too much. Because it symbolized too much.

From the silence in the other room, she figured Cord had gone to bed. It was just as well. She was so raw she wasn't sure what she'd say, what she'd *do,* if he came back. Five days avoiding even his slightest touch had her craving him the way a junkie craves drugs.

She got ready for bed like a robot. Everything reminded her of Cord—the red satin underwear that slid off her skin, the fluffy green comforter on the bed that he'd once wrapped around her, even the mirror where, one night, he'd undressed her, pointing out his favorite body parts and exploring each one.

Clothed in an eyelet nightgown, she stepped toward the bed. Visions of them entwined there—him on top of her, him thrusting into her, him whispering he loved her—made her shrink back. She couldn't sleep in that bed tonight. She just couldn't. And the sitting room, where he'd slept, was definitely off limits.

She glanced at the door. No, she wouldn't go anywhere else. She *was* still mindful of her safety. Her gaze settled on the green chaise nestled by the front windows. Crossing to it, she sank down, stretched out flat on her back and pulled the end pillows under her head.

It was safe here. They'd never made love here.

And now they never would. They'd never make love again, anywhere. He'd never kiss her spine again. He'd never nibble at her ankles. He'd never, ever again call out her name as he came inside her. It was too much—the loss of him, the loss of all her dreams for a future with him.

Suddenly, there was a rustle at the door. She looked up to see Cord bracing his arm on the archway. A muted light she'd left on in the far corner illuminated the outline of his powerful thighs, encased in snug denim cutoffs; the loose cotton shirt accented his wide, stiff shoulders.

"I thought you'd gone to bed," she said softly.

"No, I was checking the backyard."

"Why, did you see something?"

"No, no, just to be safe."

"Oh."

She studied his face. It was drawn and hollow. "You look exhausted."

He ran a hand through his hair. "I haven't gotten much sleep this week." He watched her closely, then took hesitant steps to the edge of the chaise. He stood above her for a moment, but finally sat down. His thigh rubbed hers. "Are you all right?" he asked.

"No, of course I'm not. Neither are you."

He hunched over, locking his hands between his knees. A sigh escaped him. He was silent, but she could feel the tension radiate from him. Finally, he said, "What are we going to do? About us?"

She stared up at the ceiling and threw her arm over her forehead. "I don't know."

"I'm not sure I can handle this." A deep, dark confession from a man who'd been miserly with his emotions for eighteen years. Stacey said nothing, waiting for more. It came, wrenched from him. "I'm not sure I can handle this revulsion you feel for me."

Oh, God, could he be more wrong? No matter what, she couldn't let him think that. "No, Cord, I don't feel that way."

His head whipped around and he stared at her. "I thought—I thought you said..."

"I was confused. I'm devastated by what happened years ago, and how you and my father orchestrated this cover-up. But I could never feel repulsed by you. I love you."

Cord's shoulders slumped and he buried his head in his hands. His pain reached out to her; she scrambled up on her knees, circled his waist with her arms and laid her cheek on his back. Powerful, strained muscles bulged beneath her.

After a moment, he turned and grasped her shoulders. "Stace...can I...I need... Oh, damn, can I hold you? Just for a little while? I need that right now."

She studied his face intently, then climbed onto his lap. His arms banded around her as he yanked her flush with his chest. She gripped his neck, burying her face in his skin, breathing in his scent.

"I miss you so much," she said. "I can't stand this separation, Cord. It hurts too much."

"I know, baby. Me, too. It hurts too much for me, too."

Slowly, she raised her head. He was looking down at her, his eyes dark as the night. Lifting a shaky hand to his jaw, she rubbed the rough stubble of his beard. She moved to his mouth. He was stock-still as her two fingers traced its outline.

Then she replaced her fingers with her lips.

It was as if something snapped inside him. He devoured her mouth with a force and possessiveness she'd never known from him. His hands were all over her, inflaming, then soothing. He massaged her hips, her buttocks, rubbing his big, masculine hands up and down her legs. Then he pulled back. "Oh, Stacey," he whispered hoarsely against her cheek, "I'll never be able to live without this." He raised his hand and cupped her breast firmly. "Sometimes I feel like I'm going to die if can't touch you again."

Delirious by his scent, by his hoarse declarations, Stacey said, "Then make the pain stop, Cord. Even if only for tonight, make it stop."

Without uttering a word, he eased her onto her back. Looming over her, he said, "I will," and covered her body with his.

Threading his fingers through her short hair, he anchored her head so he could master her mouth. He pressed his lips firmly to hers. His tongue probed hard, making her open to him. He invaded and claimed. "Oh, love," he said against her mouth. Trailing his lips to her ear, he glided his tongue along its inner recesses. She jerked against him, so he ground his hips into hers. "That's it, show me...show me how you feel..." At her neck now, he kissed, and sucked and she knew he'd leave marks.

She felt his hands move to the lace at the neckline of her gown. He fumbled with the pearl buttons; when they didn't give way quickly, Stacey felt pressure, then the material came apart. His frantic need to get to her made her heart pump fast. His hands were warm as he slid the garment off her shoulders, then took her

breasts and massaged them. As if accepting an offering, he lifted one to his mouth. He suckled, hard and
long, and Stacey squirmed beneath him. "Cord, it's
not enough. Do more."

"Why?" he mumbled, burying his face in her
cleavage.

Raising her hand to his head, she grasped his hair
and yanked it up. "You know why, dammit."

Blue eyes stared at her. "I want to *hear* why."

"I need you. I need you to touch me."

Sparks shot out of his eyes like the heart of a blue
flame, burning her everywhere. "Say you'll always
need it. No matter how far apart we are, say you'll always need it." He thrust his lower body against her,
sending shock waves to every extremity. "Say it."

"I'll always need it."

Released by her hoarse confession, he moved his
mouth from her breast to her ribs, outlining each one
with his tongue. She groaned. He dipped into her na-
vel and she pushed her hands against his shoulders,
urging him down. She moaned low, long, the sound
stringing out when he nuzzled her curls. "Cord,
please . . . please . . ."

Finally, he closed his mouth over her sensitized nub
and her whole body jerked in reaction. His tongue
flicked once and Stacey felt it burn through her,
singeing her nerve endings. She gripped his shoulders
for grounding, but the lightning of his touch continued, and soon her hips were bucking. Callused fingers anchored them to the cushions as he continued
with his clever tongue, increasing the pressure by de-
grees. All at once, pleasure shot through Stacey like a

runaway train, derailing all thought, all awareness, except for the crashing explosions that kept coming and coming until she thought she'd die. So sensitized, she knew he had to stop, she couldn't stand it, but he was relentless for long, exquisite minutes.

When she finally came back to reality, he edged up on his knees. Looking into her eyes, he cupped her, sending jolt after jolt of aftershocks through her. "Remember this," he said.

Stacey came up on her elbows. Her sultry eyes studied him, the short curls a tangle around her face. Beads of sweat on her forehead and over her lips testified to her pleasure—to the pleasure only he had ever given her. Savagely, he forced back the knowledge that some other man would give it to her someday. He ground his hand against her. "Tell me, no matter what, you'll always remember."

"I'll always remember," she said, underscoring his satisfaction and his terror at the same time. Then she sat up, reached out and unzipped his cutoffs. Releasing him, she took his long, hard length into her palm. He sank back on his haunches, between her spread thighs as she squeezed him, then ran her hands up and down him. He closed his eyes, wanting to give thanks but only able to feel the strength of her fingers on him.

When she let go, his eyes flew open; she scrambled off the couch and knelt on the rug. She urged him to sit. Drawing his legs on either side of her, she yanked at his shorts. He raised his hips so she could pull them off, along with his briefs. Placing her hands on his knees, she ran her tongue down the side of each thigh. "Stacey—oh, Sta-cey..."

She lifted her eyes to him. "What? Tell me."

"Dammit, take me . . . in . . . your mouth."

When she did, he groaned, bracing his arms on either side of him. All sensation, all pleasure, converged on the center of his body, pulsing and pulsing and finally erupting into the most searing pleasure he'd ever experienced.

When he could breathe again, he looked down at her head resting on his thigh. She was taking in air fast, too. He knew that making him come had aroused her, so he brought his hands to her shoulders and gently forced her back onto the rug.

Wide eyes watched him tear at the buttons of his shirt, whip it and his gun off, and bend to kiss her—starting with her forehead, journeying down her body and back up again. By then, she was panting, and his breathing had picked up. He was hard again.

"Come inside me," she whispered.

He heard the unspoken *one more time* tagged on.

That was all it took; he thrust inside her and kept thrusting and thrusting until he heard her scream his name and felt her nails dig into his back.

Then he joined her.

One more time.

CHAPTER FOURTEEN

ON THE ANNIVERSARY of Helene's death, the Webb household was eerily quiet.

Gifford locked himself in his den to deal with his ghosts. He stood by the high, arched windows and looked out at the water glistening on the pool that Helene had loved. Every August seventh had been tough for him, remembering his folly, regretting his haste. This year, given what had occurred with Cord and Stacey, the renewed sorrow and bitter frustration of losing the only woman Gifford had ever loved smothered him. Almost unable to bear the grief, he covered his face. He was committed to a black-tie dinner at Canfield Country Club that evening, or he would have taken off to his cabin and spared everyone his foul mood.

Stacey was holed up in her room. She lay on her bed, staring up at the skylights, willing herself not to feel anything. She'd never let this date have any significance for her in the past; but today, it was an excruciating reminder, not only of the mother who had been taken away from her, but also of Cord's past history with Helene. The thought was still too much to internalize. It had been three days since she and Cord had made love for the last time. She couldn't banish the images of his mouth on her, or forget his whispered words of love, so instead she wallowed in them.

Cord paced the upstairs hall like a caged animal. He'd seen Gifford go into the library hours ago and not come out. He knew the man was suffering a deep sense of loss and guilt today. Staring at Stacey's closed door, he recalled what it had felt like to be in there three nights ago. He could still feel her clenched around him when he was inside her—one last time. If he hadn't been convinced of the end of their relationship before, the poignancy of their lovemaking that night did the trick. Stacey had touched him as she never had before, and though he'd reveled in her ministrations, he knew she was saying goodbye. The thought made him kick the spindles of the railing, sending shocks of pain through his leg.

Something had to give, or they'd all go crazy being thrown together, haunted by the past.

THE SKY WAS STARLESS and blue-black at nine o'clock that night when Cord swerved his truck into a parking space behind Lauren Sellers's green Taurus. Thank God, she was home. Under the flickering street lamp, he inspected each car in the area, searching for Mark Dunn's rusted black Mustang.

Satisfied, he exited the truck, took the porch stairs two at a time and leaned on the doorbell. He waited. No answer. He rang again. Peering around the corner, he noted the dim lighting in the front room. Then he heard the snick of the lock.

Lauren pulled open the door; she was dressed in a muddy brown linen shirt and a short beige skirt. Though tailored and tidy, the outfit did nothing to enhance her attractiveness.

"Cord?"

"Hello, Lauren."

Her eyes darted around the open porch. "Where's Stacey?"

Shifting restlessly, he dug his hands into his pockets, knocking his wrist on the beeper attached to his belt. "She's not with me."

Lauren's unusual eyes widened. "Not with you? Why? You haven't gone anywhere without her in three months."

"I know. But I had to talk to you alone." Cord sighed. "Can I come in?"

Slowly, Lauren opened the door wider. Without speaking, she led him into the front parlor. "I assume you've left her well protected," she finally said when they were both seated.

"Yeah. Joe Ferron's with her. She'll be okay for a half hour."

"What's up?"

Cord scanned the cramped living room with its flowered couch, faded green chairs and battered piano. Then he glanced out the archway to the hall leading to the back of the house. "Lauren, is anyone here? Are you alone?"

"Of course," she said quickly. "I usually am."

"All right. I just don't want to be overheard." He looked up at the ceiling, wondering where to begin.

"Stacey's a mess. I don't know how much she's told you...about us."

Lauren's gaze turned icy. "I'm not going to discuss Stacey behind her back. I will tell you I think what you did to Gifford eighteen years ago was unforgivable. That man is a saint to let you into his house again."

His jaw clenched, Cord steeled himself against the guilt. "Your disgust with me isn't any greater than what I feel for myself."

"Does Stacey believe that?"

"Stacey doesn't know what to believe. That's why I'm here. She needs someone to talk to. I'm afraid she's letting all this eat her up inside. I came here tonight to tell you how much she needs...a friend. One like you, who's never let her down."

Lauren studied him before she said, "She told me the same thing last week. That you and her father had let her down badly. That I was the only one she could count on."

The restatement of Stacey's feelings toward him twisted his gut, but he forced himself to continue. He'd come here with a purpose. "She needs you. Tonight more than ever."

"Why tonight?"

"It's the anniversary of Helene's death."

"Oh poor...poor Stacey. Is her father with her?"

"No, he—"

Suddenly, Cord's beeper went off, silencing him. Clearly irritated, Lauren glared in the direction of the shrill noise. "Sorry," Cord said. "I need to call home. This beeper is for my mother. Can I use your phone? It must be important."

Lauren pointed to the extension in the hallway. "Sure."

Nervously running his hand through his hair, Cord hurried to the foyer and dialed his house. When Nora picked up, he asked, "Mom? What is it?"

"It's Megan. She has bad pains in her lower right abdomen. We're on our way to Canfield Hospital. I just called the ambulance."

"*What?*"

"The doctor thinks it's appendicitis and they might need to operate. You've got to get there right away." His mother's voice shook.

"Oh, God. All right. I'll meet you at the hospital. Hang on, Mom."

Cord slammed down the phone and turned to find Lauren behind him. "Is something wrong?" she asked.

As he headed for the door, he said gruffly, "It's Megan. She's had an appendix attack. I'm going to the hospital." He took Lauren by the shoulders, his grasp harder than it should be. "Call Stacey. Tell her what happened. Make sure Ferron stays with her. I'll phone her as soon as I can."

Lauren blinked. "Cord...I don't..."

But he was out the door before he heard the rest of her statement.

He could think of nothing but the crisis at hand.

FROM THE BUSHES, the man watched the house for twenty minutes before he set off the alarm on the police car. Sure enough, Ferron exited the front door and trotted to the black and white that was stationed in the driveway. It was almost too easy. He laughed to himself, careful not to rustle the leaves. Quiet, unnoticed, he observed Ferron duck his head into the front seat. The brick was heavy, but the man lifted it with one hand. Ferron went down without a whimper. The dumb cop was as easy to trick tonight as he had been months ago when the man had lured the jerk away from Stacey with a false-alarm accident.

He dragged Ferron out of sight. Though it was pitch-dark—he'd defused all the outdoor lights—he wasn't taking any chances. Nothing would go wrong tonight. She wouldn't escape him tonight. He licked his lips. Soon, very soon, he'd have her on her knees and begging.

Quickly, he strode to the front door and turned the knob. It didn't open. But that was all right. Sliding his hand into his pocket, he felt the outline of the key through his thin black gloves. Careful—always careful—he stalked to the back of the house.

He climbed each of the twenty-eight wooden stairs like a cat, with stealthy, silent footfalls. It was easy to slip open the door. He didn't even have to dismantle the alarm; Ferron had turned it off when he'd gone outside to check out the noise.

Inside, the sitting room was dark except for the slivered moon casting long thin strips of light on the Oriental rug. He crossed halfway, then halted. Water was running in the shower. Perfect. He'd surprise her as she bathed—as she rubbed her breasts and washed between her legs. He could picture the warm soapy water caressing the intimate parts of her. A familiar rush of blood to his loins galvanized him. Leaning down, he eased the knife out of his boot and gazed at the sacred metal instrument.

Soundlessly, he took another step.

"Not so fast," he heard—clearly, coldly—from the left.

He spun around. "What the f—"

The light switched on, and he saw Cord McKay poised on the arm of the couch, a cocked nine-millimeter aiming outward.

With his other hand, the bodyguard held a cordless phone. He said into it, "I've got him. Red-handed. I need the unit now."

His arms and legs trembled . . . chalky yellow rings appeared before his eyes. McKay's face wavered and in its place, he saw his father. *"You stupid moron,"* the old man said. *"You're a damn fool to get caught by such a simple trap. You're no son of mine."*

He shook his head. "No . . . no . . . I'll show you."

He lunged toward his father. A noise exploded the air. Pain shrieked through him, just as his beloved knife connected with flesh.

AS STACEY JUMPED out of the squad car, two attendants bent over a stretcher on the driveway. Another black-and-white—the one that had radioed that the perpetrator had been caught—was parked at an angle next to the ambulance. Stacey's heart somersaulted as she raced to the supine form lying on the cot.

Joe Ferron was just regaining consciousness and looked up at her. "I'm sorry, Stacey," he said when she took his hand. "I got caught. I didn't think . . . Is Cord okay?"

"Don't try to talk, Joe," she managed to get out. "And I don't know about Cord."

But she had to find out. Leaving Joe to the capable hands of the medics, Stacey whirled to go into the house...just as a group of people appeared at the door.

One of them was Cord.

His bloodied shirt was ripped open, and huge bandages covered his right shoulder. A sling held his arm in place. His face was pale, his mouth set in a grim, uncompromising line as he talked to the uniformed officer with him.

When he looked up and saw her, his expression transformed into something so intense, so relieved, her knees weakened. She flew to him; he caught her with his good arm, dragging her to him. She gripped his neck. "I was so worried."

His mouth in her hair, he said, "I'm all right."

"Actually, he's not," Wayne Valentino muttered beside them. "I think his shoulder needs stitches. He should go to the hospital, but he won't."

"Dammit, Valentino, I said I'd go later if I needed to."

"Cord, you should listen to him," Stacey said.

Cord's protest was forestalled as another police car pulled up to the curb. Her father, dressed in a black tux, was out the door almost before it came to a halt. Striding to them, he asked, "What the hell happened here?"

Before anyone could answer, another stretcher appeared at the door. Cord and Stacey stepped aside as the attendants stopped to get around them.

Stacey glanced down into the twisted face of Mark Dunn.

He was strapped in and restrained, his shoulder bandaged, and his skin pasty. Bitter black eyes stared up at her.

"Oh, God," she said, burying her face in Cord's chest.

Grasping her with his solid left hand, Cord said, "It's okay, sweetheart. It's finally over."

A curdling laugh slithered up from Dunn, drawing everyone's attention to him. "It's not over, bitch. Ask your good friend Lauren."

"Get him out of here," Cord bellowed.

As Stacey stared openmouthed at the retreating backs of the medics, she asked, "What does he mean?"

"Will someone tell me what's going on here?" Her father stood rigidly by, his features tense, his hands fisted.

Cord sighed heavily, then leaned against a pillar in front of the house. His face was ashen now. "We trapped Dunn."

"You *what?*"

"I set it up earlier tonight with the police. I had a hunch it was Dunn. I went over to Lauren's, guessing he'd be there tonight. I planned for my mother to call me there, ostensibly to get me to the hospital for an emergency with Megan. I hoped he'd be listening, see his shot at Stacey without me around and take it. The police gave me Ferron to help, and were going to send in a unit, if the plan worked. Even though they thought it was a long shot, I persuaded them."

"Why wasn't I told about this?" Gifford's expression was grim.

"I didn't want you to worry," Cord told him. "And besides, you'd already left when I decided to do this."

"How did Joe get hurt?" Stacey asked.

"He went outside to check out the alarm. Dunn jumped him there."

"So that's how Mark got in?"

"No, Stacey, he had a key to the door of your suite," Cord told her.

"Where did he get it?" Silence. "Cord?"

"Who had a key to that door?" Gifford asked.

Stacey's eyes widened. "He stole it from Lauren." She scowled. "Cord, what did he *mean* about Lauren?"

"I...I'm not exactly sure."

"Not exactly?"

"I think we should all go talk to Lauren," Cord said, his gaze locking with her father's. Some silent message telegraphed between them. Stacey let it go, her concern about her friend taking precedence. Lauren had to realize by now that Mark had been involved somehow.

Gifford nodded. "All right. I'll drive. But for the record, I think this was a pretty dangerous thing to do."

Cord's jaw set. "Stacey was at the police station, well guarded."

"I didn't mean for Stacey," Gifford said softly, shaking his head. "I meant it was too dangerous for you."

Tears clouded Stacey's eyes. Her father's comment stayed with her as they climbed into the car and drove to First Street.

They reached Lauren's house in ten minutes. No lights shone from the front, but her car was there, parked in the shadows. Stacey worried as they pulled over to the curb. How would Lauren react when she learned she'd inadvertently given her boyfriend access to Stacey? Mark must have stolen her key after he'd overheard Cord's staged conversation with his mother. Her friend cared so much about her. Stacey would have to be sure to be there for her.

Gifford rang the doorbell as Cord held tightly to her hand. No answer. He rang several more times before he tried the door. Unlocked, it creaked open. The house was scary-story dark; and it was still, except for voices coming from the rear.

"What's back there?" Cord asked.

Stacey frowned. "Lauren's bedroom is off the kitchen."

"This feels . . . odd," Gifford remarked.

The three of them entered the foyer, switching on the overhead light. They made their way carefully to the back of the small house; the lilt of voices became increasingly louder. "They sound familiar," Gifford noted.

Slowly, the three of them skirted furniture and approached Lauren's bedroom. The door was ajar. Cord pushed it aside so Gifford and Stacey could see in.

Candles lit the room, casting an unearthly glow around Lauren's serene face. She sat quietly on the bed, legs crossed, surrounded by what looked like scrapbooks, an open box of memorabilia, her journal. She was staring at the TV. Stacey tracked her gaze and froze. Flicking across the screen were scenes of Stacey's youth... a birthday party, a soccer game, graduation from high school. Stacey shivered. Her father must have felt it because he put his arm around her and stepped farther into the room.

The motion distracted Lauren. Her eyes swung to them, but rested on Gifford. A delighted smile broke out on her face. "I knew you'd come."

"Lauren?" Stacey said.

It was as if she hadn't spoken. "I knew you'd come, Gif. I knew that if I did all the right things, you'd finally come to me."

"What do you mean, Lauren?" Her father's voice was hoarse.

"Eventually, I knew you'd see." Her eyebrows furrowed. "But it didn't work out like I planned."

Cord stepped in front of Stacey, as if to protect her. She edged out from behind him. "What didn't work, Lauren?" he asked coldly.

Still staring at Gifford, she picked up a picture. "This is when you won that skiing championship. You were thirty-five and you beat out all those younger men."

"Lauren, what didn't work out?" Gifford reiterated Cord's question.

"And this?" She held up some faded gift paper. "Do you remember the necklace you gave me for graduation? It was wrapped in this."

Stacey's heart began to beat faster. "Lauren, what's going on here?"

"I did it all for you, Gifford." Lauren clasped her hands in her lap. "All of it." She scowled. "But... Mark, he got carried away. I paid him just to grab Stacey for a little while—maybe a day or so. Then I was going to lead you to her, and you'd—" she smiled again at Gifford "—you'd be so grateful that you'd finally, *finally* see me as a woman."

Stacey's knees gave out. Cord and her father grabbed her from either side. "Oh, God, no, Lauren, you weren't in on this whole thing?"

Speaking as if she and Gifford were alone, Lauren said, "Helene was a horrible woman to betray you. With that boy. I'll never betray you, Gifford. I'll love you forever."

Stacey blinked back tears. "I...I can't believe this. Lauren, you wouldn't...you didn't...you're my best friend." Stacey covered her mouth with her hand, fearing she'd be sick. "You, too," she whispered. Then she glanced at Cord and her father, seeing the concern and sorrow in both their faces. Her eyes went back to her friend...her very sick friend sitting on the bed surrounded by remembrances of her father. "Not you, too."

CHAPTER FIFTEEN

STACEY STARED OUT the window of the library as the workmen settled the big black cover over the pool, blanketing it for the winter months ahead. The mid-September sun challenged their actions, but she could feel the nip in the breeze that blew through the open window, testifying that it was time to pack up for the winter.

"What was that sigh for?" Her father came up behind her and rested his hands on her shoulders.

Stacey took a sip of her steaming coffee, hoping it would warm her. "I hate to see the pool close."

"So did your mother. She used to stand here just like this and watch them end the summer."

Turning to look up at her father, Stacey said, "I'm more like her than I ever knew."

Fleeting shadows skittered across Gifford's face, but he managed a grin. "Yes, honey, you are."

"Does it hurt, Dad?"

"That's a better question for you."

Stacey pivoted back to catch the men dismantling the diving board. "Yes, it hurts. But I'm learning to deal with it."

"This counselor? Is she helping you?"

Stacey nodded, thinking of Melissa Fox, who had saved her sanity at the end of August. After the initial numbness had worn off, Stacey had been immobilized by Lauren's involvement in the kidnapping attempt. Though it came out later that she hadn't participated in the stalking—Mark Dunn had literally flipped out and acted on his own—Lauren's defection still hurt. "I don't know what I would have done without Dr. Fox," Stacey told her father. "She helps to sort things out."

Ruefully, Stacey smiled at the understatement. First, there had been the denial, the refusal to accept the fact that the three most important people in her life had let her down. Then there had been the anger. Stacey had offered to pay for the small vase she'd broken when she stomped around Melissa's quiet office on the Parkway and raged at all of them. Now, she was working on acceptance.

Staring at the the men hosing down the deck, Stacey asked, "What are you doing at your desk?"

Gifford's grip tightened on her shoulders, signaling that he knew she was trying to change the subject. And, in his consistent effort to treat her like the adult she was, he let it go. "I was looking over the hospital's report on Lauren."

As always, Stacey hated to hear the strain in her father's voice when he talked about Lauren. She turned and faced him squarely. "Dad, don't blame yourself. Lauren's sick. The people at St. Joe's said she should have had help as a child. It's not your fault."

"I know that here," Gifford said, tapping his head. "It's here—" he indicated his chest "—that I can't quite get it."

"Paying for the sanitarium and not pressing charges is a good way to make any amends, and help you to accept it here." She pressed lightly on her father's heart.

Smiling at her, he asked, "When did you get so smart?"

An arrow of pain shot through Stacey as her father's question recalled other softly whispered words. *"How did you get so smart for someone so young?"*

That remark had led to a challenge and a kiss that had changed her life.

Stacey no longer tried to banish all thoughts of Cord. Melissa had urged her to let the feelings come. Stuffing them away would only delay the pain and roadblock the healing. And above all, Stacey wanted to heal.

"Have you seen him lately?" she asked her father.

With his usual perceptiveness, Gifford gave her a knowing look and went to sit behind the desk. "Yesterday."

"How is he?"

Gifford's forehead creased.

Stacey walked over, leaned on the edge of his desk and prodded. "Is it his shoulder?"

"No, his shoulder is good—as good as it will ever be after a severe dislocation and a deep knife wound from that maniac."

Mention of Mark Dunn still sent chills through her.

"Don't, honey," Gifford encouraged. "He's locked up, and it will be a long time before he sees the light of day. We need to focus on that fact."

Rubbing her arms for warmth, Stacey agreed. "What about Cord? The truth. Like you promised, Dad."

"Yes, yes, I know. All right—he looks like hell. He's lost weight and I'd be surprised if he sleeps four hours a night. Of all of us, I think he's suffering the most overwhelming sense of guilt. Next to how you were hurt by this, I feel the worst about McKay."

Stacey swallowed hard. "I don't want him to hurt. I want him to go on with his life."

"Funny, he told me almost the same thing about you. After he asked how you were."

"Well," she said, "at least he accepted your offer to back him in his new security business. I saw the storefront yesterday."

"Yeah. It looks great. We're hiring someone to do the lettering on the plate glass. Know anyone with artistic talent?"

"Dad, I'm not sure I need that kind of proximity to him." Stacey remembered the sharp stab of emotion that lanced through her when she'd accidentally bumped into Cord at the Labor Day parade, at the market, and then again at the video store. She couldn't see him, look at his mouth or his hands, without remembering what those firm lips felt like on hers, or the grip of those strong fingers anchoring her hips when he thrust inside her.

"Well, think about it. And remember, Megan's at the office a lot. You'd get to see more of her than the occasional visits you allow yourself."

"You fight dirty, Dad."

"I'm on your side, honey, I always have been."

Stacey smiled, then set her mug down, effectively ending the talk. "Are you going up to the cabin today?"

Gifford nodded. "What about you?"

"I'm going to get my hair cut. Then, I've got a date tonight," she said firmly, attempting to convince herself as well as her father that this wasn't a colossal mistake. "Joe Ferron and I are seeing a movie."

"Ah. Well, have a good time."

Smiling with false bravado, Stacey said, "I'll try."

IT WAS a colossal mistake. Cord knew it as soon as he walked into Cutter's with Eileen Martin hanging on his arm. Five weeks was apparently too soon to start dating.

In the flurry of activity following Lauren's confession, Cord had weakened and had to be taken to the hospital, after all, for stitches. He'd lost a lot of blood and Dunn's knife had done severe muscle damage. During his convalescence he had become more and more morose as he became more and more certain that he didn't deserve Stacey. Twice now, he'd torn her life apart.

He shouldn't have come, he thought, as he and Eileen slid into a booth in the crowded bar. Even though this hadn't been his idea. When Eileen had stopped by the office today, he'd agreed to a few drinks between friends.

"What's that grim expression for?" Eileen asked after a waiter brought popcorn and took their drink order.

"Um...I think I wrenched my shoulder hanging drywall today." He reached up and massaged the phantom ache.

"How is the business shaping up?"

"Great. As a division of Anderson's of New York, we have a reputation already established."

"Are you going to be able to do actual bodyguarding with that shoulder?"

He shook his head. "No. I'll handle all the administration and training and hire the security people. I'll also be offering sessions to the Canfield Police Department."

"Hi, everybody. Small world isn't it?"

Cord looked up to see Joe Ferron standing at their booth, his left arm casually draped around Stacey's shoulders.

The breath left Cord in a whoosh. He was poleaxed. Stacey peered down at him, biting her lip.

"Hi, Joe," Cord finally said. "Hi, Stace."

"Hi." She cleared her throat. "Cord, Eileen."

Eileen nodded. "Out for the night?"

"Yeah, we went to see the new Costner flick at the mall."

I think you're much more attractive than Kevin Costner.

As if she'd spoken the words from long ago, Cord heard them echo above the low murmur of the bar's patrons. A quick glance at Stacey's face told him she did, too.

Ferron looked around at the people packed three deep at the bar, and jammed at the tables. "Geez, it's hoppin' here tonight. Mind if we join you?"

Cord felt every muscle stiffen; his heart constricted and his mouth went dry. He couldn't be with her, close like this.

"Of course," Eileen said diplomatically.

Cord began to rise, intending to move to Eileen's side of the booth. Ferron, who'd never win any awards for perceptiveness, missed the maneuver and plunked down next to Eileen, forcing Stacey to slide in next to Cord.

All at once, he was painfully aware of her closeness. Her slight form next to his big one; the way the top of her black dress accented her breasts; the downy hair visible on her nape of her short, short haircut. Most of all, the scent of lemons and baby powder and that fresh after-bath splash she used almost overwhelmed him.

"So, how's the new business going?" Ferron asked after a waitress took their drink order.

"Ah, good, good," Cord answered, struggling to keep his voice neutral. He was a wreck, his emotions careening out of control every time Stacey moved: when her arm brushed his, when her thigh rubbed against him, when she accidentally kicked his foot. He thanked God when Ferron asked her to dance.

Until he had to watch her on the floor. The black dress was short and tight and hugged every curve he knew so well. As she undulated on the dance floor in soft, sensual rhythms, he thought he might swallow his tongue.

Finally, a slow song began. He was thankful when Eileen stood and tugged him out to the floor. Now he wouldn't have to watch Stacey sway to the music. Unfortunately the song was one that had played over and over on the patio on the night he'd courted Stacey. He closed his eyes, trying to block out the vision. But it bombarded him, was more acute behind closed lids—Stacey in the blue dress, crushing her body to his; Stacey bringing his head down for a long, slow kiss.

When the song ended, and another one began, he was ready to jump out of his skin with the memories. Which was why he didn't control the impulse to say, "You don't mind if I dance with Stacey, do you, Eileen? Joe?"

"Of course not, you two are old buddies," Ferron said, grabbing Eileen from him for a dance, and handing Stacey over.

Cord noticed Stacey came to him without a struggle. He tried to keep his face inscrutable as she all but melted into him. One of his arms banded around her waist—it felt thinner—as he took her right hand in his. Her left hand went familiarly to his neck and locked onto it.

After a minute, he murmured into her ear, "You feel like heaven."

"So do you." No coyness here, not his lady.

"Oh, God, I miss you."

"I miss you, too." Unconsciously, or at least he thought so, she arched her lower body into his.

"I miss that, too," he confessed. "What are we going to do, Stace?"

"Nothing tonight," she said, bonelessly swaying into him. "Hold me for a little while and forget about everything else."

He did. Just for tonight.

CORD SLAMMED the file down hard and turned to the carpet installer. The sound echoed around the empty interior like a gunshot. "I don't care how busy you are. This was supposed to be finished today. I painted until three this morning so it would be done in time for you to get in here and finish up."

Cord had gone to school with Jack Summers, who now owned Canfield Linoleum and Carpet Center. He'd been an acquaintance, not a friend, but Cord had never had a problem with the guy. He didn't know why he was yelling at him about something so stupid as a delay in the carpet installation.

Except that he was yelling at everyone these days.

Jack said, "All right. I'll call my wife and tell her to go ahead to Parents' Day without me."

Cord felt like a slug. "Parents' Day?"

"At my daughter's dance school. We get to watch today."

Cord rammed a hand through his hair. "Aw, hell, I don't want you to miss that. Go on, go, you can finish up on Monday."

"You sure?"

"Yeah."

After Jack left, Cord went to the boxes that had been delivered this morning and were stacked against the back wall. He opened the one from National Art Supply, only to see that they had not had the color paint he'd ordered for the window. "Dammit," he said just as the front door opened.

"Daddy," Megan yelped as she streaked across the floor and into his arms.

An unopened bottle of paint fell onto the newly installed carpet. He saw a sleek hand pick it up as he scooped his daughter into his arms. "Got a problem?" Stacey asked.

Yeah, and she's standing right in front of me. The sight of her frayed his nerves further. "Do you have a lifetime?" he asked. Stacey cocked her head. "Sorry. I didn't mean to be sarcastic." He looked at his daughter. "How was your afternoon, Meggie?"

"Fun. Stacey and I made cookies and read books and played with my new bead kit."

"Sounds wonderful."

"It was." She put her arms out to Stacey, who took her from Cord. "Will I see you tomorrow?"

"Soon, love. I promise."

"I miss you, Stacey," Megan said, nestling into Stacey's shoulder.

"I miss you, too." Stacey's voice was hoarse.

Cord felt a lump in his throat.

After a hug, Stacey set Megan down, and his daughter danced away into the empty space of the store. Taking in a deep breath, Stacey looked at the bottle of paint she held. "What's this?"

"I finally got someone to do the lettering, and now they send me the wrong paint."

Stacey looked back at the bottle in her hand. "Why is this wrong?"

"Damned if I know. The supply store said they didn't have the order the artist placed."

Examining the paint, then looking at the invoice, she said, "It's not the color you ordered, but it's pretty close." She unscrewed the cap and looked inside. "Get me some paper and a small brush."

Cord went into his office, retrieved the materials and returned to Stacey. He spread a small drop cloth on the floor and they both sank onto it. Fascinated, he watched Stacey take the brush and letter McKAY SECURITY on the paper.

"The guy we hired was going to use the gold to outline the logo."

"Open that for me," Stacey said absently, still working the brush.

Cord picked up the gold paint. Of course, it was stuck. It strained his shoulder—like everything did these days—so he yanked hard.

The bottle opened. All over his navy blue T-shirt.

"Son of a bitch," he said, and jumped up. Gold lamé soaked him. He saw Stacey turn her head, but not before he caught the wisp of a smile. "Damn," he said, whipping off his shirt.

The amusement on Stacey's face died quicker than a fall sunset. Confused, Cord tracked her gaze. It riveted on his chest—or rather his shoulder.

Raising moist eyes to his, she stood and ran her delicate fingers along the five-inch scar caused by Dunn's knife.

"It's so red and puckered. God, it must have hurt badly."

"It's okay," Cord said, trying to ignore the feel of her hand on his bare skin for the first time in weeks.

"I . . . I've never seen it. Does it still hurt?"

"Right now it feels like a million bucks." He smiled sheepishly.

She held his gaze. "Cord, I . . ."

"Daddy, look, there's a clown out on Market Street." Megan had stopped her gymnastics to stare out the window. Then she whirled, and flew across the room to him.

Right into the open paint nestled on the rug. Her foot was little but had momentum behind it. She managed to kick both bottles, one after the other, sending them flying across the brand-new carpet, and spattering one entire newly painted white wall.

No one spoke for a few seconds. Then Megan's eyes snapped to her father. "Oh Daddy . . . I . . . I . . ." The little girl choked with sobs.

Cord bent down and dragged her into his arms. His knees landed in a puddle of gold, coating his blue jeans and hers. "Meggie, it's okay. Honey, it's only paint. It can be fixed."

Burrowing into him, he felt little hands grab him tight. "Can it?"

"Sure," he said, smoothing her hair. "Everything can be fixed, Meggie."

"Even big mistakes?"

Cord looked over Megan's shoulders, at Stacey. "Yes," he said firmly.

"Are you sure?"

Never taking his eyes off the woman he loved, Cord said with resolve, "Yeah, pumpkin, I'm sure. Even big mistakes can be fixed. If people want it bad enough."

Stacey's eyes misted and she turned away.

Cord phoned his mother to come and get Megan, then Stacey stayed and helped him clean up the wall and carpet as much as they could.

Cord walked Stacey to the door when she was ready to leave. "Thanks for helping. You didn't have to stay."

"Are you kidding? I was afraid you'd put your hand through the window once Meggie wasn't around to see you lose your temper."

He grinned and leaned against the wall. It had gotten darker and the lights from Market Street cast intimate shadows into the office. "I might have."

"Been on edge lately?"

He frowned. "Did Megan tell you that?"

Stacey reached out and touched his arm. He felt the gentle pressure right down to his groin. "No, she didn't. You're a wonderful father."

He swallowed hard. He wanted to touch her so bad he thought he'd go crazy. Lifting his hand, he rubbed his thumb along her full lower lip and felt a shudder go through her. "So, what do you think, Stace? Can anything be fixed if you want it bad enough?"

She took in a deep breath. "I don't know, Cord."

He could have let the comment blindside him, indicate that he hadn't made any headway with her. But he chose not to. Perhaps it was time to fight for what he wanted. "Maybe this will help you figure it out."

Sliding his hand to her neck, he lowered his mouth to hers. He brushed her lips with his, back and forth, back and forth until she stirred restlessly. Then he pulled her to his bare chest, and teased open her lips with his tongue.

He reveled in the familiar taste and touch of her. It had never been this right with anyone else, never would be with another woman. He pressed his mouth and his body to her, and took the kiss he'd been dreaming about for six weeks.

He was the one to break off the contact. He'd use what he could to sway her, yet he wouldn't overdo it. They had more going for them than sex. He drew back and smiled. "Good night, Stace. Think about me."

She stared at his face, then her eyes fell to his shoulder. "I will, Cord," she said huskily.

Well, he thought as he watched her go, maybe even big mistakes can be fixed.

SOMETIMES A FATHER *had to do what he had to do.* Gifford entertained the clichéd thought as he climbed the stairs to Stacey's apartment. She and Cord were trying, but he'd given them eight weeks and as far as he could tell, they hadn't made much progress. They needed a nudge.

The door was ajar to the sitting room. His daughter perched at a small desk in the corner, poring over some paperwork.

"Hi. Back from the hairdresser's already?" he asked from the entrance.

She looked up at him, brushing the locks out of her eyes. "I . . . um, didn't go."

"You said you were overdue for a haircut."

"Yes, well." She fidgeted with the papers. "I decided to let my hair grow out for the winter."

"Ah, I see." Gifford came into the room and his eyes strayed to the catalogs she held. "What are those?"

"Some information Melissa Fox got me from Elmore College. She teaches a course there."

"Going back to school?"

Stacey nodded. "They're just starting an art therapy program. It's connected with their Teacher Education division, so the course is mostly about art therapy for young children."

"You'd be great at it, honey. You're so good with Megan."

"Well, I'm going to try it out. Part-time, anyway." Stacey stood and stretched, then leaned back against the desk, facing him. "Where is the little rascal, anyway?"

"She's eating some chocolate chip cookies in the kitchen. I have to drop her off in a half hour."

"Did you find the gypsy stuff she wanted for her school play?"

"Yes." He gripped the book he held tighter. "In the basement." He drew in a heavy breath. "I found something else, honey. Something you should see."

Stacey looked down. "Another sketchbook?"

Gifford slid one hand into his pocket and fingered the paper there. "Among other things."

She smiled. "Mine?"

"No. Another of Helene's."

"I thought we looked at all of hers."

"No, this one was packed among her personal things. I don't know why it wasn't with the others." Gifford handed her the pad. "Look at it, honey."

Stacey sat back down and opened the book. Gifford stepped closer to watch over her shoulder.

"This is Grandma," Stacey said. "She looks mean."

"She was, sometimes."

Stacey flipped past three more pages of Ana. "Who's this?"

"Our housekeeper when you were young."

"And this?"

"A friend of your mother's. I think her name was Suzanne."

Suddenly, Stacey gasped. "Oh, Dad."

Looking down, Gifford saw the eighteen-year-old face of Cord McKay staring up at him. His throat clogged. Cord looked so real—with his square jaw and windblown hair—that Gifford thought he might speak right from the paper.

"He looks so *young*," Stacey said, devouring the sketch with her eyes.

"There's more."

Stacey turned the page. Another sketch of him, next to his motorcycle. "I used to think he looked like James Dean," Gifford said.

She chuckled. "He looks like a kid with a new bicycle."

"Yes, Stacey, he does."

His somber voice made his daughter look up at him. "Dad?"

Reaching out, Gifford squeezed her shoulder. "He *was* a kid. Just a boy."

Stacey glanced back down at the pad and slowly ran her fingers over the sculpted cheek of the charcoal sketch. "And my mother saw him like that."

For a moment, Stacey stared at the impression of Cord, flipped through and saw only blank pages, then closed the book and stood. "Why did you show me this? It can't be easy for you to remember it all."

"No, it hurts. Because it reminds me of how I blew it. How foolish I was."

"So why torture yourself with the memories?"

He folded his arms across his chest and plunged in. "Because I never had a second chance with your mother. And you have one with Cord. I don't want you looking back at your life and regretting what you did or didn't do." He felt his eyes mist.

His lovely daughter reached out and gave him a huge, comforting hug. Again. Gifford wondered what he had done in his whole misbegotten life to deserve her.

When she pulled away, he scrubbed his hands over his face, and she did, too. "Well, I've got to drop the squirt off on my way to Judith's."

"Oh, I thought I'd take her back," she said.

"No, I've got some business to discuss with Cord, anyway," Gifford told her.

"All right. Tell Megan to come give me a kiss before she leaves."

Heading for the door, Gifford stopped when he heard his daughter say, "Dad?"

Pivoting, he looked at her.

"You're quite a man," she said. "I wish you wouldn't be so hard on yourself."

He smiled sadly. "Someday." *Maybe when this is all settled.*

GIFFORD WAS GLAD the child kept up her usual stream of chatter as he maneuvered the short distance to the McKay residence.

Cord scooped Megan up when she bolted out of the car and sped to where he was raking leaves. "Hi, Daddy, can I jump in those?"

"No way, kid. I've spent all afternoon piling these up."

"That's what you always say. Then you jump right in with me."

He laughed, then looked up at Gifford. "Thanks for bringing her back." His gaze strayed to the car.

"She isn't with me," the older man said.

Cord put Megan down then leaned on the rake. "Oh."

These two were a pair. "I wanted to come by myself."

Cord whipped off his sunglasses, revealing worried eyes. "Go into the house and talk to Norna, Meggie," Cord said. When she scooted off, Cord asked, "Is Stacey okay?"

"That depends. She's unhappy."

Cord threw down the rake and walked to the porch. "Look, I know Stacey's unhappy. So am I."

"Well, maybe I can help. I came here today to shed a little light on something. Maybe it will get you past this hump of self-flagellation you can't seem to cross."

Temper flared in the young man's eyes. *Good,* Gifford thought. They both needed a kick in the pants. Gifford withdrew a piece of paper from his pocket and held it up.

"What's that?"

"A letter. I found it when I was looking for something for Megan."

Cord stared at the paper again, then his eyes whipped to Gifford's face. "That isn't . . ."

"Yes, it is."

"I don't want to hear this."

"Yes, you do."

Gifford saw Cord swallow hard. "No, Gif, I can't."

"Yes, Cord. I'd like to read some of it to you. Not everything, because a lot of it is personal." He held the younger man's stare. "Trust me."

Sinking to the step, Cord nodded. Gifford propped his foot up on the step, and carefully opened the pink parchment. He took a quick glance at Cord. The younger man's jaw had tensed and his neck muscles throbbed. Gifford lowered his eyes and again felt a stab of pain as he began to read the last words Helene ever had for him.

Dear Gif,
There are things that must be said before this goes any further. You're in a rage and can't think clearly. But please, please read this, for all our sakes.
    I have much to say to you about this, but first I must set the record straight on Cord McKay. Of the three of us—yes, Gif, you bear some guilt in

this too—Cord is the most innocent. He's simply a young boy who got caught up in a volatile and emotional situation. When you left for the airport today, I feared our relationship was over, that you might do as you threatened and not come back. I felt—and have felt for a long time—that our marriage was in serious trouble. I was overwrought. For Cord's part, he'd just had a wrenching argument with his family, and he was questioning whether anyone cared about him. He turned to me at the exact moment I needed him. We came together, not in passion but in desperation. Not in love. Not even in lust. What happened was not rational, not premeditated. I know this doesn't excuse what Cord and I did. As the adult, I bear the guilt and the shame for it. Though you'll never forgive me, you must forgive Cord. Please do not punish him.

When Gifford looked up, his eyes were watery. So were Cord's.

Blinking back the moisture, Cord sighed. "Why did you show me this?"

"Because Helene was right. You were a young boy. She was the adult. And she was married. She was at fault."

"Gifford—"

"No, Cord. This is how it was. You remember it differently because of your guilt. But it's there in black and white and you can't deny it."

"I can't believe you'd tell me this."

"It's time to settle things. For all of us."

"I'm sorry, Gifford."

"I am, too."

Cord eyes widened. "You...you didn't show this to Stacey, did you?"

Still protecting her, Gifford thought. He was giving his daughter over to the right man. "No. I didn't show the letter to her. It would serve no purpose. I realize I said I wouldn't keep anything from her, but it would be cruel for her to read this."

Cord's whole body sagged. Gifford lifted his hand to squeeze the other man's shoulder. "Let's bury it all with this letter, Cord. The blame. The guilt. The self-recrimination."

Cord squinted up at him. Gifford thought he saw a lightening in the sad shadows of his eyes.

"Well, I'd better go." Gifford straightened. "Oh, and one more thing. I want to say out loud how sorry I am for running you out of town that day. I was terribly wrong. Your father was right when he said—"

"My father?"

Gifford cocked his head. "Didn't you know?"

"Know what?"

"Your father came to see me after the funeral."

"Why?"

"He said he'd waited a decent amount of time to let the shock wear off. But he had to talk to me."

"About what?"

"You, of course."

"Why did he come to you?"

Gifford shook his head. "I'm not exactly sure. He said you left town the day of the funeral. That you two had had a fight the week before, but somehow he thought your leaving Canfield was connected with me.''

"How could he know that? I never told a soul."

"That doesn't surprise me."

"How did he know?"

"He said it was a hunch. First, he asked if I knew where you were. Then, when he picked up on my...my animosity, he said he hoped I hadn't done anything to you. He said you were a good kid, hotheaded at times, but a son he was proud of."

Cord sucked in his breath. Gifford sensed this was some kind of revelation to him, though Gifford didn't quite understand it.

"And you know what, Cord? He was right. I'd be proud to have you as my son." Gifford smiled. "Or my son-in-law."

HE'S RIGHT!

Stacey stepped out of the shower and knew that her father had been wise and knowledgeable in what he had told her. She *did* have a second chance with Cord. You had to take what you were given today and run with it. If she was honest with herself, living the rest of her life without Cord in it was utterly impossible.

If only it isn't too late. If I can convince him.

She'd go over there right now. Or, better yet, she'd call him. Ask him to come here, where they could be alone. And she'd show him that they belonged together, if it took her the rest of her life.

Determined, she headed through the bathroom door to the phone in her room. But she stopped short three feet from the bed.

Sprawled on it was Cord McKay, legs stretched out, hands linked behind his neck, and the cockiest grin she'd ever seen on his face.

And suddenly Stacey knew. Her dad had talked to him, too.

"Well, hello," she mumbled huskily.

"Hi, Stace." His eyes took in the thigh-length robe that gaped at her chest. She shifted a bit, letting it fall slightly off her shoulders. A tightening of his body made her sigh inwardly.

"This is a surprise." She scowled. "How did you get in here?"

Reaching into his pocket, he produced a set of keys and held them up like a little boy revealing the key to his sister's diary. But he didn't look like a little boy, in tight, wheat-colored jeans and a cotton, baby blue sweater that turned his eyes the color of the sky.

"You still have the keys to the house?"

"Yup. And I'm not giving them back."

Purposely arching an eyebrow, and willing herself not to pounce on him, she said, "Oh, why?"

"Because I want unlimited access to you until we get our own place."

Stacey gulped. "Our own place?"

He sat up and reached for a box at the foot of the bed. Without warning, he tossed it to her. "Open this."

Stacey caught the prettily wrapped package, stared at him for a minute, then tore off the paper. The logo said Keeler's, the store where she and Cord had gotten separated the night Mark had attacked her. She ripped off the cover, and bit her lip to keep from crying when she saw what was inside. There would be no tears today.

"Where . . . when . . . how did you get this?"

"I ordered it right after the incident with Dunn." His eyes scanned her. "Put it on."

"Getting pretty bossy, aren't you?"

"No sass, lady."

As he watched, Stacey slowly untied the belt of her robe. His eyes were riveted on her hands. Letting the sides part slightly, giving him only glimpses of her naked body, she reached up and unwound the towel from her hair. He gulped. As she finger-combed the curls, the robe fell open even more. His hands fisted. First, she let the cloth fall off one shoulder, then the next. Every single muscle in his body clenched.

As provocatively as she could, she drew the lavender lace minidress over her head. Then she locked her eyes with his. "I thought you didn't want me to have this."

"That was when I believed we'd never be together again."

"And now?"

His face sobered. "Come here, Stace." He patted the mattress next to him.

She crossed to the bed and sat down on the edge. Before she could speak, he flipped her to her back and covered her body with his. "What are you doing?" she asked.

"Using every trick in the book to convince you."

"Convince me of what?"

Slowly, he traced her cheekbone with his knuckles. "We were meant to be together, Stacey. I know what happened in the past hurt you, will always hurt you, and I'll do everything I can to deal with it. I'll talk it out every day for a year if that will help. I'll go to counseling with you. But I can't let you go. I *won't* let you go. I'll dog your every step, I'll pester you every day." He bumped his middle with hers. "I'll seduce you if I have to."

Cord saw the moisture glaze her eyes. Not once since he'd jumped in the shower, dressed quickly and raced out of the house had he let himself entertain the thought that she might not agree, might never be able to forgive him. Now, the idea scared him to death.

He caught a renegade tear between his fingers. "Don't, love. Please. I promise I'll make it work." He'd beg if he had to. He didn't care.

"Oh, Cord, it's not that."

He continued, not listening to her protests. "Look, your father really needs us to be together. He's felt guilty all his life for what happened. He can't tolerate our being apart."

The tears receded and she looked indignant. "Cord McKay, that's hitting below the belt."

"And Meggie needs you, too. Sometimes she cries at night and calls for you."

"That's blackmail."

"I know. I don't care. I'll do anything to keep you in my life. I'm warning you." He peered at her intently. "I deserve this. I deserve you. Now that I know that, I'll bulldoze my way into your heart every chance I get."

He became aware of her hands at the base of his neck. They slid over his nape, sending goose bumps through him. "Will you support me when I go back to school?" she asked.

His heart lifted and pounded so hard he feared an attack. "Only if it's for art," he managed to get out.

She pouted those full lips. "I want our baby. Soon."

He felt his own tears threaten. In an unsteady voice, he said, "Okay. A boy, though. We'll call him Gifford Nathan McKay."

Then Cord sobered. It was important for her to see how much this moment meant to him, how sacred it was. Just like the first time they'd made love.

Tugging her left hand from his neck, he took her third finger and massaged the spot where his ring would go, fusing her life with his. He looked at her face, and asked, "Will you marry me, Anastasia? Will you be my wife, my lover, my soul mate, forever?"

And shining in those brown eyes he loved so much was the greatest gift he had ever received. "Yes, I'll marry you. I love you, Francis. I always will."

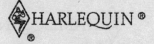

Merry Christmas, Baby!

A romantic collection filled with the magic
of Christmas and the joy of children.

SUSAN WIGGS, Karen Young and
Bobby Hutchinson bring you Christmas wishes,
weddings and romance, in a charming
trio of stories that will warm up your
holiday season.

MERRY CHRISTMAS, BABY! also contains
Harlequin's special gift to you—a set of
FREE GIFT TAGS included in every book.

Brighten up your holiday season with
MERRY CHRISTMAS, BABY!

Available in November at
your favorite retail store.

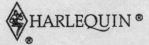

HARLEQUIN ®
®

Look us up on-line at: http://www.romance.net   MCB

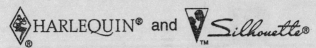
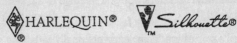

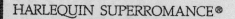

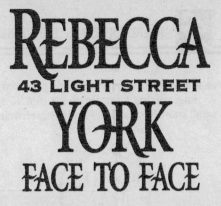

REBECCA

43 LIGHT STREET

YORK

FACE TO FACE

Bestselling author Rebecca York returns to "43 Light Street" for an original story of past secrets, deadly deceptions—and the most intimate betrayal.

She woke in a hospital—with amnesia...and with child. According to her rescuer, whose striking face is the last image she remembers, she's Justine Hollingsworth. But nothing about her life seems to fit, except for the baby inside her and Mike Lancer's arms around her. Consumed by forbidden passion and racked by nameless fear, she must discover if she is Justine...or the victim of some mind game. Her life—and her unborn child's—depends on it....

Don't miss *Face To Face*—Available in October, wherever Harlequin books are sold.

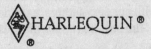

HARLEQUIN ®

®

43FTF

HARLEQUIN SUPERROMANCE®

WOMEN WHO *Dare*

They take chances, make changes and follow their hearts!

SUGAR BABY
by Karen Young

Little Danny Woodson witnessed a murder, and now the killer is after him. Claire Woodson will do anything to protect her son. Even if it means staying with the enemy. Danny's uncle—the wealthy Louisiana sugar plantation owner who's fighting Claire for custody—swears he can keep the boy safe. Suddenly *Claire's* the one in danger. She could lose her son...and her heart.

Available in October.

Be sure to watch for upcoming titles in Harlequin Superromance's exciting series WOMEN WHO DARE. Each story highlights our special heroines—strong, caring, brave and passionate women who know their own minds and dare anything...for love.

Available wherever Harlequin books are sold.

Look us up on-line at: http://www.romance.net

WWD96-7